THE DECEPTION YOU WEAVE

USA TODAY & WALL STREET JOURNAL BESTSELLING AUTHOR

TRACY LORRAINE

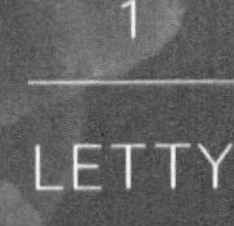

1

LETTY

"Kane," I cry, racing down the stairs after him.

Tears cascade down my cheeks, my chest aching from my confession and the memories that threaten to pull me under.

"Kane, stop. Please." My legs move faster than my body and I stumble at the bottom of the staircase, crashing into the wall.

Pain shoots through my shoulder as I collide with the exposed brickwork, but I don't stop.

I can't.

I need to tell him the truth.

"Kane," I scream once more as I run to the parking lot, but it's too late. His car is already wheelspinning out of the lot, tires screeching as he goes.

"Noooo," I scream, wrapping my arms around myself, trying to hold myself together so I don't shatter all over the sidewalk for all the students at MKU to witness.

A sob erupts from my throat but just as my knees are about to give out, a strong set of arms catch me.

"It's okay, Let. I've got you."

Hearing his voice, the concern in his tone shatters the little control I had left on my emotions and I break down, ugly sobs erupting from me as fat tears drop down onto my cheeks.

Leon sweeps me into his arms, clearly sensing that I'm not going to be able to walk. With my head tucked into the crook of his neck, he carries me back inside and up to my dorm room.

I have no idea if anyone stops him, if anyone says anything as we pass them, the only thing I can focus on is the pain. The loss. The grief. The emptiness that I've only recently managed to somewhat put behind me.

Another sob erupts as the reason for the loss of that feeling hits me.

It was him.

He made it disappear.

I hold on to Leon tighter as he kicks my door closed and lowers us to the bed.

He doesn't say anything as he holds me close and gently rubs his hand up and down my back in silent support.

His body trembles beneath mine. I can only imagine what he must be thinking, feeling, after watching me run after Kane like that.

I know how much they both hate him. But what they know is only the tip of the iceberg. I have no doubt that when they discover the truth, their anger is only going to get more ferocious.

I have no idea how much time passes with him just holding me. I'm grateful that no one else tries to come in and check on me. I don't want to see anyone right now and I don't want to talk. I just want to vanish.

He thinks that I... I sob again.

"Cupcake, you're scaring me," Leon whispers so he doesn't startle me.

"I'm okay," I sniffle.

"Lying to me won't help."

Lifting my head from his shoulder, I eventually look into his concerned eyes.

He gasps the second he looks over my face.

I can only imagine the state of my appearance.

I looked like a car crash even before Kane stormed his way inside here.

His eyes drop from mine in favor of my neck and chest.

"Fucking hell, Let. What did that motherfucker do to you?"

His grip on me tightens as his anger resurfaces.

"No, no, that's not—" I start but soon realize that I have no idea where I'm going with it.

"He did this." It's not a question. I guess it doesn't need to be. We both know the answer. "What's going on, Cupcake? Talk to me, please."

I swallow nervously as Leon attacks his bottom lip as he waits.

"I..." My eyes find his once more, before they drop to his lips again.

"Letty," Leon warns, clearly sensing where my thoughts are going.

I shift until I'm straddling him, and his eyes darken at my move.

"Make it go away," I mutter, crashing my lips to his.

"Letty, this isn't... we shouldn't... fuck," he mumbles against my lips as I pull the bottom one into my mouth and sink my teeth into it.

His hand lifts to my hair as he loses control, his tongue delving into my mouth to tangle with mine.

I focus everything on him, on every stroke of my tongue, on the roll of my hips as I grind against him. Everything else falls away until it's no longer consuming me, shattering me into a million pieces.

Desire surges through me as he matches my intensity move for move until suddenly, he's no longer there.

"What the—" I look up to find I've been deposited on the bed. Leon is pacing the small space of my room with his hands in his hair, a conflicted look on his face and a bulge in his jeans.

Coldness engulfs me and I pull my knees up to my chest and wrap my arms around them, suddenly very aware that I'm only wearing a tank and booty shorts.

"Lee?"

He stops at the sound of my voice this time and turns to look at me, his eyes sweeping over what he can see of my bruised body.

"I'm sorry. I shouldn't have..."

"No. It wasn't you. I'm sorry. I just..." I let out a long sigh. *I just wanted it all to go away.*

Commotion out in the living area has us both looking up before the door flies open and a panicked looking Luca fills the doorway.

"What's going on, I had a voicemail that said—" His eyes land on me. "Fuck."

I'm swept up into another pair of arms, but this time, I'm stronger and manage to rein in my emotions.

"I'm okay. It's okay."

He places me back on my feet and looks at my body.

"It's really fucking not. Look at you."

"I'm fine."

He lifts his hand and moves my hair away from my neck.

"Tell me it wasn't," he warns, his voice terrifyingly low.

I swallow nervously and it's all the answer he needs.

"Motherfucker," he roars, spinning away from me and planting his fist into my wall.

"Luca," I scream, diving for him and wrapping my hands around his solid upper arms. The answer to all of this is not for him to hurt himself and damage his arm. "Stop it, please. P-please." My voice cracks when I see the blood on his knuckles and he immediately relaxes in my hold.

"Fucking hell, Letty. What have you got yourself into?"

He wraps me in his arms again, holding me tighter than I think he's ever done before.

The air around us becomes heavy and I wiggle for him to release me.

"I need a drink," I mutter, reaching to the chair for my hoodie to cover up.

"I'll go get something," Leon says.

"Make it strong."

He nods before slipping out of the room.

Lifting my hand to my lips, I recall our kiss.

That was a mistake. I knew it the second I did it, but fuck.

Lowering my hand, I press the heel of my hand against my chest right above my heart that feels like it's shattering into a million pieces.

Luca watches my every move as I curl myself back up on my bed once more.

I don't look up at him, but I feel his stare, feel his concern.

"The blonde had whiskey in her room," Leon says, walking back in with a small bottle.

"Ella," I say, although my voice is empty. "Her name is Ella. She's the one you were dancing with Friday night."

"Yeah, yeah, that's the one. Here," he says, passing the bottle over.

Twisting the top, I lift the bottle to my lips and swallow down a huge mouthful.

My bed dips as Luca sits beside me while Leon takes the chair opposite me.

The whiskey burns all the way down until it begins to warm my stomach. It's more than welcome but it barely takes the edge off.

The image of Kane's devastated face as I confessed what really happened after Skye's party eighteen months ago haunts me. The reason that my life imploded and I found myself here instead of Columbia.

"Let, I get that you probably don't want to talk right now. And if you just want to sit here in silence, then we can totally do that for as long as you need to, but..." I look up into Luca's soft green eyes. "Did he hurt you? Like... really hurt you?" His jaw pops as he asks the question.

"No," I whisper. All of the marks and bruises on my body were more than consensual. "Not physically."

"What did he do, Let?" Leon asks, earning him a warning growl from Luca who's surprisingly got a little more patience right now.

"N-nothing," I admit, dropping my forehead to my knees as I remember the minutes before he fled my room.

"But—"

"There are things that he—that no one knows." I wince because I hate to admit that I'm keeping secrets from them.

"Okay."

"God, this is such a mess. I don't even know where to start."

"The beginning," Luca urges.

I open my mouth to say something, although I'm not entirely sure what was about to come out when my door once again flies open.

The three of us look up to find Zayn standing there. His eyes wide and his chest heaving as if he's just run across campus to get here.

"Your cell fucking broken or something?" he mutters.

"What's wrong?"

He glances at both Luca and Leon.

"It's okay."

He nods. "It's Kane. He's in the hospital."

"What?" I screech, jumping up from my spot on the bed. "What happened?"

"I don't know. Harley just called to tell me she and

Kyle were on their way to Maddison ER. Her cell cut out before I got the details."

"Holy shit," I breathe. My body moving on autopilot as I pull on a pair of Chucks and grab my purse, reaching for my car keys. "Fuck. I don't have a car." I look between the three of them, half expecting them to point-blank refuse my next request. "Can one of you take me to the hospital?"

"You want to go to him?" Luca asks, disbelief written all over his face.

"I need to. This is my fault."

"I hardly think—"

"It's my fault," I say firmly.

He was so angry. He never should have got behind the wheel.

I should have stopped him.

If he'd just let me explain.

"I'll take you," Leon says, "I drove here." He flicks a look at Luca knowing that he didn't. "But you need to put some pants on." He nods to my thighs, his lips pressing into a thin line at what he sees there.

I look down at my bare legs. The hoodie is covering the worst of the marks but they can all clearly see the evidence of the time Kane and I spent together.

If I weren't so numb, I might be embarrassed by it.

"Fucking hell, Let," Zayn mutters, taking in the marks.

"Leave it, Zayn," I bark. Really not in any mood to get into it with my brother.

Dragging on a pair of leggings, I shove my feet into my shoes once more and walk to the door.

"Come on then," I snap at Leon.

"Uh..." He looks at Luca and Zayn.

"Leave them. I need to be there now."

I stalk out of my room on shaky legs.

Every set of eyes turn toward me, but I keep my eyes focused on where I'm going. It's not until I start running down the stairs that I realize that Leon is actually following me.

He steps up beside me and threads his fingers through mine.

Silently, we make our way down to the parking lot but I come to a grinding halt before we get to his car.

"What? What's wrong?" he asks the moment he realized I've stopped.

"My car." I lift my hand and point as if it isn't obvious.

"Uh... right?" I glance at him, seeing his creased brow.

"It doesn't matter. It was getting fixed and I wasn't expecting it back yet."

"Oookay."

"Come on." I march up to Leon's car and drop into the passenger seat.

Thankfully it's only a fifteen-minute drive to the hospital, although it feels like it takes about fifteen hours when Leon pulls into a parking space.

The second the car comes to a stop, I'm reaching for the door handle.

"Let, wait," Leon says in a rush.

I glance back at him, begging him to say what he needs to say fast because now that I'm here, I need to know what's going on.

"Whatever is going on here. I just want you to know that I won't judge. You can tell me anything, okay?"

Emotion clogs my throat as I stare at his dark green eyes.

"I don't deserve you," I force out.

"Aw, Cupcake. I'm the lucky one. Come on, let's go and see what's going on."

I know this is probably the last place that Leon wants to spend his Thursday night, but his loyalty to me wins out over his hatred for Kane and together we race toward the ER.

I head straight for the reception desk the second the doors open for us but I don't get there.

"Letty," a familiar voice shouts and when I turn, I find Harley, my little sister, running at me.

She throws herself into me and wraps her arms around my waist.

"Is he okay? What happened? Where's Kyle?" All the questions come tumbling out of me at once.

Taking my hand, Harley leads me over to where she was sitting when we walked in.

"He's going to be okay," she assures me, and I feel like I can breathe for the first time since Zayn showed up and dropped the bomb. "He was in a car accident."

My heart sinks. I was right. All of this is my fault.

"He was on the wrong side of the road apparently."

"Christ," Leon mutters, scrubbing his hand down over his face.

I appreciate that he does actually care and isn't standing there wishing the outcome was worse.

"There's Kyle." Harley nods to a set of doors behind us. "He'll be able to tell you more."

"Hey," he says.

"Is he okay?" I ask in a rush despite the fact Harley just told me he was.

"Come with me and see for yourself."

2

___

KANE

Everything feels fuzzy when I come to.

The last thing I remember was driving away from training and flipping Luca and Leon off as they emerged from the building.

Everything after that was a blur.

I know I was exhausted, but fuck.

I twist my head to the side and pain shoots down my spine. It's so sharp that it makes me suck in a breath.

"He's waking up," a familiar voice says.

Am I still dreaming?

"Kane? Bro, can you hear me?"

"K—" My throat is so dry I can't get any more out.

"Do you need a drink? Here." A straw is pressed to my lips and I suck down some water. My eyes still refusing point-blank to open.

"Th-thank you," I whisper as everything begins to get hazy again.

Darkness engulfs me and the reality that I was trying to grasp once again slips away.

I hear her voice and I fight to wake up, to see her, to touch her.

When I manage to get my eyes to work, we're in my bedroom at the house and she's standing in the doorway to the bathroom with just my towel wrapped around her.

My body grows hot as I take in the marks on her body.

The bruises around her throat, the angry red marks down her chest and poking out the bottom of the towel on her thighs.

My cock swells as I stare at her.

So fucking beautiful.

"Princess," I growl, holding my hand out for her and throwing the covers back so she can join me. I've certainly not had my fill yet.

Some movement on my arm drags me from thoughts of Letty. That touch certainly isn't hers and the blood running through my veins cools almost immediately.

"Are you going to wake up for us soon, young man?" a strange voice says, although it sounds like she's a million miles away. "Your brother and girlfriend are here waiting on you."

"Oh no, I'm not—"

At her voice, I fight like hell through the fog but the darkness is too strong and I slip away again briefly.

Is she here? Wherever here is.

"Bro, calm down. It's okay." A warm hand lands on my forearm. "Kane. It's okay."

Kyle.

His hand slides down to my hand and he squeezes. But it isn't his hand I want.

Mustering up every bit of energy I have, I force my eyes open.

The fluorescent light from above burns my eyes and they immediately start watering, making everything blur that much more.

"Kane." The hope in his voice keeps me fighting to come back. "Hey," he says, and finally my eyes clear enough to see him staring down at me.

He looks terrible, like he's been awake for a week.

That thought forces me to look away from him.

The sterile room comes into view along with the line that disappears into the back of my hand.

Holy shit.

"W-where am I?" Each word feels like it rips my throat wide open.

"Here." He moves a cup toward me and presses the straw to my dry lips.

I drink down the entire cup, forcing him to refill it so I can have more.

"You're in the hospital."

"H-hospital?"

"Kyle, you should call for the doctor."

My entire body tenses at the sound of her voice.

I try to see her but Kyle is blocking my view.

Reaching out, I press my hand weakly against his stomach, tapping to make him stand back.

The second he does and my eyes land on her, all the breath races from my lungs.

She's curled up in a chair in the corner. Her hair is piled on top of her head, her face is bare of makeup, her eyes dark with lack of sleep, and her teeth are attacking her bottom lip. She's cuddling a takeout coffee cup as if she needs it to survive.

Dragging her eyes from my brother, they land on mine and widen in surprise despite the fact she just heard me talking and was the one to tell Kyle to get the doctor.

For the briefest of moments, I'm relieved to see her.

Then all my memories come rushing back to me.

They hit me like a fucking tsunami, and if I weren't already lying down, then I swear they'd take me to the floor.

"Get out." My words are low and so quiet I doubt anyone actually hears them.

Kyle stills beside me.

"Get. Out."

Her lips part as if she's going to argue, her eyes exhausted and full of tears.

I don't give a fuck about how she's feeling right now.

She's the one who did this.

"Get. The. Fuck. Out," I spit, my fists clenching. The cannula in my left hand stings and the muscles in my shoulders ache from the movement. I have no idea exactly what happened or what's wrong with me but right now, the only thing I need is her out of this room.

She uncurls herself from the chair.

"No, stay," Kyle insists.

She hesitates and looks between the two of us.

"If you knew what she'd done, you wouldn't be saying that. I need her out of this room." I don't bother looking at her as I say those words. "She's a liar and I don't want her here."

Her gasp of shock rings out around the otherwise silent and sterile room.

Kyle wants to argue, I can see it on his face but he wisely keeps his mouth shut as he looks to Letty with something akin to an apology in his expression.

The sound of her feet moving drags my eyes away from my brother so I can watch her walk out of the room and away from me.

My heart slams in my chest, as it feels like it's cracking wide open all over again just like when she finally told me the truth.

She pauses at the door and I panic.

My hands tremble and my chest heaves, trying to drag in the air I need.

A little machine beside me starts beeping but I pay it little mind as her eyes finally lock with mine.

"It's not what you think. You need to let me explain."

I shake my head, the insistent beeping continuing. "I'm not interested in anything you have to say. Get the fuck away from me."

She's forced to move aside as a nurse comes running in.

"Mr. Legend, as good as it is to see you awake, you really need to calm down."

Narrowing my eyes in warning at Letty, she finally gets the idea and rushes from the room.

Falling back onto the bed, I close my eyes and suck in a few deep breaths while the nurse checks my vitals and chastises me for getting worked up.

"You were very, very lucky young man. But that

doesn't mean you're in any state to get yourself worked up. You need to rest, your body has been through a lot."

I don't say anything, I don't even look at her as I assume she checks my vitals then promises to be back later.

"What happened?" I ask once I know it's only Kyle and me in the room.

He hangs his head, running his fingers through his hair and stares down at me.

"You were on the wrong side of the fucking road, Kane. What the fuck happened?"

I shake my head. "I wasn't paying attention."

"You fucking think. You nearly drove headfirst into a fucking truck."

"My car?"

"Jesus fucking Christ. Someone needs to come back and check your fucking head. You should be glad you're fucking alive." His voice gets louder as his own fear begins to get the better of him. "If you'd have died then I—"

"I'm sorry," I whisper, guilt flooding through my veins at the look on his face. "I'm sorry, shit just got messed up and I wasn't thinking. I shouldn't have got in my car."

He raises a brow at me as if to say 'you fucking think.' But I had to get away from her.

Even as I think about those few minutes before I fled, my anger begins to take over.

"She hasn't left this room since she first got here."

"I don't care," I shoot him down. "I don't want to think about her. Talk about her. She's nothing."

"Right. So it's safe to assume that she's the one who caused all of this?"

"She never should have come back here," I mutter.

"It's her home, Kane... kind of."

"I don't give a fuck. I've worked too hard for all of this to have her fuck it up."

He drags a chair over and sits beside me.

"Are you feeling okay?"

"No," I answer honestly. "Everything fucking hurts." Although I don't tell him that the worst pain is in my chest and I don't think any amount of drugs will help with that.

"You managed to escape a concussion or any broken bones, but you're pretty beat up. The meds have kept you under for almost twenty-four hours."

"You've been here all this time?"

"Yep, Letty too."

"Don't," I mutter. Just hearing her name right now is too much. "I guess that explains why you look like such shit."

"Cheers, Bro." He rolls his eyes at me, settles back in his chair and props his feet up on the edge of my bed. "So come on then. I want to know about college, seeing as you've been there almost two weeks and I've had nothing more than a few shitty conversations with you."

"Don't pretend like you haven't been too busy with Harley to talk to me."

His cheeks heat a little and a smile plays on his lips.

As happy as I am, a little part of me dies inside. I'm always going to be connected to Letty, whether I like it or not. Something tells me that my little brother isn't going to be letting her little sister go anytime soon.

"Moving to Rosewood was the best thing that could have happened," he admits.

"Funny, you should have seen your face that day I picked you up from juvie and dropped that bomb on you. I thought you were going to be going straight back inside for murder."

"Hey, I had faith in you."

"Did you?" I raise a brow at him.

"Well, I do now. I just wish you didn't have to put your life on hold for me."

"It's done," I say, although the lie tastes bitter on my tongue. "We're all where we're meant to be." My words become slower as my exhaustion once again kicks in. "I need..." I fall back under before I even finish the sentence. Although the second the image of Letty holding a baby appears in my mind, I wish I could have fought it longer.

"Are you sure you wouldn't rather go home?" Kyle asks as he walks slowly beside me toward the Harris house.

"I'm fine." It's a lie. Every fucking inch of my body hurts but I'm not running back to Rosewood. This is where I need to be. Plus, like fuck am I telling him that the thought of sitting in the car while he drives us all the way back to Rosewood makes me want to cry. The journey from the hospital to here was bad enough.

"I've got your bag," a soft voice calls from behind us.

I wince, knowing that the second I look at the owner, it's going to be like a bat to my chest all over again.

Harley's eyes are so like a pair I never want to look into again it hurts.

"Thanks, Kitten. I'll take that."

"Okay, I'll get a drink so he can take his meds."

"He is right here and more than capable of looking after himself," I snap.

"We know, Bro. Just let us help, yeah?"

"Whatever," I mutter, wrapping my hand around the handrail and using it to haul my body up the stairs.

Why the hell is my room on the second floor?

Kyle hesitates behind me, I can sense his need to help but thankfully, he hangs back and lets me do my thing.

By the time I push through to my bedroom, I feel like I've run a marathon. I fall down onto my bed and will the pain surging through my body to subside.

The bed dips by my feet and I prop myself up on my pillows to look at him.

"You need to talk to her."

"Are we really going there again?"

"Yes. Harley is worried."

"Not my problem, Bro. Sorry."

"It fucking is and you know it. She sat there all fucking night waiting for you to wake up. You didn't see how terrified she was."

"I don't care. She has no right to be concerned about me."

He groans, pushing from the bed and paces across my room.

"You're fucking unbelievable," he mutters.

"Our paths weren't supposed to cross again."

"So that makes everything okay?"

"We're done talking about this."

"You know, I really fucking hate you sometimes."

"You're just worried about Harley holding out on you because she's pissed at me."

Kyle's face turns beet red with frustration.

"This has nothing to do with me and everything to do with you. You're hurting Letty. You're hurting my girl. All because you're too fucking pigheaded to talk to her, to put the past behind you."

"It's not in the past though, is it?" I slam my lips shut the moment the words fall from my lips.

"I wouldn't fucking know. You shut me down every time I even mention her name."

"I hate her. There's nothing more to talk about."

"Right. Of course." He shakes his head at me before a soft knock sounds on the door and Harley joins us.

The second she steps inside the room her eyes jump between the two of us.

"What happened?" she asks, clearly feeling the tension as much as we are.

"Nothing. He's just being his usual stubborn self."

"Pfft, takes one to know one," Harley snarks, earning herself a spank on the ass from my brother.

"You can both leave," I say, staring up at the ceiling.

"Wow, you really are an asshole, you know that?"

"I do. I'd hate to ruin my rep."

Thankfully, after letting me know that they've instructed Devin and Ellis—who are both downstairs— that they're to check on me every hour and ensure I've taken my meds, they leave.

I love my brother more than anything. Every single

thing I've done has been for him and our futures, but right now. I really just need to be alone.

I'm grateful for his support but I haven't had even a minute to myself since I woke up in that hospital room late Friday night. I really just need to take a breath.

I stare up at the ceiling, recalling the events that led to me getting in my car and fucking myself up.

I might not have broken anything or caused any serious damage but I already know I've fucked up playing the first game of the season. It's going to take a fucking miracle for me to be in shape by Saturday.

I bet Luca and Leon are over the fucking moon about that.

My fists curl as I think about the two of them. Did they know all of this? Did everyone know what Letty was hiding? Was I the only one in the dark about what she's done?

My body heats as the anger I felt in the minutes after those words fell from her lips consumes me once again.

She got pregnant the night of Skye's party.

Pregnant.

By me.

My heart races.

I've always been careful. I always use protection and never take anyone bare. Until her.

Like with everything else, I lose my goddamn mind when I'm with her.

My teeth grind as I think about the fact she never once tried to reach out to me. She never even tried to tell me.

You wouldn't have listened or accepted it, a little voice shouts in my head but I shut it down.

I'd like to think that if she'd shown up at my door explaining she was pregnant that I'd have done the right thing.

But I never got the chance.

She took care of her little issue.

She made it go away.

"Scarlett, where is my fucking baby?"

"G-gone."

"Gone?"

"I'm sorry. I'm so sorry."

"Argh," I scream into the silence of my bedroom. My muscles pull tight with my need to go to her, to wrap my hand around her fucking throat and force her to explain herself. But even if I could, I don't have a fucking car. Just another thing of mine she's ruined.

"You okay, man?" Devin's head pops into the room.

"Oh yeah, fucking great."

"You want some company?"

I quirk a brow at him and he puts his hands up in defense.

"Alright, I was only offering. I'll leave you to it."

"W-wait," I call before he disappears. "What happened with the cameras?"

"Nothing yet. You ended up in the hospital and we kinda put it to one side."

"It was her."

He nods. "We know. Question is, why?"

"Any of you tried asking her?"

"Nope. Thought you might like a second shot at that."

"Victor said anything?"

"Nope."

My brows pull with confusion. "They came from him though, right?"

"Well, I'm pretty sure your girl isn't actually spying on us, so yeah."

"She isn't my fucking girl."

"Sure. Sorry. Shout if you need me."

"Are you sure you've got everything?" Mom asks as she passes me the bag I threw a few things in before I hightailed it from MKU in the early hours of Saturday morning.

I walked back into the dorm to find everyone awake and waiting for me. They couldn't have known that Kane was going to send me away like he did. It makes me wonder just how long they'd have waited if I didn't show when I did.

Every single one of them jumped up at my arrival but it was Ella who raced forward and swept me into her arms. Brax and West quickly followed until I found myself in the middle of a group hug.

After excusing myself, I packed a bag while Ella watched from my bed. She asked zero questions and with another hug, she watched as I drove out of the parking lot.

They've been messaging me all weekend, checking if I'm okay and I've assured them that I am. That I just needed some space after everything.

They heard the argument between Kane and me, although I have no idea if they actually *heard* the words we spat at each other.

I really hope not.

It's bad enough I told him like I did. I really don't need my entire dorm knowing what I've been hiding.

"Yeah, I'm good," I say sadly, wishing I could stay here longer.

Mom must see that I'm only holding on by a thin thread because she gathers me up in her arms and tries to help hold me together.

"He's going to be okay," she whispers in my ear and I crack.

An ugly sob rips from my throat as I picture him lying in that hospital bed.

Kane has always been such an enigma. Larger than life. So to see him lying there totally helpless with machines and tubes... a shudder races through me.

Sucking in a steeling breath, I release Mom and give her a smile that I hope convinces her that I'll be okay, even if I feel like I'm shattering all over again.

"Everything will be okay," she says softly, squeezing my hand in support. "Give him some time and then tell him everything."

I nod at her, afraid that if I open my mouth all I am going to do is break down.

'Thank you,' I mouth before stepping away and pulling my door open.

Dropping into the driver's seat, I breathe in the clean scent. Not only did Kane get my tire fixed, but he had the entire thing detailed as well.

The keys were on the counter in the kitchen in my dorm and I had no idea.

I shake my head as my tears threaten to drop once more.

You can do this, I tell myself. *You are stronger than this.*

With my little pep talk done. I give Mom a little wave and set off on my journey back to MKU.

I know that he's been discharged and is at home now. Harley has kept me informed of his condition, which isn't actually as scary as it looked when he was in that bed. He was lucky. So very lucky. But that doesn't mean he's going to be able to continue with life as if nothing happened.

Hopefully, that means I'll get at least a few days to find my footing once again before I need to face him and tell him everything.

My hands tremble at the thought of looking into his hard, angry eyes and relaying the hell I went through in the months following that party.

I know I made a mistake by not telling him as soon as I found out I was pregnant. But I was terrified, and every time I stared at his contact in my cell I chickened out for some reason.

I had a feeling that he wouldn't believe me, that he'd convince himself that I was just trying to trap him or something.

I don't bother turning the stereo on, I drive in silence with just my thoughts to keep me company.

Getting away this weekend was the right thing to do.

Not only did I need to put some distance between

Kane and me, but I knew that the Harris brothers would be after me.

He might not have said the words, but I soon realized that he was too angry just from me sneaking out in the middle of the night.

They'd found the cameras already and they knew exactly who had planted them.

My grip on the wheel tightens as I consider what the Harrises will do to get their revenge.

All I can hope is that Victor got what he needed before they found them or I'm in a whole world of shit right now.

Long before I'm ready to face reality, I'm pulling up in the parking lot behind our dorm building.

I kill the engine and stare out of the windshield at the students that are loitering around looking like they don't have a care in the world.

I blow out a long breath, wishing like hell my life was like that. I've forgotten what it's like to be a student with no worries other than getting assignments in on time.

I look up at the building and then down at my purse.

A part of me wants to message him, ask him if he's okay. But I know he doesn't want to hear from me. Hell, after the way he sent me away from the hospital, I doubt he ever wants to see me again.

He thinks that I—I can't even think the words.

I need to talk to him. I know Mom is right. But how am I going to do that when I already know he's going to refuse any attempt I make.

Feeling defeated by life, I throw my car door open and climb out.

Time to re-enter my life once again.

The dorm falls silent the second I walk into the communal area.

"Letty!" Ella hops up and comes over to hug me before I've even shut the door. Everyone else's concerned eyes burn into me. "We weren't sure if—when—you were coming back."

"I'm sorry I bailed," I say once I'm released.

"S'all good, right guys?" Ella turns to the others.

"Of course. Nothing to apologize for," West says, with a wide smile.

"How's he doing?" Violet asks with a wince, while everyone shoots her a death stare. "What? Am I not allowed to be concerned for a fellow student?"

Everyone ignores her and turns back to me.

"He's going to be fine. He's out of the hospital. I'm just gonna go settle back in." Their eyes follow me as I walk around the table where they were all sitting, enjoying their dinner, and pull my key out.

"It wasn't your fault," a soft voice says from behind me.

I pause in the middle of my room.

"It was though."

"Letty," Ella sighs. "Please don't blame yourself for this. He was the one who showed up here having it out with you."

"Yeah, because of me. All of this is because of me."

Kane is right. Everything is my fault.

"No, I refuse to let you believe that."

I drop my bag to the floor with a thud and lower my ass to the edge of my bed.

"How much of our argument did you guys hear?" I ask, my eyes locked on my feet.

"Not much. It wasn't very easy to make out the words through the door." The bed dips beside me and she reaches for my hand. "Whatever it is. I'm here. You can tell me anything and it won't go any farther."

I glance over at her, her liquid honey eyes hold compassion I've never seen on her before and I wonder just how honest she's being with me about what she heard.

"I really appreciate it. But it's still too raw."

"I understand, and that's totally fine."

"I need to talk to him. I need to explain."

"Just give it some time."

"He's never going to forgive me," I admit.

"I thought you hated him?" Ella asks, but there's no judgment in her tone.

"It's complicated."

"Isn't it always." She blows out a breath, making me think she's dealing with something herself right now.

"Do you want to talk about it?" I offer.

"I... uh... I slept with him again."

"Colt?"

"Uh-huh."

"But I thought he didn't do repeats."

"Apparently I broke the rule."

"So what's the issue?"

"Once he realized what he'd done, he kicked me out."

"Ouch."

"Right? It was cold. His swimmers were still inside me and everything," she deadpans.

"Oh my God." I bark out a laugh and when I recall her words again, my giggles only get worse.

I lose myself for a good two minutes laughing at her expense.

"Fuck, I'm so sorry, but I really needed that," I say through the tail end of my giggle as I'm wiping the tears from my eyes.

"I'm glad something good came out of it."

"Oh, come on. Don't pretend like you didn't *come* out of it."

"Okay, yeah. There was that. It wouldn't be so bad if he wasn't so damn good at it."

"You like him, don't you?"

"I like his cock, if that's what you mean."

I wrap my arm around her shoulder as she pouts, glad to be able to comfort her instead of the other way around. "You'll figure it out. If you're lucky, they'll win on Saturday and he'll want to celebrate."

"There's a party at the Delta house. Apparently, they're all going."

"Yeah? So you've got a week to figure out how you're going to show him what he's missing. Assuming he doesn't booty call your ass in the meantime."

"We should go shopping, get me a killer dress." Her face lights up and I can't help but feel a little of her excitement trickle through me as well.

"Sounds like a plan. Tell me when and where and I'm there."

"Yes." She hops up. "Are you going to be okay? I've got an assignment that I really need to finish for the morning."

"Yeah, I'm good. Thank you for this."

"Anytime. If you need anything, you know where I am."

I watch her walk to my door and she's almost gone before I call her name.

"Yeah?" she says with a wide smile.

"You heard, didn't you?"

She blows out a slow breath as she finds the right words. "I was standing right here ready to storm in and beat his ass for taking things too far." She gives me a sad smile. "When—if—you're ready. I'm right here." She blows me a kiss before closing my door behind her.

I thought I'd hate knowing that someone knew my secret. But as I sit there thinking about her confession, I realize that actually, it's like a weight has been lifted that someone knows. That she's accepted that I don't feel strong enough to talk about it. I have no idea what I did to deserve Ella in my life but I'm grateful because I think she's going to become a very good friend.

I shower and spend ages blow-drying and straightening my hair just to give me something to do so that I don't find myself in my car and heading to where I know Kane is. I curl up in bed with my laptop to go over a paper I wrote at Mom's this weekend for tomorrow.

I'm halfway through when there's a knock on my door.

"Come in," I call, assuming that it won't be him coming back for a repeat of Thursday night. Although when the door starts opening, I suddenly panic that I might be wrong.

"Hey, Ella said you were back," Luca says, stepping

into my room, closing the door behind him, and sucking all the air from the room.

He looks terrible.

"Luc, what happened?"

"This?" he says, pointing to his face. "Lee and I got into it."

"You were fighting? Why?"

He shrugs, kicking off his sneakers, pulling his hoodie over his head, and crawling into bed with me.

"Not important. Missed you," he murmurs, throwing my computer to the end of the bed and pulling me into his arms.

His scent surrounds me along with his heat and I immediately relax in his arms.

"I was only gone for the weekend."

"I know, but I only just got you back."

Guilt once again swamps me knowing that I had a hand in allowing us to go our separate ways for a couple of years.

"I'm back now."

"I'm sorry for Thursday night. I kinda lost it a bit."

He releases me, and I reach for his hand, vaguely remembering him punch my wall. Although, most of my memories of what happened after Kane disappeared is kind of a blur.

"Did you even clean this?"

"It'll be fine. You should see the guy who was at the other end." He smiles, but it's forced.

"Tell me you didn't beat the shit out of Leon because of me."

His eyes bounce between mine but the words that finally fall from his lips don't make me feel any better.

"Don't worry about us, Let."

"But—" He presses two fingers against my lips and shakes his head so slightly that I almost miss it.

I'm so lost in his sparkling green eyes that I don't even notice his fingers slip from my lips.

"About this?" he asks, his fingertip circling one of Kane's marks.

My temperature soars as I think about him sucking on my skin and I hate myself for it.

"What's really going on here? I thought you hated him." Luca's words are forced, his movements controlled as he waits for my answer.

"Um..." I hesitate, averting my eyes so I don't have to look into his kind ones. Ones that should make my blood boil and my body come alive.

Why couldn't it have been him? I ask myself for the millionth time.

It would have been so much simpler.

"I do hate him. There is nothing going on. It was an exorcism."

"It was... right," he sighs. His brows pulling together as he struggles to understand.

I get it. It makes no fucking sense in my head either.

"Is it... is it over?"

"It never started. It was... a mistake."

Luca lays down and pulls me with him until we're almost nose to nose on my pillow.

He studies me in silence for the longest time. Although I'm totally comfortable in his company, the longer it goes on, the more my heart rate begins to pick up.

"Scarlett," he whispers, lifting his hand to tuck a lock of my hair behind my ear. "I rea—" He stops himself and my breath catches in my throat.

"Luc," I breathe, desperate for him to continue but equally terrified that he's about to confess something that I'm not ready to hear.

His eyes drop to my lips as I say his name and his hand comes to rest on my waist. His touch heating me from the outside in.

He swallows almost nervously. It's a weird look on him because he always seems so sure of himself. After a second, his eyes find mine once more.

"I really hate that he did this to you."

"I gave as good as I got." The second the words are out of my mouth, I realize I've made a mistake.

His entire body tenses. "Motherfucker," he breathes. "It was you."

"W-what was me?" The thought of Kane bragging about what happened between us in the locker room with the team—with Luca and Leon—makes a shiver wrack my entire body.

"Fucking hell." He scrubs his hand down his face. "It was nothing. I confronted him and... it doesn't matter. Tell me you're done with him," he begs.

"O-of course. We've never been anything."

"So why?"

"Remember Riley?" When I first moved to Rosewood and met Luca and Leon, Riley and I were still together. We were for a few months until I realized that one, I had a mega crush on my best friend and was thinking about him more than my boyfriend, and two, the long-distance thing—even if it was only about thirty minutes—was never going to work. I'd left the Creek and was becoming a different person with an actual future ahead of me. "He was Kane's best friend."

"Oh," he says, not needing any more words from me to explain why Kane might have such an issue with me. "He blames you."

"For that and a few other things."

"Shit."

"Yeah, shit."

4

KANE

"Tell me you're not," Ellis begs the next morning after it's taken me about a million years to get my ass downstairs.

"I've got classes. I'm already falling behind."

He stares at me with his eyes wide in shock.

"You almost died."

"Over exaggeration much?" I mutter, pulling the chair out opposite and trying to sit down without showing him quite how much pain I'm in.

"If that truck didn't swerve, you'd be in a wooden fucking box by now. You were lucky as fuck that he only clipped your back end."

"I know," I mutter, wishing I had a better memory of that fateful moment.

I remember the panic, the fear, the anger that was driving me forward. But I don't remember anything past seeing the truck's headlights.

"Did the doctor say you could get back to it so soon?"

"I don't give a shit what the doctor said. I've got a few bruises. I've come off a football field worse than now and spent the night partying."

Okay, so it's stretching the truth slightly but there's no way I'm staying in bed all day and fucking up my first year at college before it's even started.

Feeling Ellis' stare burning into the top of my head, I look up at him as his lips part as if he wants to say something.

"Spit it out," I bark, irritated that he's holding back.

"W-what happened?"

"What do you mean?"

"What happened with Letty that you ended up driving headfirst into a truck."

"I didn't do it knowingly," I snap.

"No. But whatever went down was bigger than those cameras, right?"

I narrow my eyes at him, wondering where he's figured this out from.

"Micah," he says, answering my unspoken questions. "They all heard you screaming at each other."

My heart begins to race at the prospect of others witnessing what went down between us Thursday night. Of hearing what she confessed to me.

Who the hell am I kidding, I'm probably the last one to know.

The one person who should have been party to the truth about the fallout of that night.

My fists curl under the table.

I need to see her.

I need to hear the truth.

Let her confess all her fucking sins so I can decide what I'm going to do with her.

"What did he say?" I pin Ellis with a look that most would reel away from, but he sits firm, not intimidated in the least.

"Nothing, just that it sounded brutal."

You have no idea.

"It was a long time coming."

"So I'm assuming it was about Riley," he correctly guesses.

"Partly."

"Right. Well, I'm guessing you need a lift," he says, downing his coffee and standing from the table.

"Yeah, my car is..." I wince, wondering what state my baby is in. "Where is my car?"

"Fuck knows. Scrap heap. Sorry," he whispers the last word when he sees the color drain out of my face. "I guess that's something else you can blame her for, eh?"

"You think I should let it all go too, don't you?"

He's halfway across the room but pauses at my words.

"Kane," he sighs, looking back over his shoulder at me. "It's not my place to tell you how to feel and how to deal with it all. What I do know is that she never would have planted those cameras off her own back, and we need to know what Vic is playing at."

"Agreed."

"A little payback might be necessary,"

"You want to bug her dorm to find out?"

I jump at the idea initially, being able to watch her

when she's no idea that I am. But then my excitement vanishes the second I remember who else she hangs out with and what they might do in that room.

"Why not?"

"Because she isn't going to tell anyone shit about Vic. She isn't that stupid. I'll get it out of her."

"A little less dramatically next time would be ideal."

"I'll see what I can do." *It would have been fine if she never dropped that bomb.*

"I'm leaving in thirty. Need me to haul your ass upstairs?"

I look down at my sweats and hoodie.

"Nah, I'm going as I am."

"You look like shit."

"I'm aware. I feel it."

It's my own fault. All of it. But also, I've only taken half the painkillers the doctor prescribed because they knock me out, and I don't want to spend the next few days sleeping.

I need to get back to life. I need to see her.

I'm finishing my own coffee when Ellis emerges twenty minutes later with his bag over his shoulder, ready to go.

"Aren't the others in this morning?" I ask when no one follows him.

"Fuck knows, I ain't their father," he spits, marching through to the kitchen to grab some food. "Eat this, you look like you need it." He throws a cereal bar at me and I just about move in time to catch it, although my shoulder fucking kills as I do so. "Are you really sure this is a good idea?"

"I'm just gonna sit in class. It's no different than sitting on the couch."

"Suuure." He looks anything but convinced. "This?" He points to the bag I dragged down the stairs with me and when I nod, he throws it over his shoulder with his own. "Come on then, you don't wanna be late, or everyone will see your battered face when you walk into class. Probably best just to hide in the shadows."

"Fuck you. You're just pissed because even like this, I'm better looking than you," I mutter.

"Oh yeah, that's totally it," he deadpans.

By the time Ellis pulls up in the closest parking lot to the Westerfield Building for my American lit class, I'm regretting not taking more pills. But I refuse to show him that I'm struggling any more than he already knows. The second he kills the engine, I throw the door open and prepare myself for the pain that's about to come.

"What?" he says before I push from the seat.

"What?" I bark, needing to just get this over with.

"If... when." He chuckles. "When you see her, go easy. We don't know the whole story. Having us grilling her ass might be the last thing she needs."

"You're right, you don't know the whole story, so let me deal with Letty, yeah?"

His eyes burn into my back as I drag myself up from his passenger seat but I don't look back. I don't need to see the concern or pity on his face.

The campus is still relatively quiet as I make my way into the building and toward the auditorium for this morning's lecture.

Everyone I pass gives me a double take as if I've

suddenly sprouted an extra head. I'm sure they've all heard the gossip about what happened, the team—the Dunns—have probably made a point of spreading the gossip about me being out of practice and missing at least the first two games of the season because of this.

The auditorium is empty and still in darkness when I push through the door and step inside.

The overpowering scent of lemon floor cleaner mixes with the musty old wood smell as I make my way deeper into the room.

I've got my sights set on the very back seat, right out of the way and where I'll be able to watch everyone enter.

Lowering myself down, it takes me an embarrassingly long time to catch my breath after the energy it took me to get myself here.

I pull out my books before dragging the cereal bar Ellis threw at me from my pocket and ripping it open.

It's not ten minutes later when voices begin to get louder out in the hallways. In only seconds students begin filling the seats around me, ready for a new week to get underway.

As the clock ticks around to the start of class, I start to wonder if they're not going to show. Then a minute before class is set to start, the door opens and Colt, one of the guys from the team, steps in, quickly followed by the Dunns who are once again flanking Letty's sides.

I ignore them and focus on her.

Her hair is flawless, as is her makeup, but I can see everything she's trying to hide.

Her eyes are bloodshot and the circles beneath them are dark despite the makeup. She chews nervously on her bottom lip as she walks into the room, but she doesn't look up. She just lets Luca and Leon guide her toward a row of empty seats.

She isn't expecting me to be here. If she were, then I have no doubt she'd be scanning the room trying to find me. Needing to know where I might appear from.

It's not until she stops on the steps to allow Colt and Luca to walk down the row that she looks up.

I like to think it's because she can feel my stare, that I affect her just as much as she does me, but it might be wishful thinking.

But then her eyes lift higher and lock on to me.

She might be at the other side of the room, but I swear to God I hear a shocked gasp as her chin drops.

A menacing smile curls at the corner of my mouth in greeting. This right now... this moment, her shock, her fear. It makes all the pain of getting here so fucking worth it.

Leon rests his hand on the small of her back to get her attention and she quickly rips her eyes from mine to stare up at him.

The way she looks up at him makes my chest ache. I can read her like a book and the feelings she has for both Dunn boys are clear.

It makes me wonder—and not for the first time—what the reality is there. I've taunted her about fucking them. But has she? Do they really think they own her in any way? Do they really believe they could take her from me? And do they think for even one second that they could give her what I can?

Thoughts of the marks I left on her body make me

smile. If they've got anywhere near as close to her as I fear they might have, then they know. They know exactly who's capable of making her lose her mind. And it sure as fuck isn't them.

5

LETTY

My heart slams against my ribs as I allow Leon to usher me forward into a seat beside Luca, ready for our lecture to start.

Everything around me blurs as the scorching heat of his stare burns my back.

He shouldn't be here. He should be at home recovering.

But—

Fuck.

"Shit," I snap as my pens all clatter to the floor at my feet.

"Are you okay?" Luca asks, snatching up my trembling hand as I reach down to grab one by his foot.

His soothing touch relaxes me a little and I lean into him, needing him to wrap me in his arms and tell me that everything is going to be okay.

"Of course." I smile at him but he can read me better than to be fooled by it.

"Let, you're shaking."

"Too much coffee?" It's not meant to come out as a question. The second Luca hears the lie, he looks over his shoulder, correctly assuming what—or who—is suddenly affecting me.

He obviously doesn't spot Kane hiding in the darkness at the very back of the room.

His concerned eyes find mine and a ball of emotion grows in my throat.

I hate this.

I know I should just tell him the truth. But I'm worried about how he'll react.

Watching him punch the wall Thursday night, and seeing the evidence of him and Leon fighting because of me will only be the tip of the iceberg if they learned the truth.

I can't do it to either of them. College football has always been their dream. The NFL has always been their dream. I refuse to be the person who gets in the way of that.

"Here," he says, picking up the pens beneath his chair.

"Thank you."

His eyes bounce between mine as he studies me. He's got a million questions on the tip of his tongue. Thankfully, he doesn't get a chance to ask any of them because Professor Whitman begins our lecture and we're forced to listen.

Dropping his left hand to my thigh, he squeezes gently in support as he picks up his pen with his right and begins scribbling down notes.

His touch feels traitorous while Kane's eyes continue to sear into the back of my head.

Unable to stop myself, I lean over to Luca and drop a quick kiss on his cheek.

He turns to me, his smile meeting his eyes and making the green sparkle with something I don't want to acknowledge.

When I woke this morning, he was gone. In his place on the other side of my pillow was just a note telling me to call him if I needed him and that he'd meet me for class.

Although I missed him, I knew he'd done the right thing.

Something had shifted between us as he held me last night. He'd wanted to tell me something, I could almost read it, but I was terrified to hear the words I think he wanted to say.

If—when—he says what I fear, then it's going to change everything once again and I'm not sure I can cope with that.

I need him right now.

I need him to be the supportive best friend he's always been. There might have been so many times in the past that I was desperate for the line to blur, but for me, now is not that time.

I lower my hand to his for a beat and squeeze before focusing my attention back on our professor. I do my best not to waste the entire lecture on thoughts of the guy sitting behind me

Before I know it, the low tones of Professor Whitman have stopped, although I've barely heard a word.

I groan as I pack away my books and pens.

"You okay?" Leon asks.

"Great. Best day of my life," I deadpan.

"Aw, we'll buy you a cupcake to make up for it."

I smile at him in the hope it rids him of the concern in his eyes. "That sounds amazing. Thank you."

"Let, what are you doing?" Luca asks as he stands, and I don't follow. Leon and Colt are already halfway down the stairs heading for the doors with the masses. I, however, ensured I hung back a little.

"I just need a minute."

"But—"

"Luca, please. I'm coming for coffee. I'll just meet you there."

His eyes plead with me to just leave with him and just when I think he's going to agree. He looks up. And this time I know he hasn't missed Kane.

"Scarlett," he growls, his jaw popping in anger.

"It's okay, Luc."

"Nothing about this is okay. Look what he did to you, how he treated you."

"He isn't going to touch me. We just need to talk."

Luca stares down at me, his nostrils flaring, the muscle in his neck pulsating.

"Luc," I whisper.

"I'll be right outside the door. Leon too. If you need us, shout and we'll take the motherfucker out."

I smile at him, appreciating his need to protect me even if it is a little suffocating.

'Thank you,' I mouth as he swings his bag over his shoulder and backs away from me.

Before he's forced to turn around, his eyes lift to what

I can only assume are a pair of furious blue ones behind me.

With his silent warning hanging in the air, Luca reluctantly leaves with the last of the students.

The second the door is closed leaving only the two of us in here, I struggle to breathe.

Silence rings out for the longest time but I can't find it in me to turn around, to do anything.

"What are you doing, Princess?" His deep voice echoes around the vast space and I jolt as it hits me right in the chest.

"We need to talk." I have no idea if he hears me because it comes out quiet and weak and I hate it.

"No, you need to leave. I can't even look at you," he spits.

Affronted by his words, I hop up out of my chair and storm to the aisle.

The second my eyes land on him, I gasp.

He's no longer sitting in the shadows, hiding from the world. He's standing at the very top of the stairs, holding on to the nearest chair as if it's his lifeline.

The bruising that I remember from the hospital down the side of his face is still dark and angry, but that's the only visible sign of what he went through.

"Where's your sling? Your arm—"

"Is fine," he barks, the words echoing around the room.

I want to argue with him but I know it's pointless.

Slowly he starts to descend, and when I say slowly, I really mean it.

Pain twists his features to the point that I feel it for

him. But I know he won't welcome my help. So, instead, my grip on my bag tightens, my nails digging into the leather strap over my shoulder.

My breathing becomes more labored the closer he gets and my muscles ache for me to run. But I refuse to.

Nothing he can say or do to me can hurt as much as what I've already been through.

The moment he's in front of me, his arm flies out faster than I gave him credit for and his hand wraps around my throat.

He leans me back so that his grip is the only thing that's stopping me from going tumbling down the stairs.

I swallow nervously, a move he doesn't miss if his wide smile is anything to go by.

My eyes beg him to let me talk, to hear me out so that I can tell him the truth but I fear that even if I did say the words right now that he wouldn't even hear them. He's too angry.

"Kane?" I manage to force out through his tight grip.

He leans over me, his cold, hard eyes piercing mine. And even with his anger, his touch might turn me on, but at this moment, I think I'm more scared of him than I've ever been.

He looks possessed. And the bruise sure doesn't help.

"It doesn't need to be like this," I whisper when his fingers release my throat a little.

"Well maybe you should have thought about that before."

With seemingly little effort, he pushes me backward down the stairs.

I can almost feel his pain with every step he takes, it's

right there in his eyes and I suspect he's totally unaware that I can read it in him.

I shriek in shock when my back hits the wall. We're so close to the door that I fear Luca and Leon might burst through at any moment.

I don't want any of them fighting. It's bad enough they've gone up against each other because of this.

Kane lowers his face to mine. For a moment, I think he's going to kiss me. My blood heats and a surge of desire hits my lower stomach.

It doesn't matter how much I hate him, how much he tells me he hates me. This heat, this chemistry is always between us, just simmering under the surface and waiting to explode.

But he doesn't make a move for my lips, instead, the scruff on his jaw scratches against my cheek before his warm breath coats my ear.

"You're a liar, Princess. A liar and a murderer. And you are going to fucking pay."

"Kane, no, I didn't—"

He pulls back and the look in his eyes immediately stops my words. A shiver races through my body. He's terrifying.

"I'm done with you. And I hope you know what's coming next is worse. Because when Victor catches up with you, he'll make me look like a fucking puppy."

My blood turns to ice at just the mention of his name.

"We're done, Princess."

He releases me and I sag against the wall, my weak legs only just holding me up.

Taking three huge steps back, he keeps his eyes on me as he moves to the door.

"So that's it? You're just going to forget all about this? Feed me to the devil and let him do your dirty work?"

His eyes flash with something I can't read but his lips twist with evil intent.

"Watch your back, Hunter," he warns, walking to the door and ripping it open.

Luca stumbles into the room, clearly trying to listen to everything.

"Keep your fucking dogs on a leash," he spits, stepping around Luca and marching for the door.

"Fuck you, Legend. You need to be the one watching your back. If I hear you threaten my girl again then I'll—"

Kane spins back around and pins Luca with his death stare. "Then you'll what, pretty boy? Huh, what are you really going to do?"

Luca's chest puffs out, his fists curling as he prepares to fight.

"Luc, no," I cry, racing toward him before he manages to take a swing at Kane. "You're better than him," I whisper, my hands wrapping around his bicep in the hope my touch cools him off a little.

Kane's eyes drop to where I'm touching Luca, his lips purse in frustration.

"You're welcome to her," he spits, tilting his chin in my direction. "Be warned, I've already ruined the whore."

The roar that rips from Luca's mouth is like nothing I've ever heard before.

Racing around him, I press my hands to his chest.

"Leave it, Luc. Please."

His chest heaves, his nostrils flare as he stares at Kane.

"You deserve better than that, Let," he seethes.

"He's baiting you and you're playing right into his hands."

Looking over my shoulder, I find Leon who's barely restraining himself and finally Kane with a smug as fuck smirk on his face.

"You won't listen to me, then fuck off and leave me alone. You're right, Kane. We are done."

Reaching for Luca's hand, I slip my fingers through his before grabbing Leon's when I reach him.

"Think what you want of me, it makes little difference to my life what your opinion is. Especially when we all know the only cunt here is you."

Before he has a chance to respond, the three of us move past him and out of the door.

"Holy fucking shit, did you just see his face," Leon booms as we get outside of the building. "I never thought I'd see the day but you, Ms. Hunter, just fucking gutted him."

"Kane doesn't care what I say. His heart and soul are black." But even as I say the words, I know they're not true because I saw the look on Kane's face just as much as Leon did. It takes every ounce of strength I have not to go back for him.

Ella: Where you at, girl?

I stare down at my cell as I sit with Luca and Leon in the same coffee shop they brought me to on my first day at MKU.

Tapping out a quick reply to get her to meet us, I sink down in my chair a little with my coffee.

Luca and Leon have relaxed slightly. I know that until I tell them the whole truth about what's happened with Kane that they're going to keep glancing at me with irritated and angry eyes.

I'm just hoping that Ella joining us will break the tension.

It's only five minutes later when the bouncy blonde appears at our table and pulls out the chair between Leon and me.

She looks at both of them, her cheeks heating before turning her eyes on me.

"How do you do it?" she whispers and all I can do is burst out laughing. "I'm serious. You're sitting here like it's just a normal day."

"It is," I say with a smirk.

"Hey, how's it going?" she says to the guys after ripping her eyes from me.

They both look at her with amused expressions on their faces.

"It's good," Luca says, making a point of dropping his eyes down her body.

Ella squirms under his attention and stares down at the table.

When Luca's eyes catch mine, he winks and shakes his head.

'Evil,' I mouth to him but he just shrugs.

"So... first game of the season on Saturday. You guys ready?"

"Puh-lease," Leon scoffs. "We're always ready."

"Ah, I forgot about the Dunn egos," I deadpan.

They both look at me with a smile, but I hear the unspoken words between them. They're now down a wide receiver. Despite how much they both hate him, they both know he's the best one to be standing up there with the pair of them. Another reason they hate him. They need him.

Thankfully, talk of football and the upcoming season distracts everyone from the elephant in the room.

"You busy tonight?" Ella asks when Leon goes to order us more coffee.

"Just studying."

"Good, we're going out."

"Oh?"

"Violet won't stop rattling on about that new Zac Efron film. Thought we could go together. So dinner and a movie?"

"Sounds like a great date."

"Plus, Thursday we're hitting the mall for dresses for Saturday night. We need to look hot to celebrate the guys' win."

"Hell yes you do," Luca agrees, his eyes zeroing in on mine.

"Sounds awesome," I say honestly. I need this, something normal to take my mind off every part of my life right now that is far from it.

6

____

KANE

"You gonna spend the night out here?" Ellis asks, looking over at where I'm sitting unmoving in his passenger seat outside the house later that afternoon.

I glance at the front door, it feels like it's a million miles away.

I'm fucking wiped. I knew going to class today was a bad idea, but nothing was going to keep me away. Even the pain I'm now in.

"I might," I admit. Right now, it seems like the easiest option.

"So now you're willing to admit you're in pain," he mutters.

"What do you want? You want me to say you were right and I should have listened?"

"It's a start." He climbs from the car and slams the door behind him.

I expect him to leave me there, but I should know better because Ellis isn't Ezra or Devin, he's softer.

"Come on then, asshole," he demands after ripping open my door and reaching in for me.

"I'm fine. I can do it."

He stares at me with his brow raised.

"Okay, fine," I conceded and allow him to assist me from the car.

I groan half in pain, half in relief the second I fall onto my bed. I feel like I could sleep for a year after today.

"I'll bring you up some dinner and your meds."

"It's fine," I argue. "I'll just lay here for a bit then I'll come down."

His lips part to argue but he decides against it and backs out of the room.

The second he's gone, I close my eyes and let the pain wash through me, letting it ground me.

The sight of her walking away from me earlier with them on either side of her plays on repeat in my mind.

I should have fought harder but the truth of it was, I didn't have the strength.

It took everything I had to go up against her, and I was crashing faster than I could control.

I hate that it made me look weak. I hate that they saw exactly how I was feeling when she got the final word and walked away from me.

I really wanted to believe the words I spat at her, that we were done, but fuck if they're true. We're not done. Not even close. And like fuck am I going to allow Victor to get his hands on her.

The only person who is getting their hands on Scarlett Hunter is me.

Just maybe not today... or even tomorrow.

I come around to the feeling of soft fingertips running down my cheek.

Letty.

My eyes fly open and I have to blink a few times to get my head to catch up with what I'm actually seeing.

"What the—"

"I heard you needed a nurse."

My entire body locks up as her fingers run down my neck and over my shirt-covered chest.

"I'm fine, thanks."

"Oh come on, sweetie," she purrs in her annoying high-pitched voice. "You know I can make you feel so much better."

"You shouldn't be here, Alana."

Her cool hand cups my cheek as she stares into my eyes. "Aw, do you need more meds?"

"No, I need—"

"Food? I can go and make you something."

"No, I need to be alone. You should go."

Looking away from her, I focus my attention on the wall instead.

"But—"

"I don't need anything from you, Alana. We're not a couple. You're married and should be with your husband."

"He doesn't want me and you know it," she spits. "But we could—"

"No. That is not what this is. You need to go."

Her lips part in shock but she swallows down

whatever her next argument is. "Okay, fine. If you need me, you know where I am."

She stands from the bed and walks to the door. It's only now I notice what she's wearing. Her little nurse's outfit barely covers her ass. The sight does nothing for me.

If it were on someone else, however... I shake the thought from my head.

"K?"

"Yes," I grit out when she's half out the door.

"Who's Letty?"

My chin drops at her question and my body heats. Why does she know her name?

"No one, why?"

She shakes her head. "No reason, you just said her name in your sleep."

"Huh, weird." *Or not, seeing as I was wishing you were her.* "Later," I say, looking away once again in the hope it makes her leave.

Her footsteps ring out in my silent room as she races down the stairs. Thankfully, seconds later, the sound of the front door slamming makes everything rattle around me. I guess that explains how she feels about my dismissal then.

I have no idea what she was expecting though.

We're not a couple. We've never been a fucking couple.

I've only ever done my fucking job. It's just a shame she can't see it for what it is.

It takes longer than I want to admit to talk myself into

crawling out of bed, but eventually my growling stomach forces me to move.

I glance at the bathroom door as I pass, desperate for a shower but know I don't have it in me. Instead, I head for the hallway in the hope of finding some food.

When I finally get downstairs, I find Devin, Ezra, and Ellis sitting around takeout pizza boxes.

"Which one of you fucking assholes let her in?" I bark the second I walk into the room, keeping my eyes trained on each of them instead of the food I'm desperate for.

"Nah, man. Don't look at me," Devin says, holding his hands up in surrender.

I ignore Ellis because this has his twin's name written all over it.

"What?" he says as if he can't believe I'd have an issue with this. "Did you not fucking see her?" He lifts his hands, mimicking her breasts as Ellis slaps him on the back of the head. "What was that for?"

"You're a pig."

"Wha—fine. If you can't appreciate a fine piece when it's in front of you, not my problem."

"I don't want her here. You got that?"

"Them meds are making you cranky. You should have considered letting her at least blow you before you kicked her ass to the curb. Ow." Ellis hits him again. "I'm just saying, you're tense as fuck."

"I don't want her anywhere near my junk. You," I say, pointing directly at Ezra. "Don't go anywhere fucking near her either."

"I know, I know, you don't share your toys unless you're involved."

"One time, Ez. One fucking time."

I roll my eyes at him and snatch the pizza box from his lap, lifting a slice to my mouth.

"You fuck—"

"Eat shit."

Ellis smothers a laugh, but Devin throws his head back and laughs at the dejected look on Ezra's face.

I spend the night shooting the shit with the guys and beating Devin's ass on the Xbox.

No one mentions the elephant in the room that is Letty and the cameras and I couldn't be more grateful, not that it means she's far away from my mind.

She's always there. Always has been.

But the less I think about the fallout from all of this with Victor, the better.

We still have no idea what he was trying to achieve with his little spying mission. I guess we can only hope that he got what he needed and has fucked off for a while.

Dread sits heavy in my stomach that whatever it is has something to do with Reid and his questioning of the guys but I don't want to bring that up with them. Devin told me he's having issues with shipments, whereas Reid thinks there's a supply issue here at MKU.

Whatever the problem is, it's really none of my fucking business.

Only it is because he got Letty involved.

I shake the thought from my head, excuse myself before I let my mouth run away with itself, and head up to bed.

"You know, your bed would have been nice and warm had you let her stay."

"I'd rather sleep in the fucking yard," I mutter, dumping my glass in the kitchen sink and heading for the stairs.

"You're pissy when you're not getting laid. You should call Let—ow. For fuck's sake, stop doing that," he bitches at Ellis.

"Well then stop running your fucking mouth. Kane knows what he's doing. And if he needed to get laid, then he fucking would. It's not like he's short of offers."

"Unlike you."

"Shut the fuck up."

I walk away before they start fighting and Devin and I have to drag them off of each other. I don't have the energy or the patience for that shit.

Despite the fact I'm exhausted, I spend hours staring up at my ceiling, every inch of my body aching like I've spent the day in the ring with Devin, or worse, Reid.

I should have taken the painkillers and allowed them to knock me out, but I hate feeling out of control.

I run the events of the day through my mind, remembering the look on Letty's face when she pleaded with me to hear her out, to let her tell me the truth.

But what good can come of the truth?

Our baby doesn't exist because she didn't deem it worthy enough to live. Didn't deem me worthy enough of being its father.

The sun is almost up when I do finally crash and when my alarm goes off for class. Ellis pops his head in to see if I'm ready, I tell them both to shut the fuck up and turn back over—albeit slowly—and pass back out again.

When I finally surface, I'm in more pain than I was

when I woke in the hospital. I have no choice but to take some of the medication prescribed to me in order to just get my ass in the shower.

I skip both my lectures on Tuesday. I know I've got no classes with Letty on Wednesday, I find I'm unable to drum up the motivation to get my ass out of bed then either.

When I finally leave the house again, it's for our statistics class Thursday morning Thank fuck, I'm beginning to feel a little more alive by then.

I follow Ellis out of the house and my heart sinks when I find the space where my beloved Skyline should be parked.

I've had her since I was fifteen. I started running jobs for Victor after our parents died when I was fourteen. Around a couple of months after, Letty decided that my best friend was the boy for her. That's when I saved every penny I earned to buy that car.

I guess it makes sense that Letty was the one to ruin that for me as well.

The reasons to hate her just keep stacking up.

My fingers clench as I imagine wrapping them around her throat again like I did on Monday. It physically hurt me to do it then, but today, I'm stronger, and tomorrow even more so.

The next time she finds herself alone with me, things aren't going to be so easy for her.

My blood heats just thinking about the things I want to do to her. The ways I want to make her pay, hurt her, punish her.

She might want to talk, explain, try to weasel her way out of it, but that is not what's going to be happening.

I don't get to class early today, I don't hide in the shadows. Instead, I walk in late, making sure that every motherfucker knows that I'm there.

She tried to ignore me when I finally walked into statistics first thing, but I felt her stare no matter how hard she tried to hide it as I walked past her to find a seat.

But it's nothing compared to our afternoon class when both Luca and Leon turn their hate stares on me the second I enter.

They follow my every move as I find a seat that gives me the perfect view of the three of them, or more importantly, Luca's hand on Letty's thigh.

My chest tightens at the sight.

Luca's entire body is rigid, his other hand on the desk clenching as if he's preparing to fight for his girl.

Pfft. His girl.

He has no fucking clue. But he will.

He might be able to cast aside the marks I'm sure he's discovered on her body by now this time. But next time, I'll make goddamn sure that he knows she's mine. Him and every other motherfucker in this place.

Because Scarlett Jada Hunter belongs to me.

7

LETTY

I want to say that classes without Kane's eyes burning into the back of my head make everything easier.

But they don't.

Instead of worrying about what he might do or say next, all I do is worry that something is wrong. That the doctors missed a concussion or something and he's back in the hospital.

My cell burns a hole in my pocket the entire time. It would be so easy to message him asking if he's okay, if he needs anything. But I already know he doesn't want that. He isn't going to make it that easy.

If I'm going to get the chance to talk to him, I need to be more clever than that.

"He'll be okay," Ella says as we walk through campus to our morning classes.

"W-what?" I ask

"Let, you don't need to pretend with me. I'm not the

twins. I'm not going to go and try to break his nose if you so much as mention his name."

"I'd kinda like to see you try," I mutter, thinking of her tiny fists swinging around.

"Not the point. If you want to talk about him, about what happened, you're allowed. Judgment-free zone, remember."

"I know, I just..."

She reaches over and wraps her arm around my shoulder. "I know. And he'll be fine, and one day soon you'll get to tell him everything."

"He doesn't want to hear it."

"He will. Just give him time. He dove off the deep end pretty bad last week. Things can't always be fixed overnight, Let. And sometimes they're worth waiting out."

"You're saying you think he's worth it?"

She shrugs. "I mean, all the clues point toward him not being. But, I know as well as anyone that when it comes to love, our heart doesn't always care."

"L-love?" I stutter.

"You like him, Letty. I see the way you look at him, and the way he gazes at you when he thinks no one is watching. Under all that simmering hate, is something so much deeper."

"No, you're wrong," I state full of confidence.

"Maybe. Only time will tell. Subject change?" she asks with amusement as Luca and Leon step around the building, both of their faces brightening at the sight of us. "And then there's these two. Scarlett Hunter is just unknowingly breaking hearts all over the place," she whispers.

I shoot her a stare before I'm swallowed up in strong arms.

"Ella." Leon nods in greeting and her entire face burns red. For someone who claims to know about matters of the heart, she sure is a goof around a good-looking boy.

"We picked you up a coffee," Luca says, releasing me and passing me the cup I didn't notice in his hand.

"Aw thank you, you didn't have to. I know how busy you are with—"

He presses two fingers to my lips and quirks a brow.

"If I want to get you coffee, I'll get you a coffee, Let."

"Thank you," I whisper, taking it from him when he hands it over. My heart constricts as our fingers brush because I just don't feel the same spark as I do when Kane and I connect. I'd give anything for it to happen with either of these boys.

They make so much more sense. They'd treat me right, love me right.

But my heart doesn't beat for them.

Only for him.

And I hate myself for it.

"You ready to get to work?" Luca asks after I've taken an awkward sip of my too-hot coffee.

"Yes, let's do it."

We say goodbye to Ella and Leon who head off in a different direction and the two of us walk toward the Baskerville Building.

We've only taken two steps when Luca's fingers brush mine and then grip my hand tightly.

I look up at him, feeling his eyes on me, and smile,

although I don't really feel it as I once again beg for that fire to erupt at his touch.

The hate stares I feel from all the girls loitering around campus burn hotter as we walk together.

"You're aware of how many hearts you're breaking right now, right?" I ask, trying to defuse the tension that's fallen between us.

"I don't give a shit about them. You, on the other hand"—he tugs me into his body as we step inside the building—"I'm worried about." He takes a step toward me and my back bumps against the wall.

"I-I'm fine," I stutter as his mesmerizing green eyes stare down into mine.

"Did you even sleep last night?" he asks, lifting his hand so his palm cups my cheek. The warmth is welcome. It settles me in only the way my best friend's touch can.

I shrug. "A few hours."

His eyes search mine as if he's going to find all the answers he needs within them. He could always read me so well back in high school. But after everything, I learned how to shut everything down, close myself off so I could look like I was surviving while inside everything was crumbling faster than I could control.

"I wish you'd talk to me, Let. I'm right here."

"I know," I force out through the lump in my throat.

I want to tell him everything, I do. But he'll go straight to Kane and... I can't let that happen.

The weight of my secrets press down on me as his eyes plead with me to tell him everything.

He drops his forehead to mine and my eyes fill with tears.

"I just want to help."

I nod, unable to say anything with the emotion clogging my throat.

"Want me to come over after practice tonight, help you get some sleep?"

He knows as well as I do that I sleep better in his arms. It's just something neither of us needs to get used to.

But despite knowing that, a very different answer falls from my lips.

"Okay."

A smile twitches at his lips for a beat before it properly emerges and lights up his eyes.

"Everything will be okay, Let. I'm here, whatever you need. All you need to do is ask."

"Don't you have some other girl's bed to be in?" I ask after a few seconds.

I know Luca's reputation, I have for years. Back then, it used to bother me. I wanted to be his one and only. Now though, monopolizing his time, stopping him from getting what he needs, has guilt surging through my body.

"No," he states firmly.

I swallow down the lump that jumps back into my throat at the unspoken words I can once again read in his eyes.

"Come on, we're going to be late."

After a quick kiss to my forehead, he steps back, taking my hand once more and tugging me toward my statistics class.

West and Brax are lingering outside the room while other students file in.

Luca nods at them, telling me all I need to know about why they're waiting.

It's not unusual for them to be my bodyguards, but the fact they're scheduling it now instead of letting it happen concerns me.

"I'll meet you after, yeah? We can go for lunch."

"Uh... sure." With one final squeeze of my hand, he nods once more at my new protection and takes off down the hall to his own class.

"Come on, girl," Brax says as both he and West thread their arms through mine and escort me into the room.

I know instantly that he isn't here. A long sigh passes my lips as my concern once again floods me.

"So..." West starts once we've found our seats. "You and QB1 were looking a little cozy when we walked in. Anything you need to tell us?"

"Nope."

Brax chuckles at my blunt answer but before I can say anything else, the atmosphere in the room changes.

I don't need to look at the door to know why, but my eyes move over without instruction from my brain.

I fight to keep them off him, to look like I don't care that he's finally emerged, but it's almost impossible.

The bruising on his face has reduced a little and he seems to move easier than he did on Monday. The concern for him that's been growing inside me settles as he walks across the front of the lecture hall and begins climbing the stairs to the side of us as Professor Richman marches inside and sets about beginning our class.

His attention remains on me throughout our entire lecture, although I never once look up at him.

You'd think that after having two days off, that he'd need to listen but I'd put money on him not hearing a word that's passed Professor Richman's lips.

The second we're finished, I pack up and get the hell out of class. West and Brax are hot on my tail as I push through the crowd.

As expected, when I emerge, Luca is already standing on the opposite wall with his foot propped up against the wall and his hands deep in his letterman jacket. His head is down, allowing his hair to fall into his face but his eyes are firmly on me.

"Looking good, Dunn," I say as I walk up to him.

"Oh yeah?" His eyes sparkle with excitement.

I roll my eyes. "Like you need me to tell you that."

"Luca," some girl behind me squeals, damn near pushing me out of the way to get to him.

"Hey," he says, barely glancing at her as she curls herself into his side and presses her hand to his chest.

"Sorry, Grace. I'm busy."

Luca's eyes remain on me as Grace follows his eyeline.

It amuses me how hard she has to fight not to let her eyes roll.

"I've got an hour before my next class. I thought we could—"

"I'm busy." He pushes from the wall and wraps his arm around my shoulder. "Hungry?" he asks, looking down at me and completely ignoring his jersey chaser.

Her face turns tomato red as she looks between the two of us. But then she looks over my shoulder and spots Brax and West, and her mood instantly flips.

Shaking my head, I look back up at Luca, remembering that he just asked me a question.

"Starved." In all honesty, I'm not hungry at all. Having had Kane's eyes on me for the past three hours, all I want to do is go and hide, but I know I won't be allowed to get away with that.

"Perfect. Pizza?" he asks me and then looks to the guys.

"Hell yeah," Brax says, wrapping his hand around West's upper arm and dragging him away from Grace.

He pouts as he trails behind us.

"Was that necessary?" he complains.

"Your brother has probably already tapped that. I didn't think you wanted his sloppy seconds."

"Brother?" I ask.

"Yeah, Colt is his older, better-looking, and more talented brother," Brax jokes.

"Shut the fuck up, man. It's all lies and Letty knows it."

I laugh at the two of them, wondering how I didn't see the likeness before.

"Where are we going?" I ask as Luca leads me toward the parking lot. Leon, Colt, Ella, and Violet are waiting there.

I can't help but laugh at the look of complete awe on Ella's face as she stands between the two guys.

"To a place off campus. Thought you might like to get away for a few hours."

"Yes," I all but shout.

"Come on then." He pulls open his car door for me

and I drop down as West and Brax climb into the back. The others pile into Leon's car and we take off.

Just before Luca turns the car out of the lot, I spot Kane emerging from the building. His eyes almost immediately finding mine through the window as if he knew exactly where I was.

A shiver runs down my spine, my blood heating from just that simple connection alone.

His face is sad and it makes me want to demand Luca to stop the car so I can talk to him. But I know he won't hear me out, he's already made that abundantly clear.

Ripping my eyes away, I try to focus on West and Brax's banter in the back seat. But it's hard to focus when my desire, fear, and concern all collide and send me into a tailspin.

"I am so ready for a bit of girl time," Ella says, her arms laced through mine and Violet's as we walk into the mall side by side later that day.

Our lit class was about as tense as I expected it to be with Luca and Leon on full alert in case Kane pulled any shit. But other than watching us, he made no attempt to talk to me or even get close.

Fine by me.

Even Colt seems to have joined in the *We Must Protect Letty At All Costs* club. I'm not sure if that's Luca or West's doing. It really could be either at this point.

But no matter how many guys I've got looking out for me, I fear it'll never be enough.

When Kane decides he wants to get to me, he will, no matter how many members of the football team are watching my back.

Kane doesn't play by the rules, he never has. He plays dirty, and he always wins.

Just the thought makes me shudder.

"So what's first, dresses or swimsuits?" Violet asks as we walk deeper into the colossal building.

"S-swimsuits?" I stutter, narrowing my eyes in Ella's direction. She never said anything about needing a freaking swimsuit for the Delta party.

"Hell yes, the Delta pool parties are legendary."

My heart sinks into my shoes. I don't want to walk around in an itsy-bitsy bikini.

"Oh... I think I'll pass on the swimsuit."

"Nonsense. Come on, we'll get those first."

I groan as the two of them draw me toward a store full of them.

"We are going to find you the perfect suit, Let. Those boys won't know what's hit them," Ella all but shouts.

I refrain from asking which boy in particular she's talking about because right now I don't want to think about any of them.

By the time we walk toward the dressing room with an armful of swimsuits each, I can't deny that a little of their excitement has started to seep into my veins.

Of course I want to be at the party. I want to celebrate the guys' first success of the season—because of course they're going to win—and if that means a few extra shots to get over my fear of showing off some skin, then so be it.

I can stand here wishing the past year never

happened. I can wish I was as confident about my body as I was when I first started at Columbia. Or... I can embrace the moment and enjoy the escape my new friends are offering me.

They usher me into a dressing room and both enter the ones on either side of me.

"Letty?" Ella calls.

"Yeah."

"Do the copper one first. I think it's the one."

I glance at the garment hanging from the hook before me.

I can't deny that it's stunning, and I suspect that she might be right. The color against my skin is going to look great. The only issue is that it's fucking tiny.

"Will do."

I quickly strip out of my clothes and pull the fabric from the hanger. The top takes a bit of figuring out with all its straps but once it's in place along with the very ass exposing bottoms, I can't help but stare at myself in the mirror with my chin dropped.

Holy shit.

"Okay, girls. Let's see the goods," Violet shouts, clearly ready to show off her first option.

The sound of both of their curtains being pulled back echoes around me.

"Letty?" Ella calls.

Sucking in a huge breath, I throw the curtain back.

"Holy fuck," Ella gasps.

"Girl, you're buying that," Violet adds.

"The Dunns will lose their fucking shit."

"N-no, that's not—" Ella pins me with a look that

makes my stomach twist with nerves.

I don't want them looking at me like that... do I?

"Those two are killer," I say, pointing at the two of them and their suits.

"I'm not sure about the color," Violet says, twisting this way and that in the mirror. "I'm gonna try the red one." She slips back into her dressing room, leaving me with Ella.

"You're getting that, right?"

"Do I have a choice?" I raise a brow.

"Absolutely not. But if you don't want to wear it tomorrow, I totally understand."

I look at myself in the full-length mirror once more, feeling my confidence beginning to grow. I'm glad that the majority of the marks Kane left on my body last week have almost vanished.

Without thinking, I lift my hand to one of the lingering bruises on my collarbone.

"You miss him?" Ella whispers so Violet can't hear.

Do I?

"I never had him to miss."

Her lips part to say something but she must change her mind because she remains silent for a few seconds.

"It's okay to miss something even if it never belonged to you. Even if it's just a memory."

Her words hit me like a fucking truck.

I know she knows something, but she doesn't know everything or just how hard those words hit me.

Tears burn the backs of my eyes and I fight to keep them down, not wanting to drown in the past when I should be focusing on my future.

I nod. I know. Although I'm not sure any of our memories are worthy of being remembered.

I quickly think back to an easier time, of playing on our bikes around the trailer park, of hot summers and wading pools and ice-cold buckets of water.

A smile pulls at my lips. So maybe they're not all worthless.

"You are getting that, right?" she asks, changing the subject.

I look back at myself and genuinely smile at what I see in the mirror.

"Yeah, I am."

"Confidence looks good on you, Let. I'm gonna try a couple of others, I'm not one-hundred percent on this."

"Okay."

I change back into my jeans and shirt, foregoing trying on the rest of the options I brought in here with me, knowing that none of them are going to compare.

We all pay for our choices before heading to look for three killer dresses.

Amazingly, in less than an hour, all three of us are swinging bags from our fingers. We laugh at the messages Brax and West are sending us demanding to get a sneak peek at the night's outfits.

"So you're telling me that you've all lived together for over two years now and none of you have screwed?" I ask them as we sit down with trays full of tacos.

"Nope. There has been no sexy times with the guys."

"Not through their lack of trying though." Violet laughs, making me think of Brax's more than blatant offer before Luca and Leon's party the other weekend.

"They're hot, I can't believe you've never even got close."

"Oh, there might have been close calls," Ella sheepishly admits before Violet bursts out laughing.

"Oh my God, that game of Twister freshman year."

"And that is the exact reason why Brax wants you. A shove in the right direction that night and he'd have just slipped right on in there."

Violet looks like she wants to argue, but after a beat, she just shrugs. "My skirt was way too short for Twister."

"And your panties covered nothing."

"Meh, good times."

"Seriously though, we're all family now. It's not like that with us," Ella says once she's finished laughing.

"So you wouldn't go there?"

They both narrow their eyes on me.

"No, why? Do you know something we don't?"

I think about Micah's reaction to Ella sleeping around in my first few days. "No, I was just curious."

"I would ask if you were into one of them but I think we all know you've already got more on your plate than you can handle."

I hold my hands up and laugh. "Guilty." It feels so fucking good to be out with two awesome girls who aren't judging me for what's going on in my life right now.

I really fucking needed this.

"Doughnuts to take back?" Ella asks once we've cleared our table and are about to make our way to her car.

"Is that even a question," Violet mutters. "The guys will disown us if we show up without any."

With three massive boxes of Krispy Kreme, we head back to campus.

I feel lighter than I have in a long time.

Scooting forward from my spot in the back seat, I poke my head between the two front seats as both Ella and Violet belt out Billie Eilish lyrics like their lives depend on it.

"Thanks for this," I say once the music has dropped out. "I really needed to just get away."

"Any-freaking-time, girl," Ella sings. "You still up for yoga Sunday?"

"Hell yes."

The guys practically pounce on us the second we step foot into the dorm.

"Back the fuck up, animals. We bought them, so we get first dibs," Violet announces, making them all do as she's told.

After taking one each, we let the starving men descend on the boxes.

I'm still laughing at them as I back toward my room.

"There's a little surprise for you in there," West says with a wink when he notices me making my escape.

My heart jumps for a minute, but then I remember just how protective they are and know for a fact that I'm not about to find the devil waiting for me.

And I'm proved right when I swing my door open to find none other than Luca Dunn sitting at my desk studying as if he lives here.

"Hey," I say, walking in and dumping my bags on the end of my bed.

"Doughnut?"

His eyes grow wide as they drop from mine to the plate in my hand.

"Um... yes."

"Take it."

"I'm not taking yours."

"Luc," I say with a laugh. "It's fine. We had tacos. I'm stuffed."

"Share?"

"Sure." Lifting it from the plate, I take a huge bite before passing it back to him.

My chin drops when he stuffs the entire thing in his mouth in one bite.

"And the girls claim you're sexy. They have no idea what they're missing," I deadpan as he chews.

"What?" he mutters, his eyes twinkling with delight. "Don't tell me you're not burning up for me right now," he says once he's swallowed.

"Oh yeah, my panties are melting right off me. You've got crumbs... everywhere," I say, waving my hand around in front of him because there are too many to just point out.

"Hmm..." He wipes them off and straight onto my floor. "So more about your panties." His eyebrow quirks in a way I know makes other girls swoon. I must admit, it does have an effect because my best friend is hella hot after all.

"Firmly in place, thank you. Check this out though." I rummage through one of my bags and pull out the barely-there swimsuit.

"Holy shit. Don't tell me that's for Saturday night."

"Might be." I smirk.

"Jesus," he mutters, running his hand through his hair. "Wanna give me a preview, you know, just so I can decide if it's actually appropriate or not?"

I hold the scrap of fabric on the end of my finger as I look like I'm considering his request.

"Nope."

"Can't blame a guy for trying."

He takes a step toward me and something crackles between us.

"Did you have fun tonight?"

"Y-yeah. Um... why are you here?"

"Ouch, Let." He covers his heart with his hand.

"You know, I don't mean it like that. I just wasn't expecting you to be here."

"Why? Got a booty call planned?" The second the words are out of his mouth, he must realize his mistake.

"No."

"Shit, I... fuck."

His eyes hold mine and my truths are on the tip of my tongue, but even still when I speak, they're not what comes out.

"You working on our lit paper?" I ask, sidestepping him to look at what he's got laid out on my desk.

"Y-yeah."

He snatches my hand and forces me to look at him. Heat races up my arm and it's enough for me not to pull away.

"I can go if you want," he offers, his eyes darkening in disappointment.

It's only then I remember his words from this morning

offering to sleep here so that I could actually get a few hours rest.

"Don't be silly. You okay hanging out on your own for a bit though, I need to shower."

"I'm easy," he says, tugging on my hand and pulling me in for a hug.

"Oh, I know, Mr. Dunn."

He barks out a laugh and I instantly feel better.

He falls back down onto my chair and I sort myself out and head for the bathroom.

My cell pings as I walk past my purse and I pull it out.

I have to do a double take at the name staring back at me because I wasn't expecting to hear anything from him.

> Kane: Spending another night with another man in your bed? You're a dirty little whore, Scarlett Hunter.

A gasp rips from my throat at his words.

"Everything okay?"

I glance over at Luca's concerned eyes and I force a smile on my face.

"Of course."

How the hell does he know?

I close the bathroom door behind me, my hands trembling as I lean back against it.

I thought he was done.

A silent laugh falls from my lips because a small part of me even believed it.

I'm such an idiot.

When it comes to Kane and me, I suspect it'll never be over. Not unless he kills me.

8

———

KANE

Letty's usual protectors are long gone as she walks into sociology Friday morning. She's just followed by one of Luca and Leon's minions, but he doesn't look like he particularly cares for the role of babysitter.

The second her ass hits the chair, her cell buzzes and she stupidly pulls it out.

> Kane: You seem to have lost your harem.

Her head twists to the side slightly before she catches herself.

Instead of replying, she locks her cell and places it on the desk in front of her.

> Kane: Now that's not very friendly of you. I thought you were all about sharing.

She glances at the preview on the screen and her shoulders tighten in anger.

Good, I'm getting to her.

> Kane: Put it wherever you want, you know I'm better.

She laughs as she reads this one and my over-inflated ego has the desired effect because she picks it up and starts replying.

> Princess: Not even you can compare to a Dunn sandwich. Enjoy your life, we're done, Kane.

She ends it with a middle finger emoji at the end and I can't help but laugh which earns me more than a few irritated glances as our professor continues on with his lecture.

> Kane: You're not calling the shots here, Princess. You're the one hiding all the secrets. We're only done when I say we're done.

> Princess: You did. Or did you forget already?

I cast my mind back to our hazy conversation on Monday but the fact of it is, I was so out of it and in so much pain that I can hardly remember anything. I know she was the one to have the last word and walk away though and that doesn't bode well.

> Kane: Doesn't count when I'm high on pain meds, because of you, I might add. We're not done until you have zero secrets, Hunter.

> Princess: I didn't make you drive into a truck, I NEVER MADE YOU DO ANYTHING. All of this bullshit is on you.

> Kane: You're a liar.

> Princess: Then let me explain.

I stare down at her words. I know that letting her do just that needs to happen. But I'm not sure I'm ready to hear any of it.

I look around the vast auditorium and suddenly feel as if the walls are closing in on me. My body heats and my chest starts to heave with my need for fresh air.

Fuck this.

Grabbing my stuff, I make the people sitting beside me move as I make my way to the end of the aisle.

The commotion I cause is enough to force Letty to turn around and look at me. The second our eyes connect, it's like someone's smashed me in the chest with a baseball bat. It's just another reason why I need to get out of here.

"Is there a problem, sir?"

"No, I'm sorry. I just..."

I march from the room, leaving the gossip behind me.

I walk to the parking lot on autopilot but when I get there, I'm reminded that my car is a fucking wreck and unless I call for a fucking Uber or one of the guys then I'm stuck.

"FUCK," I bellow, my voice echoing around the silence around me.

Deciding against leaving, I suck in a lungful of air and head for the coffee shop.

Coffee fixes everything, right?

I find an empty table in the back, hoping that I can hide for a bit.

I pull my cap down low and sink down but apparently it isn't enough because not ten minutes later does a shadow fall over me.

"Is this seat taken?"

Reluctantly, I look up, finding a familiar face.

"Yeah, it is."

"And lucky for me, they don't seem to be here yet, so..."

She drops her ass to the chair and rests her elbows on the table as she stares at me.

"Hi." She smiles, but it's forced as her eyes scan my face. "I don't think we've been formally introduced. I'm Ella."

I keep my face blank as I stare at her.

"Right?"

"I live with Letty."

I widen my eyes, hoping it'll encourage her to get to the point.

"R-right well," she stutters, her nerves starting to get the better of her under my stare. She swallows and squares her shoulder. "You need to sort your shit out."

"I'm sorry?" I rear back a little, unsure if I'm pissed off or impressed with her little outburst.

"Letty is my friend and you're hurting her with your games and bullshit. Stop it," she warns in her harshest voice.

A smirk tugs at my lips but I just about manage to stop it from spreading.

"Or what?"

"Or..." She blows out a long breath as she tries to come up with a threat. "I don't know, just stop it. She's been through enough and you're making it worse."

"Oh yeah, and what do you know about what she's been through?"

"Honestly?" she asks, slumping back in the chair. "Not much. But she's suffering, that much is obvious, and you're not helping her start over here."

"It's not my responsibility to make her life easier."

"And it isn't your job to make it harder, either."

Touché.

"You know nothing about what's happened between the two of us, so I suggest you keep your nose out of it." I sit up as if I'm about to get up and walk away. I want to, this chick is pissing me off. But there's a big part of me that wants to hear her out. Hell knows I'm not ready to do the same to Letty, but this might get me some of the information I need.

"I heard the two of you arguing the night of your accident."

"So? That makes you an expert, does it?"

"No, not in the slightest. It just tells me that you need to talk. She's drowning, Kane, and I suspect that you're the only one who can stop her from going under."

My lips part to respond but I soon find I have no words.

"And I think you are too."

"You're wrong," I spit, twisting to get up.

"You need her but you're too pigheaded to admit it."

"You don't know fuck all."

Our eyes meet in a battle of wills. She's begging me to admit that she's right and I'm pleading for her to let it go.

"Okay, fine. Keep living in denial without the one person who could make it any better."

"Great. I would say that this has been fun, but really, it hasn't, so..."

I stand, swiping my bag from the back of my chair.

I've got my back to her about to walk away when she speaks again.

"Talk to her, Kane. Find out the truth. I think you might be surprised by what she has to say."

I suck in a breath, a question on the tip of my tongue but I swallow down the words and walk away.

I don't want to talk to her friend about this, I don't even want to talk to Letty about this.

Reluctantly, I hang around campus until my afternoon class. Knowing it's business with Ellis makes it easier, plus once we're done, he'll take me home.

I really need to go buy a new fucking car. Is it fucked up that it feels too soon? I'm still grieving over my last one.

"Party tonight at the Kappa house. You in?" Ezra calls the second Ellis and I step through the front door later that afternoon.

"No," I bark, marching through the living area and straight to the kitchen to get a drink and something to eat.

"Oh come on, the Kappa's get the best pussy."

"Don't give a fuck," I shout over my shoulder.

"He's still in a pissy mood about Letty," Devin mutters,

"Fuck you, asshole. This has fuck all to do with her."

"Riiight. So, come and prove it."

"You're fucking with me, right?"

With a bottle of water and a sandwich from the fridge in hand, I come to stand in the doorway and stare at him.

"Do I look like it? You need to have some fun. Come with."

"No."

"Fuck, man. You really need to get laid," Ezra mutters.

Without instruction from my brain, my arm moves and a second later, my water bottle collides with his head.

"What the fuck, Legend?"

"You're coming," Devin states, standing from his chair and throwing his plate into the sink. "I'll even help you get dressed if it'll help." He winks at me and my fists curl.

"I'm not a fucking cripple," I mutter.

"Fucking drink this and quit your bitching." He passes me a bottle of vodka with the top already off.

I probably shouldn't have any with the pain meds that are still in my system, but fuck it.

Lifting the bottle to my lips, I swallow down two shots, letting the alcohol warm me from the inside out.

"Better?" he asks with a smirk.

"Fuck you." I punch him lightly in the shoulder, although he whines like a little bitch about it.

After drinking half of the bottle with the guys while we shoot the shit, I shower and get ready to head out.

Do I really want to party? No, not particularly, but it sure beats sitting here alone and being miserable.

The party is already in full swing when Devin pulls up outside the Kappa house. There are people loitering in the front yard drinking and having a good time, but I don't feel even a trickle of excitement that I should right now.

I'm at college. At a frat party. And I really couldn't give a shit.

My mind is stuck on her final message to me earlier along with her friend's words.

But then I remember seeing Luca at her dorm window last night as I left the library with Ellis and I throw the car door open and climb out.

She's clearly forgotten everything and moved on.

Eyes fall on the four of us as we make our way to the house.

I know exactly why. The Harrises have just shown up, which means the party is really about to start.

People don't even give them a chance to get a drink before they come over to start sweet-talking them. I have no idea what they expect. Handouts, maybe? But I really don't give a fuck and no sooner have I found myself a drink, I leave them behind in the kitchen.

"Kane Legend," a voice says before a delicate hand wraps around my bicep.

Looking over, I find the same blonde girl who stopped me outside of class the other week. I smile at her, but it isn't because of her, it's because of Letty's reaction to her flirting with me that day.

"It's about time we got a little more time together, don't you think?" She steps right into my body, pressing her breasts against my arm.

She's pretty, sure, but there's not even a hint of interest on my part right now.

"No, not really," I state coldly.

"O-oh."

"Is there anything you wanted, or can I continue?"

"I just want to get to know you a little better." Her fingers walk up toward my shoulder and I just about manage to refrain myself from slapping her hand away.

"I'm good, thanks. Have a good night." Shrugging out of her hold, I march toward the backdoor in the hope of escaping.

Why exactly did I think coming here tonight would be better than being home alone?

I get more than a few curious glances as I step down off the deck but thankfully, no one else tries to talk to me. If anything, they take a wide berth. Probably for the best. My fists curl at the thought of swinging it into some motherfucker's face.

Only problem is that the football team—our captain—isn't here seeing as it's the first game of the season tomorrow. They'll have been under strict instructions from Coach to be good little boys and go to bed early.

I find an empty chair and fall down into it, lifting the bottle to my lips.

My cell buzzes in my pocket. Pulling it out I see a message from Ezra, opening it, I find a video above his message.

Ez: You didn't waste any time.

I hit play on the video to discover a replay of what just happened in the house as whatever her name pressed herself up against me. Only, it ends before I shoot her down and instead lingers on me looking down at her.

"Fucking hell," I mutter, putting it back into my pocket.

I don't have the patience to deal with desperate jersey chasers tonight.

By the time my bottle is empty, I've got a nice buzz going but I'm still not in the mood to party. Not even a little bit.

Throwing the bottle across the yard, I watch as it shatters against the wall, making a few girls scream in shock but I don't hang around long enough to see what anyone does about it.

My body still aches with every step I take, but it's much easier to move than it was at the beginning of the week, the vodka sure helps too.

It's not long until the sound of the music behind me begins to fade and the darkness of the street beyond engulfs me.

When I finally drag my eyes open the next day, the sun is already high in the sky and my head steadily pounds while my muscles continue to ache. If I didn't know better, I might think I partied hard last night. But the truth is far from that.

The walk back here last night took me longer than I want to remember. I should have called a car, but the silence was welcome, so I just kept going.

I didn't look at my cell again for fear of the video blowing up. It looked bad. I shouldn't care. But I can't help thinking that Letty is going to see it. Again, I really shouldn't care.

With a groan, I roll over and shove my head into my pillow. What the fuck is wrong with me?

Reaching my arm over the side of the bed, I find my pants and pull my cell out.

As predicted, my screen is full of notifications from all the tags. Clearing them all away. I look at the time.

Almost two.

I fall back and stare up at the ceiling.

The game is going to start soon. I should be there in the locker room with the team getting a pep talk from Coach about starting the season the way we mean to go on.

They won the championship last year, and there's no reason not to go all the way this year either. Although it would probably help if I were there and not having a pity party for one in bed instead.

Part of me wants to go and experience the game. But there's a bigger part of me that just wants to hide. If I can't play, then what is the fucking point.

Instead of getting up and heading to the stadium to cheer my team on, I climb out of bed and go in search of coffee.

The house is in silence. No surprise there. I heard someone come in at some point during the night, but I have no idea if they're all back yet.

Shutting myself back into my room before I have to talk to anyone, I grab my laptop and set about doing some homework.

I get lost in my lit paper that's due next week and I

don't realize how much time has passed until my door flies open.

"What the fuck, Dev?" I bark, looking up to see him standing in my doorway with his eyes wide.

"What? You're not jerking off," he says as if that could be the only reason why I don't want him barging in on me. "Seen it all before anyway, man."

"What the fuck do you want?" I ask, slamming my laptop closed in frustration. I was so close to the fucking end.

"You need to come downstairs."

"Why? Is the house on fire?"

"No. Just... just do as you're fucking told for once."

"Alright, Jesus."

Climbing off my bed, I swipe my hand through my hair, pulling it back from my brow and I follow him downstairs.

"I swear to God if I have to help you clean up after some sex fest gone wrong, I'm gonna be really pissed."

"No sex fest. Well... not that happened here anyway. That girl who was searching you out last night was fucking wild though."

"I don't want to know."

"Your loss was certainly my gain, man."

"Glad I could help."

"Help?" he asks, sounding affronted. "I don't need your help to get laid."

"Whatever. What am I here for?" I ask, looking around the living area at nothing.

"Not here. Outside."

"If this is—"

"Just go with it. It'll be totally worth it, I promise."

"Fine."

I walk down the hallway toward the front door and throw it open. Trying to prepare myself for whatever bullshit might greet me on the other side.

It won't be the first time, or the last, that Devin will have pulled some bullshit prank on me. I know he's pissed that I'm moping about, but he needs to get the fuck over it.

Lifting my eyes from the doorstep, they widen in shock.

"Holy fucking shit. Is that—"

"Yep." I can hear the smile in his voice.

"Holy shit," I repeat, running from the house forgetting that I have no shoes on and the driveway is covered in fucking gravel. "Ow, shit."

"Here." Devin throws me a pair of slides that were by the front door. I slip them on before making my way over to something I never thought I'd see again.

I run my fingertips over the spotless gunmetal gray hood, not really believing what I'm seeing.

"Do you need me to give you a minute alone?" Devin asks as I continue walking around the car, my hand on the paintwork.

I ignore him, too confused to form an answer.

"H-how? How is this possible?" I look at the plate on the back. Yep, it's mine.

"You mean... you didn't organize this?"

"Do I look like I fucking knew?"

"No, you look like you need to get her in the garage for some private time together."

I flip him off.

"This wasn't me. I thought she was totaled."

"Well, clearly someone worked some magic because she looks pretty good to me."

I know the truck only hit the tail but Kyle told me she'd been picked up and was gone.

"Yeah," I breathe, continuing my tour around my car, focusing on the spot where I know the truck hit it.

She's perfect. As if it never actually happened.

The second I get to the driver's door, I pull the handle and climb inside. I suck in a deep lungful of the clean car smell and I can't wipe the smile off my face.

Maybe all isn't lost after all.

Closing my eyes, I rest my head back for a beat, trying to let this settle in.

Shaking my head, I find that Devin has slipped back inside the house, probably to give me the privacy he teased about.

It's not until I look to my right to check out the rest of the inside that I find a white envelope on the passenger seat.

Picking it up, I hold it in front of me but the second my eyes land on the writing, my hand trembles.

Letty.

9

—————

LETTY

I walk into the Delta house with Ella and Violet on either side of me, feeling better than I have in a long time.

I'm rocking the swimsuit under the black bodycon dress they insisted I bought. I teamed it with some huge hoop earrings, a small choker necklace, and ridiculously high strappy sandals.

I feel like the old me and it feels really fucking good.

Add the fireballs we had while we were getting ready and the buzz from the guy's epic win this afternoon and I feel like I'm on top of the world.

"Let's party," Ella shouts, throwing her arms over her head and rolling her hips as we get inside just as the beat drops.

"You two dance, I'll get drinks," I offer, making my way through the crowded house until I find the kitchen.

Grabbing three Solo cups, I fill them with vodka and soda before making my way back again and attempting not to spill them all over myself.

Heated stares follow me as I move through the crowds, I see a few faces that I recognize from my classes but no one stops me as I pass.

"Here you go," I shout to the girls as I join them in the middle of the living room where they're dancing.

"The team here yet?"

"Nope."

"Good, I love it when they arrive at a party after a win."

I smile, pride for what Luca and Leon achieved this afternoon, making my chest swell.

We drink and dance and laugh while waiting for them to make their entrance, but they don't seem to be in any rush to get here.

"I need to pee then we need to head outside. That pool is calling my name," Violet shouts, breaking away from us.

"We'll come with, right, Let?"

"Sure."

Dumping our now empty cups in the trash, we head upstairs and join the line for the bathroom.

Thankfully, it's quick and only ten minutes later, the girls are leading me outside.

"Oh my God, why didn't we come out here first?" I ask, looking around at the Hawaiian-themed backyard.

There are beach huts, a bar serving cocktails out of coconuts, girls—and guys—in grass skirts. The pool is almost full with students enjoying themselves as the same music from inside pumps through speakers that line the space. There are lights along the fences that run the length of the yard and then strung up in the trees at the end.

I look around, trying to take it all in, my chin dropped in shock. When they told me it was a pool party, this was not what I had in mind at all.

"Now do you understand why you needed a swimsuit?"

"Yeah, I get it." And I actually feel a little overdressed right now looking at everyone.

"Come on then, what are we waiting for?" Violet asks, placing her purse on the table beside us and peeling her dress up her body, much to the delight of some of the guys surrounding us.

"Take it off girl," someone calls and she immediately turns to the voice and wraps her arms around his shoulders.

A loud cheer erupts inside the house and a wide smile curls at Ella's lips.

"The guys are here."

In a flash, she has her dress over her head and is dropping it to the table. She doesn't get a chance to fix her hair because Brax and West come running out of the house and tackle her until the three of them go crashing into the pool.

I crack up laughing as they throw her around as if she's no more than a rag doll.

"Come on, girl. Take it off. Take it off," she shouts when they let her up for air.

Turning to me, both West and Brax join in her chant until almost everyone out here looks my way.

My cheeks heat under everyone's stare. I'm grateful for the alcohol that's surging through my system because it gives me the confidence I need to drop my purse to the table with Ella and Violet's and shimmy my dress down my body.

"Yes, girl," Ella cries while the guys whistle, helping me feel less self-conscious about showing so much skin.

"Holy fucking shit," a deep voice barks behind me, sending a shiver racing down my spine.

Spinning, I turn to Luca and all but throw myself into his arms.

"Congrats," I squeal in his ear, making him pull back a little.

His hands land on my waist, the heat of them sending my temperature soaring.

"Thanks, it was a good game."

"Good? You were on fire."

"You were watching me?"

"I always watch you at games, silly." I swat his shoulder. What else am I going to be watching aside from him and Leon? It's not like I actually like football.

It's not until the wall of the house hits my back that I realize he's moved us.

"W-what are you doing?" I ask, noticing that he's caged me in.

His eyes bounce between mine for a beat before they drop to my body.

My heart races at his attention, my previous blush burning so hot I feel it race down to my chest.

"L-Luc?"

When his eyes meet mine once more, the green has

almost vanished in favor of the hazel that emerges when he's excited, drunk or... horny.

My mouth waters and I quickly swallow, my body reacting to his proximity and clean manly scent while my brain tries to keep us in line.

"You need to get dressed." His voice is so low that I almost don't hear it.

"What? Don't be crazy, it's a pool party."

I look down to see that he's wearing blue and white boardshorts, proving that he knew exactly what this party was.

"I know. But you can't walk around like that."

I look down at myself and then back up to him.

"Don't you like—"

"Don't ask a question you're not ready to hear the answer to, Let."

He takes a step closer, his body heat burning my skin, as he rests his forearm against the wall beside my head.

"O-okay."

Our eyes hold, something I'm not used to crackling between us.

"Luc, man. Put the girl down and come and get a fucking drink," a voice booms from behind him, but I can't see who because he's hiding me with his huge body.

"Unless you want me to break some motherfucker's nose tonight, you need to put your dress back on."

"Stop being such a caveman. It's not even that small."

He shakes his head. "No, it looked small hanging off your finger. On your body, it's fucking sinful."

"Luc," the guy tries again and this time, he takes a step back from me to allow me to see who's waiting for him.

Colt rolls his eyes at his captain before I look over his shoulder and find Leon staring at me as if he wants to devour me whole.

This swimsuit was a really, really bad idea.

With one last look at me, Luca marches over to Colt who leads him inside. Luc stops very briefly to say something to his brother before they both look at me.

Luca disappears inside but Leon keeps his eyes trained on mine.

After a second, he moves toward me and allows his eyes to drop.

Right before he comes to a stop, he shakes his head at me, a knowing smirk playing on his lips.

"What? It's just a swimsuit," I say, throwing up my arms. "I'm not dressed any different than any other girl out here."

"I know, Cupcake." He pulls me into his arms and I welcome his support.

"You killed it out there tonight."

"I'm glad it looked easy, truth is, we were missing someone."

My breath catches at his unspoken words.

"Oh?"

"I might hate the dick, but he's fucking good on the field."

"He'll be back soon. He's too stubborn to stay away longer than necessary."

"Cheers, man," Leon says, releasing me and taking two drinks from one of the freshman team members I recognize as one of their personal waiters from their party two weeks ago.

"Thank you," I say, taking the cup from his hand.

"Come on, let's enjoy ourselves."

Taking my hand, Leon guides me toward an empty lounger. After I sit down with my feet still on the ground, he pulls me down to sit between his legs and wraps his arm around my waist so I have no choice but to lean back into him.

He might not have demanded I put my dress back on like his brother, but something tells me that being wrapped in him is having a similar effect.

No guys are now looking at me. As I glance around the backyard, I find that most have actually turned away. It's only the girls who are now staring daggers at me for taking one of their beloved kings away from them.

"I don't need a babysitter, you know."

"I'm just hanging out with my friend, there's nothing wrong with that."

"There is when you've got an ulterior motive."

"I—"

"Don't," I say, cutting off his argument before he even starts.

They might be a little overbearing but to be honest, I'd rather be sitting here with Leon than being hit on by any of the guys out here.

"Where have you been all week? It's almost like you've been avoiding me." His arms tense around me at the question. "Wait?" I ask, spinning around so I can look at him. "Have you been avoiding me?"

"No, I haven't," he answers honestly, holding my eye contact. "You don't need me to tell you that Luc and I got into it last weekend, I was just giving you guys some space."

"So you were fighting because of me." I sigh, remembering the bruise on Luca's cheek. "Because I kissed you?"

"No, Let," he says, lacing our fingers together. "It had been coming for a while. We just needed to let off steam. You don't need to worry about it."

"But I do. I don't want you guys fighting."

"We're brothers," he states. "It's what we do."

"I remember," I mutter, casting my mind back to all the times they ended up fighting in high school.

"You done?" he asks, nodding to my cup.

"Yep."

"Come on then, let's party. I've got a win to celebrate."

We dance, we drink, Brax and West finally get their hands on me when Ella mysteriously vanishes around the same time Colt disappears too. Leon's attention has been stolen by some redhead who's batting her eyelashes at him despite the fact he's clearly not interested.

Luca is sitting with some other members of the team, including my brother on the deck. His eyes burn into me constantly despite the fact I'm just hanging out with friends. Every time our eyes connect, something crackles between us, but at no point does he come over to join us. He just broods from his seat while knocking back drink after drink.

I finally manage to break free of the guys and after swiping one of the towels that are helpfully rolled up on one of the tables in front of the trees at the end of the yard. I dry myself off and step back into the shadows to watch everyone enjoying themselves.

There's noise behind me, but I don't think anything of it as West, Brax, Zayn, and a couple of his friends bomb in the pool soaking everyone who's sitting close by.

I'm laughing at them when I sense movement behind me but I don't get a chance to alert anyone because a hand covers my mouth as an arm clamps around my waist and I'm hauled back into the trees.

All the air rushes from my lungs as I'm slammed up against a tree and stare into an all too familiar set of blue eyes.

"Enjoying yourself?" he seethes, ripping his eyes from mine and dropping them down my body. It's dark out here so I doubt he can see much, but something tells me that he's been watching me and knows exactly how little I'm wearing. "Dirty little whore," he growls, sending tingles straight to my clit.

How does he do that?

I bite back my response. It would be pointless anyway seeing as his hand is still covering my face.

"I've been watching you—" *As I suspected.* "Letting *them* put their hands all over you."

I shrug and look away from him as if I don't care. *I don't.*

He steps closer, his heaving breaths fanning over my face and making my skin erupt in goose bumps.

His angry, cold eyes stare into mine as I hold strong. The alcohol in my veins is still bolstering my confidence.

"Why?" he spits. "Why did you do it?"

When he first lowers his hand to my throat, I'm still

thinking he means the guys back at the party, but they didn't actually do anything. It takes a few seconds for my brain to catch up.

Realization dawns as I remember getting a message this afternoon to tell me that his car had been delivered almost as good as new.

"Why not?" I ask, causing a muscle I rarely see begin to pulse by his temple.

"I don't want anything from you." His voice is low and gravelly, and I can't help but think he's trying really hard to hold himself back right now. His fingers tighten around my throat as his eyes drop to my lips.

Feeling sassy, I stick my tongue out and lick it across the bottom one.

"What are you going to do, Kane? Punish me and send me back to the party fully fucked over?"

A growl rips from his throat at my words.

"They already want to fuck me. Imagine the looks on their faces when I reappear after you've done me over."

I shouldn't be baiting him, but my mouth seems to have a mind of its own right now and I can't stop the words pouring out.

"Isn't that what you want? For them all, for Luc and Leon, to know that I'm yours?"

"Princess." His warning would probably terrify most girls, but I know Kane. He might be the one full of anger and wicked intentions, but right now, I hold all the power.

"So what are you going to do, big man?"

His hand reaches out, his fingers wrapping around the top of my swimsuit, tugging harshly at the fabric until it falls around my waist.

His giant hand roughly grabs my breast, kneading it in the most painfully delicious way.

"Oh God," I whimper when he pinches my nipple hard enough to hurt.

My core throbs for him as he continues.

"Did I say you could enjoy this?" he barks, pinning me against the tree at my back with his hips, allowing me to feel his hardness at my stomach.

"Kane," I moan as his other hand joins in, teasing me until I wonder if he'd be able to get me off from this alone.

"No," he barks. Although I have no idea what he's telling me not to do. Enjoy it?

Lowering down, he bites the side of my breast, making me scream as the burn from his teeth turns the entire top half of my body hot.

My fingers find his hair and they twist until I know it hurts. I want to say I'm holding him in place as he laves at my breasts, but I don't think I could actually pull him away right now if I tried.

"Oh fuck," I breathe as his teeth sink into my nipple. Pain blooms, my entire breast throbbing, making me wonder if he just bit the fucking thing off. But then I forget all about it as his hand pushes inside my bottoms, finding my soaked pussy.

"I told you not to fucking enjoy this," he murmurs against my breast.

"No, you didn't," I say between my heaving breaths. "Fuck," I cry as he pushes two of his fingers inside me. Rubbing at my walls and reaching up to find my G-spot. "Shit, shit, fuck."

His mouth latches on to my neck and he sucks hard

enough to break the skin.

"Kane," I cry as my orgasm crests, but before I get to fall, his fingers are gone and I'm being turned around.

"Hold on," he barks, and I reach out to hold the tree as he drags my bottoms down my legs.

My knees barely hold me up as his pants rustle behind me.

In seconds, he's kicked my legs wider and is running the head of his cock through my wetness.

A moan rips from my throat but I just manage to stop the plea that's on the tip of my tongue.

"I'm taking you fucking bare, Princess."

He surges forward before I've even registered his words.

"Oh fuck," I cry as my arms give way and my face flies toward the tree.

The rough bark grazes my cheek before he catches me, his fingers digging into my hips ensuring that he's going to replace the bruises that have only just faded from my body.

He ruts into me over and over, hitting me so deep it hurts but it only makes my release return stronger than ever.

"Kane, Kane," I chant.

"Don't. Fucking. Talk," he spits between thrusts. "All lies. Everything you say is lies."

"No," I complain, earning myself a strong slap to my ass.

"You think fixing up my car will make up for everything. Make up for everything you've done to me. All the lies, the deception, the pain."

"No, Kane. No, it wasn't—"

"Stop," he bellows, fucking me even harder until my orgasm slams into me without warning.

I cry out, although I have no idea what I actually say as wave after wave of pleasure races through me, turning my muscles to mush and making me lose my damn mind.

I'm vaguely aware of him tensing behind me before a guttural roar rips from his throat and his cock jerks violently inside me, filling me with his seed.

My heart jumps into my throat remembering the consequences of the last time this happened.

Tears burn my eyes as memories threaten to overtake me.

The second he's done, his hands release my hips and I collapse on the ground at his feet. Pain shoots out from my knees and hands but it's nothing compared to the agony that rips through my chest.

I scramble around, pulling my bottoms up and flipping over.

He's already dressed once more and staring down at me with menacing eyes.

"Stay out of my business, Princess."

"Like you stay out of mine."

He takes a step toward me, but if he thinks I'm going to cower, then he's going to need to think again.

A squeal falls from my lips as he reaches out and grabs me by the throat, lifting me from the dirty ground. His jaw pops as he stares at me before his eyes move to my lips once more.

"Kiss me," I growl. "I dare you."

"Fuck you," he spits, dropping me and storming into

the darkness.

"Holy shit," I breathe, my trembling hand coming to my throat where his fingers just were. "Fuck."

The sound of the party just a few feet away comes back to me and reality comes crashing down.

"What did I just do?"

It takes me a good five minutes to get my body under control enough to be confident that when I stand my knees won't give out.

I right my bikini, covering myself up, but I already know I can't just walk back like nothing happened.

I'm covered in mud, I've got scrapes on my knees and cheek and I'm sure red, angry marks all over my chest and neck.

Luca or Leon—hell, any of the team—will take one look at me and all hell will break loose.

In hindsight, it's probably not the best thing to do. But under the influence of alcohol and with aftershocks of that earth-shattering orgasm still making my limbs twitch, I turn on my heels and walk away.

The twigs and stones cut into my feet, but I figure it's the lesser of two evils as I make my way toward where I think the road is.

We're not that far from campus, it'll take me twenty minutes tops to get back. If I'm lucky, someone will abduct me and put me out of my misery before I get there.

Shaking my head at my depressing thoughts, I square my shoulders as the streetlights come into view through the trees and continue forward.

I'll just tell the others I got drunk and found a lift

home.

I pause, thoughts of my purse, cell, and wallet sitting on the table around the pool hitting me. But it isn't enough to make me turn back.

I wince as I step out onto the sidewalk. The ground might be more even, but the rocks cut just as badly as the twigs.

I hurry down the street and I swear I don't breathe until I turn the corner and away from the frat houses that line the previous one.

Pushing my hair out of my face, I hold my head high and walk with confidence I really do not feel.

The street thankfully is empty as I make my way past the houses. I have no idea what time it is, but many of the windows are in darkness. I look back over my shoulder. Their residents are probably partying in the house I just left.

The rumble of an engine makes my spine straighten. My heart rate picks up but I refuse to look over my shoulder in case I have to watch it come to a stop, ready to do or say something.

I know this area is full of students and finding a girl doing the walk of shame in only a bikini probably isn't the most unusual thing they've ever seen. But I could really do without knowing that anyone has noticed me.

Thankfully, the car passes without any drama, although I can only imagine there was pointing and laughing from whoever was inside.

The next time I hear a car in the distance, I panic less. Although I really should have been more alert because it slows behind me.

Assuming it's just a couple of guys probably making the most of ogling my almost bare body, I keep going.

Refusing to turn back, I pick up my pace when they make no effort to pass me.

My breaths come fast and my entire body begins to tremble as my thoughts about being abducted rush back to the forefront of my mind. But something tells me that I'm not that lucky. It's probably just Kane about to tell me that I look like a whore.

Deciding that the latter option is probably more likely, I keep going. A car door closing behind me is like a gunshot through my chest. I'm just about to take off running when arms wrap around me and I'm pulled back into a strong chest.

I scream, but it's muffled by a huge hand. A hand that I already know doesn't belong to Kane.

My arms flail around and my legs kick, trying to connect with whoever is holding me, but it's pointless.

He spins me around and I'm thrown into the back of a black Town car.

The second my eyes lock on the vehicle, my hackles rise even more. There's only one person who'd turn up in a car like that to take me.

The instant I look up, I'm met with the smug yet evil eyes of Victor Harris.

"Scarlett, what a surprise. You even dressed for the occasion."

I open my lips to respond but I don't get the chance because something blunt connects with the side of my head and everything goes black.

Everything hurts when I start to come to, but nothing more so than my head.

I try to open my eyes but they're so heavy, it's almost like my eyelashes are stuck together.

I groan as I try to fight the darkness that wants to claim me once more. But then someone talks beside me and I'm immediately awake.

"Dad?" I ask, forcing my eyes open and looking to my right. "Oh my God, Dad," I cry when I get a look at him.

Both his eyes are dark and swollen, dried blood coming from his brow, his nose looks crooked as if it's broken and his lips are split.

"What happened? Where are we? What is going on?"

My blood runs cold as I recall the last face I saw before everything went dark.

Victor Harris.

"I have easy access to people you love, Scarlett. You should never forget that."

His words from his car two weeks ago comes back to me.

"Oh my God," I sob.

I failed and now my dad is going to pay.

I try to move my arms and soon realize that they're bound behind my back, my fingers numb as I try to move them. I shift one leg and find that I'm unable to do that as well.

Fucking hell.

I hang my head for a second, trying to get my brain to wake up to really focus on what's happening here.

I look around the room but there's nothing to give me any clue as to where we are. The room is bare, the walls are gray and covered in dark stains. Stains I don't even want to look at, let alone consider what they might be.

There's one window high up on the wall to my left but it's been boarded up, not allowing any light in at all. I have no idea if it's still night or if I've been out long enough for the sun to rise.

Memories of how I found myself here have me looking down. I find I'm not just in my swimsuit but someone has pulled a dirty shirt over my head to cover me up. I'm not sure if I should be grateful or not because it smells like the last person who might have worn it could have died in it.

I shiver as I appreciate for the first time just how fucking cold I am. The bright spotlight that shines on both of us gives off some warmth but it isn't enough and before long my teeth start chattering.

"W-where are we?"

"I don't know." I fight the sob that wants to escape my

throat at my dad's cold tone.

I look over at him but he doesn't move. His eyes remain fixed on one spot in front of us, but when I look to see what's holding his attention, I don't see anything. That end of the room is in darkness.

"I'm so sorry," I whisper, my voice cracking with emotion.

"Y-you... you're sorry?" He turns to me for the first time, giving me my first full look at his face and I fight to not allow my reaction to show.

"Y-yes. This is all my fault," I all but cry.

"Oh, sweetheart. It's not, please don't think that."

"He... he gave me a job and I failed."

"He what?" Dad roars, his voice bouncing off the silent space around us.

"It doesn't matter now. He told me that if I failed, then he would go after my family, and here we are."

Dad thrashes against his restraints.

"Where are you, you fucking cunt," he screams, pulling so hard at the bindings at his wrists I'm worried he's going to rip his hands clean off.

I have no idea what mine are tied with but Dad's are bound tight with cable ties. Cable ties that are cutting into his skin and causing a puddle of blood on the floor beneath him.

"Calm down," I demand.

"Calm down? Calm fucking down. That cunt has my baby girl bound to a fucking chair." He looks at me, his eyes lingering on the side of my face. From how much it hurts, I hate to think how it looks. "And he fucking hurt you."

"I'm o—"

He pins me with a look that cuts my words off immediately.

"Get out here and face me, you fucking cunt."

I stare at my dad with my chin dropped. It's like he's an entirely different man to the one I grew up with right now. I think I can probably count on one hand the number of times I've heard him swear in my life but he's like a man possessed right now.

I narrow my eyes at him, studying him as spittle flies from his mouth and his body trembles with barely contained rage.

Do I even know my dad at all?

Heavy footsteps coming from the darkness that stops his shouting and after a nerve-wracking thirty seconds, he appears.

Fear races down my spine and Victor's eyes land on mine before they drop in favor of my body.

"That's a shame. I did love what little you were wearing."

Dad's chair rattles as he once again tries to break free.

"Calm down, William. You should be proud of your girl, here. It seems she's a chip off the old block."

Dad's eyes burn into the side of my head, but I refuse to look away from the monster staring at me.

"Let him go," I demand.

Victor holds my eyes for a beat before the skin around his eyes crinkle and he throws his head back laughing.

"Wow, Scarlett. You've got bigger balls than I ever gave you credit for. It's such a shame Mummy ran away with you when she did. You could have been a real asset to me." His eyes once again linger on my body and my stomach churns with disgust.

"Leave her alone. This has nothing to do with her," Dad cries.

"Oh but, William. It has everything to do with her. You see, it hasn't just been you that's screwing me over, but both of you. And you can bet your fucking asses that I'm going to get to the bottom of it."

"I've got nothing to do with this. I did what you wanted, I planted your cameras," I spit. "It's not my fault you didn't get the intel you wanted."

"No, but it did result in one of my best men in the hospital, didn't it, Scarlett."

"What's he talking about?" Dad demands of me but again, I refuse to look at him.

"Kane's accident had nothing to do with that."

"Oh, but it was. He was angry and you pushed him over the edge."

"His actions are beyond my control."

He tuts and shakes his head. "This seems to be a regular occurrence with you, isn't it? First Riley and now Kane. You're a curse, Scarlett Hunter."

Dad gasps but we both ignore him.

"So why did you come near me? Do you have a fucking death wish, too?" I smirk.

He chuckles, it's cold, evil and I feel it right to my toes.

"So..." he says, finally turning his eyes away from me and to my dad. "Daddy, did you want to tell your daughter why you're both really here, or shall I do the honors?"

"Fuck you." Dad spits in Victor's face.

He pulls a handkerchief from his pocket and wipes the spittle away before rearing his arm back and punching Dad square in the face. His nose explodes once again, sending a river of blood spilling from his chin.

"Stop it, please," I cry. "Stop it. This isn't his fault."

"Oh but, Scarlett. It is. You see," he says, taking a step back from my dad and pulling his handkerchief out once more to clean up his knuckles. "Daddy here isn't just a dumbass mechanic that he led you to believe. He's the one who runs most of my supply chain."

"What?" I ask, rearing back in shock. "No, you're lying. There's no way. No w—"

"I'm sorry, sweetheart." My dad's voice breaks through my shock and I sit there staring at him with my mouth hanging wide open.

"What?"

"It's true. I work for this cunt."

A growl rips from Victor's throat at Dad's words.

"It was never my intention but, fuck, some bad shit happened and I didn't have another option."

"But someone bought the garage, they paid the debts, they..." Realization dawns. "That was Victor."

An accomplished smirk appears on Victor's face.

"Dad, how could you?" I cry. He sold his fucking soul to the devil.

"It was that, or make you all homeless and I would never do that to my family."

"You let us go though. When Mom decided she was done, you just stood by and let us walk away."

"Okay, as fun as this is," Victor says, stopping

whatever else I was going to say. "You've both got a very important lesson to learn."

My body trembles with the silent threat in his voice.

"No one disrespects me, goes behind my back, tries to steal"—he stares right at my dad—"hurts my boys"—he turns to me—"without learning the consequences."

"I haven't stolen a fucking penny from you, Victor," Dad pleads.

He takes a step toward me, pulling a pair of pliers from his back pocket as he makes his way around my chair.

"No," Dad bellows, clearly knowing where this is going. "Don't touch her, please. Take it out on me."

"Dad, no. You just said you haven't done anything."

Victor hesitates behind us, although I'm confident it isn't because he can't decide which of us to hurt. He's a twisted motherfucker and he'd more than happily torture both of us without a second thought.

I know that many of the rumors that run rife around the Creek about his behavior are exaggerated, but they come from some truth, I know that for a fact.

Tears cascade down my cheeks at the thought of him turning his wrath on my dad when he's innocent. Victor might not believe him, but I do.

My dad would never have done any of this willingly. I believe he had no choice and did it for his family. That's the man I know. The father.

Victor moves and I watch every step over my shoulder as he moves to my dad.

"No, please. I'll do anything, please. Don't hurt him." Now that gets the sick fuck's attention.

"Anything," he snarls.

"Yes, anything."

His eyes run down my body as if there's no chair blocking my view from him at all.

"You know, as tempting as that is, I can get better whores than you at a snap of my fingers."

"Don't you dare talk to—argh," my dad screams as Victor bends, clamping the pliers down on one of his fingers.

"No, please, NO," I cry as Dad's body jolts in pain.

I don't hear the footsteps approaching as Dad's groans of agony fill my ears until he's standing before me.

My breath catches as my eyes find him.

I haven't seen him in years, but those years have been good to him, if you ignore the fact that he looks like a younger, hotter version of his wicked father.

"Enough, Victor," he barks, and Victor stills.

"What can we do for you, Son?"

"William isn't the answer. I've found the mole."

My lungs deflate faster than I've ever known as a huge rush of air passes my lips.

"Oh my God," I breathe, my head spinning.

"Oh?"

"It's taken care of." He nods toward his father and Victor comes to stand beside his son and second-in-command.

"Okay. Good. So, William is free to go?"

"Yes. I've been assured he was unaware of the situation. But we will be watching you," Reid warns my father. "Any more fuck-ups and you won't walk out of here so easily."

"And Scarlett?"

"I'll deal with her." His eyes bore into mine and the same level of fear shakes my bones as it did when his father looked at me.

I would be foolish to believe that just because he's younger that he'll be easier to convince to allow me out of this mess.

We might have gone to school together. He might be Kane's friend. But he has no loyalties to me and everyone in the Creek knows exactly what Reid Harris does to his enemies.

He pulls a blade from his waistband and steps toward me.

"Please, no," I beg as he gets closer.

Something akin to amusement shines in his eyes before his lips part a beat before they brush against my ear.

"Be fucking scared, Scarlett," he warns, his deep voice sends chills racing over my skin.

I hold my breath as he disappears behind me, and a second later I sigh in relief, bringing my arms around to my front and inspecting the damage on my wrists. Thankfully, they're in better shape than Dad's are, but it doesn't make me feel any better about this situation.

Next, he slices through the bindings at my ankles and pulls me to my feet.

My knees barely hold me up and if it wasn't for his arm around my waist, then I'd be a pile on the ground right now.

It makes me wonder just how long I was tied there and not aware of it.

"Let's go," he snaps, his harsh grip digging into my waist.

"But my dad," I cry.

"Your dad and I have things we need to discuss, *Princess*." Victor growls as Reid pulls me away.

"P-please don't hurt him," I beg.

"How about you just worry about yourself. My son knows exactly how to punish a woman, isn't that right, boy?"

"No," Dad cries, the chair wobbling so much with his escape attempt that it topples over, making his head collide with the cold concrete floor beneath him.

"No," I scream, trying to break out of Reid's grip to get to him.

"Let's go," he demands, lifting me into his arms as if I'm a small child.

I fight to get away but his grip is too tight and in the end, my muscles give in and I fall still while he carries me away from whatever fate my dad is about to meet.

Reid doesn't speak until we are outside what I now realize is the Hawks clubhouse.

Almost every set of eyes turn our way as he marches through the communal areas where all the members hang out. The fact there are so many still awake gives me my first hint that maybe I'd not been out of it all that long.

That thought is confirmed when he kicks the door open and we emerge to the sight of the sun just starting to appear over the horizon.

He comes to a stop by his truck and places me on my feet.

Ripping his door open, he pulls a black hoodie from inside and hands it to me.

"Here, put this on. That stinks."

"Oh... um..."

"It's okay, I'm not going to hurt you."

"But you said—"

"I know what I said. Now do you want to change or not?"

"Y-yes." Without thinking, I quickly pull the disgusting shirt over my head and throw it to the ground.

"Lucky motherfucker," Reid mutters as I take the hoodie from him.

"What was that?"

"Fuck. N-nothing."

Swiping the fabric I discarded from the ground, he opens the backdoor and throws it in.

"Get the fuck in," he says, glancing into the back seat of the truck.

"Oh... uh... sure."

I scramble in, in two minds as to whether I actually want him to take me away. On one hand, I want to be as far away from this place as possible but on the other, my father is inside and I've no idea if he's going to be able to leave as easily as I seem to be.

The second I'm inside, Reid slams the door closed on me and climbs into the driver's seat.

"What about my dad?" I ask, poking my head between the seats.

My body screams at my sudden movement but I push it aside. My need to know if my dad is going to be safe or not is more important.

"Your dad can look after himself, Letty, He's been a part of this life for years, he knows the drill."

"Yeah, about that."

"Letty," he sighs, pulling out of the compound parking lot and turning toward the highway that leads toward Maddison County. "It's not my place to tell you about your dad's life. You should talk to him."

"Well, you're helpful," I huff, sitting back and resting my head against the window. "What time is it?"

"Six a.m."

My eyes feel heavy as I stare out at the passing traffic. The effects of the alcohol I'd consumed before my night turned into a living hell has long worn off. My head throbs but I think that's more to do with the fact that Victor knocked me the fuck out more than anything else.

The longer Reid drives for, the more I feel my body begin to shut down. My need to fight, my adrenaline drains from me and leaves me exhausted and broken. It's not a feeling I'm unfamiliar with, but one I'd quite happily never feel again.

"Here," Reid says, and when I look over, I find he's holding out my purse, shoes, and dress that I abandoned at the party.

"How'd you—"

"How about just a thank you?"

"Thank you," I whisper, taking them off him and placing them on my lap, too exhausted to do anything else with them.

I'm not sure how much longer I last, but eventually, my heavy eyelids flutter closed and the vibrations of the car send me to a much-needed sleep.

11

KANE

I lay on my bed with Letty's still unopened letter in my hand and staring out the window at the orange glow that's beginning to light up the sky.

I need to sleep but my body is still buzzing from our few moments in the woods behind the Delta house.

I shouldn't have gone, I knew that. But I also couldn't stop myself.

The thought of her celebrating with the team, with the Dunns, was too much to ignore. I found myself getting back into my car for the first time since the accident and heading across town.

What I wasn't expecting was what happened next.

I thought I'd be forced to watch her from a distance. Well, I did. For quite a long time but when she moved to watch everyone else, I knew I had to strike or I'd probably regret it for the rest of my life.

I barely react to the front door slamming closed. Ellis was here when I got back but Devin and Ezra were still out at some party or another. I was invited to wherever they were going but I didn't even listen. After Friday night, I was done. Plus, I knew where Letty would be and there was no way I was going to be at a different party.

Footsteps thunder up the stairs, getting closer to my room and I pull myself up in bed a little knowing that they're either coming to me or Ellis if they're making the effort to come to the top floor.

Two seconds later, my door flies open but the person standing in the doorway is not who I was expecting, nor is the passed-out body in his arms.

"What the fuck?" I jump from the bed, pulling the sheets back so Reid can lay her down.

Her legs are covered in scratches and mud, she's wearing a man's hoodie but neither of them are the most concerning things because that is the dried blood that's covering the right side of her face.

"What the hell, Harris?" I bark, dropping to my knees beside her and gently moving her hair to get a look at her injury.

Reid only responds with one word and it makes my blood run cold.

"Victor."

"Motherfucker," I spit.

"Why?"

"Why do you think? She didn't get him the intel he wanted on the shipments."

I glance over my shoulder as Reid drops into the chair at my small desk.

"This is bullshit. It's got nothing to do with her."

"Victor pulled William in for it."

"Oh shit. Does she know?"

He nods and I blow out a long breath.

"Yeah. He had them both tied to chairs. If I didn't show when I did... well..."

He doesn't need to say any more, there's already a shiver running down my spine. I'm more than aware of what Victor is capable of.

"How'd you get her out?"

"William hasn't done anything wrong, he just got caught up in the bullshit."

"Did he expect you to hurt her?"

"Probably. I didn't touch her though." He holds his hands up in surrender.

"I know, man. Didn't even think it."

She stirs in my bed and I wonder if she's conscious enough to be aware of where she is.

"I should go," Reid says, pushing from my chair.

"Wait," I call before he opens the door.

"Why'd you bring her here?"

"Because I knew you wouldn't want her to be anywhere else."

A sad smile twitches at the corner of my mouth.

"Thanks, man."

He nods in acceptance and then slips through the door. I hear his footsteps down the stairs before the front door closes behind him.

I watch her for a few minutes, desperate to crawl into the bed beside her. I want to pull her into my arms, but I know I need to clean her up first, check her head properly in case she needs stitches.

I make quick work of running down to the kitchen to

grab the first aid kit I've seen hiding under the sink and a bowl of warm water.

The second I'm back in my room, I drop to my knees once more and dip a cotton ball into the water and begin to clean up her face.

She moans when the warmth hits her skin.

"It's okay, Princess. You're safe." I almost laugh at my words. She might have been through fuck knows what tonight, but it started with me dragging her into the woods and brutally fucking her against a tree. I should be the last person she feels safe with. Yet she's here, and I'll do anything I can right now to make any of this better.

Once I've cleaned off the blood, the cut that's in her hairline at her temple doesn't look so bad. I place a couple of sutures across it just in case before discarding everything I've used and finally crawling in beside her.

I lay on my side and just watch her as she peacefully sleeps. My need to wake her to find out exactly what she's been through tonight is strong, but I know I need to let her rest.

Needing to be close to her, I press the length of my body against hers. I tell myself that it's for her, to keep her warm, but I know it's bullshit the second sparks shoot out from our contact.

She must feel it too because her entire body tenses before her eyes flutter open.

Her loud gasp fills the silent room before she tries to sit up in a panic.

"Where the hell—"

"It's okay, Princess. You're safe," I repeat my words

from earlier. But when she turns her wide, terrified eyes on me, she looks anything but reassured.

"I need to leave." Her arm shoots out to fling the sheets off her, but I wrap my hand around her upper arm and she immediately stills.

"Letty, you've been through a lot tonight. Just lay back and rest a minute, yeah?"

She blinks, blows out a long breath and nods.

Slowly, she lays back down, clearly not having the fight in her to really want to get away from me.

She stares up at the ceiling with her walls built so high, I'm not sure if I'm going to be able to scale them.

"Look at me, Princess."

She refuses, her jaw tensing and her tiny hands balling into fists around the top of the sheets.

"Letty, please."

My breath catches when she does as she's told—possibly for the first time ever—and I find her eyes full of unshed tears.

"Everything's okay. You're safe now."

"M-my dad?"

"He'll be okay," I soothe, reaching out and cupping her jaw, brushing my thumb over her cheek, catching the lone tear that escapes at my words.

"B-but... h-he's..."

"Working for Victor. I know, baby."

A deep frown line forms between her brows.

"How long have you known?"

"A while. But it wasn't my place to tell you, not that you'd have listened if I'd tried."

She opens her mouth to argue but must quickly

realize that I'm right because she closes her lips once more.

"Did he hurt you?" I ask softly.

"J-just my head when he knocked me out."

"So he didn't touch you?"

"Not that I'm aware of. W-when I woke, I was wearing this gross shirt. Someone put that on me, but I don't know who. I have no idea how long I was out for, so..."

Every single muscle in my body pulls tight as I picture all the things that he could have done to her while she was unconscious.

"I don't feel like anyone hurt me. T-touched me." Her eyes widen as if a memory has just hit her. "A-apart from you. Fuck." She lifts her hands and covers her face. "I need to go home. Everyone is going to wonder where I went. They're probably going out of their minds."

"I'll sort it out," I assure her. "You just need to rest."

She nods, clearly not having the energy to fight with me.

"Do you have any painkillers? My head..." She trails off, really not needing to say anymore.

"Of course. I'll grab you some and a glass of water."

The second I pass her the tablets, she throws them back before settling back under my covers. And fuck if the sight of her there doesn't stir something inside me.

Laying back down beside her, I stare straight ahead.

"Tell me what happened," I demand.

"I didn't think you wanted to talk?"

Her words make my chest ache.

"I—someone hurt you."

"Yeah, you did."

I open my mouth but all that comes out is a long exhale.

"Why did you do it?" I continue, despite her reluctance.

"You're going to need to clarify," she mutters.

"The cameras." I decide to start with the easiest part of all of this.

She blows out a breath before answering quietly. "Because I didn't think I had a choice. He threatened my family so... little did I know that my father was already tied up with him."

"I'm sorry."

"For him being a part of it or for not telling me?"

I shrug. "Both. Not that I had anything to do with him being a part of it."

"W-what does he do?" she asks hesitantly.

"You really should get some rest," I say, trying to steer the conversation away from this topic.

"Tell me," she snaps, the harshness in her tone enough to make me look over at her.

She's laying with her eyes closed, so I've no idea how she's really feeling right now.

"He organizes distribution. The garage is a cover."

"Jesus. I can't believe he ended up tangled-up like that."

"From what I heard, he didn't have much of a choice. His family was at risk."

"Right," she sighs.

"What about... what about the rest?" I ask, although

I'm still not sure I'm ready to go there, but I feel that I need to make the most of this little truce between us.

"Have you read my letter?" I glance at the floor where I know it fell when Reid stormed in.

"No," I admit.

"I wrote it for a reason."

My lips part, but once again no words come out. All I feel is guilt and pain. Regrets swamp me for all the things I could have done differently, all the mistakes I've made. Almost all of which have involved Letty.

"Okay," I whisper.

She never responds and when her breathing evens out and her body finally relaxes. I breathe a sigh of relief that she's getting the rest her body needs.

I, on the other hand, just sit there staring at the wall trying to drum up the courage to read what it was she needed to say to me.

I have no idea how much time passes, but when I finally climb from the bed and pick up the envelope, the sun has long risen and is streaming through the gap in the curtains.

Before I do anything else, I grab her purse and dig out her cell.

It's dead, so I put it on a charger and wait for it to power up.

It only takes two attempts to get through her passcode. Seems I know her too well.

She's got messages and voicemails from both Luca and Leon, and all her roommates.

I hesitate, trying to figure out the best way to handle this situation. I can hardly message the Dunns back as her, they'll see right through it. Equally, I can hardly tell them that she's with me, that won't reassure them.

In the end, I open one message and hit dial.

"Where the fuck are you?" a sleepy, husky voice comes down the line.

"It's Kane," I whisper, not wanting to wake Letty up. "She's with me. She's... fine."

"You really expect me to believe that?" There's rustling in the background before the deep rumble of a guy's voice.

"Yeah, actually I do. She's asleep in my bed, so can you please call off the search party?"

"Why would I do that?" she snaps, suddenly sounding very awake.

"Because you're a good friend, Ella."

She huffs out her frustration.

"You promise me you haven't hurt her."

"I promise. When she's awake, I'll get her to call you. But I need you to call the others off but—"

"Let me guess, don't tell the Dunns that she's with you?"

"I mean, feel free if you want to deal with the wrath. But I'd maybe keep it to yourself somehow."

"Fine," she sighs, sounding exhausted and exasperated. "Fine. I'll do your dirty work this time. But only this once."

"I appreciate it. Look, I know things are..."

"Fucked-up."

"I was going to say complicated, but that works. But I'd never hurt a hair on her head, I need you to believe that."

"What's happened, Kane? You're scaring me."

"It's not my story to tell, but she's fine and I'll have her call you."

"Fine. Okay. I'll just have to trust you, I guess."

"I know it'll be a challenge," I deadpan. "But I appreciate it."

"Can I go back to sleep now?"

"Once you've delivered the news, yes."

"Good. Bye."

She hangs up before I've even parted my lips.

Okay then.

I knew she'd be pissed, but shit.

Placing her cell on the side, I lift the letter from my lap once more and stare down at her writing.

Sucking in a breath, I flip it over and slide my finger under the flap, opening it.

My heart races as I pull out the paper inside. I have no idea what she's going to have written in here but the last thing I'm expecting is for a small square to fall from the folded letter.

I pick it up and gasp.

"Holy shit." My hand trembles as I stare at the fuzzy black and white image.

I stare down at the easily recognizable baby and my chest constricts at the sight.

Is this my baby?

Needing to know more, I place it gently on my thigh and open the letter.

Kane,

I was scared.

I was so fucking scared. There are no words I can write here that could truly express how I felt the day I stared at that positive test.

I'd had all my dreams come true. I was living my best life. And then you'd barged in once more and turned everything I'd worked for upside down.

I've never hated you as much as I did in that moment. And let me tell you, I'd really hated you before that even happened, so it's really saying something.

I should have told you. I knew that then, and I know that now. All I can do is apologize and say that I was too scared.

I was scared you'd think I was lying, trying to trap you, trying to punish you. There were a million and one things I came up with as to why telling you would be a disaster.

That night never should have happened. You weren't supposed to be there. But you were, and look what happened.

There was never any choice for me. I might have hated you with every fiber of my being at that point, but I could never have gotten rid of our baby.

I was fully prepared for you not to want anything to do with us. Honestly, I was expecting that to be the case, and I mentally prepared myself to be a single mom.

Although I never told anyone.

I guess I was ashamed for not being more cautious.

I was embarrassed. I was on birth control, but apparently it wasn't enough and I felt like I'd failed. Failed you. And, yeah, you guessed it, I was scared.

I knew how Mom was going to react, and I hated the idea of disappointing her.

So, I just... carried on hoping that the time would come where I'd find the strength to do all the things I needed to.

Everything was great.

I didn't get sick. Having my first scan and then hearing the heartbeat was two of the best things I've ever experienced in my life, although I was ridden with guilt. You should have experienced that too.

I was making plans to come clean. My belly was growing, and I wasn't going to be able to hide much longer.

I told myself that I'd have my next scan, find out the gender and then I'd be able to tell everyone what it was and it would be easier to take.

Well, my plan failed.

I walked into that room so excited to see him or her, to listen to the heartbeat, to learn how big it was, to walk out with a photo that I could keep forever to remember.

But that's not what happened.

I knew something was wrong the second the sonographer looked at the screen. Her face said it all.

To this day, I have no answers.

Only regrets.

But there was no heartbeat.

That little baby I thought was happily growing in my belly... wasn't.

"Fuck." I cover my mouth with my hand as my eyes fill with tears.

She lost our baby.

I pick up the scan picture again and notice the date.

This is a picture from that scan.

She lost our baby, and... and she was alone.

I scrub my hand over my face, rubbing at my eyes, and when I look up, they lock with hers.

"Fuck," I breathe. I had no idea she was awake, let alone watching me.

She pushes herself up as the tension gets heavy between us.

She sucks her bottom lip into her mouth and looks at the floor.

"I'm sorry," she whispers. It's so quiet that I almost think I imagined it, but when she finds the strength to look up once more, I know she said it, I can read the pain in her eyes.

"Fuck, Princess."

I'm out of the chair before I've even registered the move. Lifting her onto my lap, I rest back against the headboard and hold her tight as she trembles against me.

She doesn't make a noise, but I know she's crying, the wetness of her tears soaking my chest as she sobs.

My own breathing is shaky as I try to get my head around what I just read. But none of what I feel right now even comes close to the agony this woman has been through in the past year.

I knew she was strong. Hell knows I've put her through enough shit to test it over the years. But right now, I'm in fucking awe of her.

"It's okay, Let," I soothe, rubbing my hand up and down her arm as sobs continue to wrack her body.

12

LETTY

Kane's warmth seeps into me and for the first time, I feel like I might actually be strong enough to take a trip down memory lane to my darkest days.

The last thing I expected when I woke up was to find him reading my letter.

I knew he hadn't. If he had, he'd have said something.

He might not have known anything about what happened, but I don't think even Kane is cold enough not to be affected by the truth.

"I'm sorry for what I said," he admits quietly, his lips pressed into my hair. "I'm sorry for suggesting you might have..."

"It's okay."

He tenses, his grip on me bordering on painful.

"No, it isn't. I accused you of... I can't even. Fuck. Letty, I'm so fucking sorry."

I shrug. I don't need his apologies now. It's too late.

Silence falls between us as my eyes find the letter and

the ultrasound picture on the floor where it fell when he jumped up.

After long, agonizing minutes he finally speaks, startling me.

"I've spoken to Ella. She's going to let everyone know that you're okay."

"You spoke to Ella?" I ask as if he just said that in another language.

"Yeah, I figured she was the safest bet."

I nod, understanding what he means.

"How are you feeling?"

Empty. Broken. In pain. I swallow all of those down.

"Hungry. What time is it?"

"Almost lunch."

His voice is rough, and I twist in his lap so I can look at him.

"Have you slept at all?"

"I'm fine," he assures me but I can tell from one look at him that he isn't.

"I'll head home and let you rest."

"No," he says in a rush, his arms tightening around me. "Stay. Let me get you some food, you can shower or whatever. I just..." He looks away from me, I suspect to stop me from reading too much in his eyes. "I need you here right now."

His confession has my breath catching in my throat.

Reaching out, I cup his rough jaw, trying to twist his head back to me but he refuses.

"Kane, I—"

"I don't know how to process all this, Princess. I'm trying, I just..."

"It's a lot to take."

A humorless laugh falls from his lips before he falls silent once again.

My heart breaks watching him trying to deal with everything he's just learned. My own grief might be threatening to drag me under right now, but I've had a lot of time to deal with this. A year of this darkness that has festered inside me since that appointment.

"I'm a shit cook, but have you got any requests?"

I want to force him to talk, but I decide against it. This is new territory for us and it's safe to say that it's a minefield. I'm more than aware that at any moment I could say something that's going to flip his switch and he could forget all about being nice and his anger could return full force.

"Nope, whatever you've got will be great."

I twist around ready to climb from his lap but to my surprise once again, he holds tighter.

"Use whatever you can find. I'll lay some clothes out on the bed for you when you're done."

"Th-thank you," I stutter, feeling weird saying those words to him when we're usually firing insults at each other.

"You're welcome."

Finally, he lets me up and I walk across his small room wearing only last night's swimsuit and Reid's hoodie.

I'm pushing the door open when he speaks again.

"Scarlett?"

I pause, waiting to see if he's going to continue.

The silence is heavy as I wait and after only a few seconds, I look over my shoulder.

He's sitting on the edge of his bed, still only dressed in his boxers. His fine body and tattoos on display with his lowered head. The confusion in his eyes stop me from taking my fill like I usually would.

"I'm... I'm sorry." The roughness of his voice, the honesty within it makes all my hairs stand on end.

"For which part exactly?" I can't help asking, knowing just how much he has to apologize for.

"I... um..." He looks away for a beat before his eyes come back to me. "For making you believe that I wouldn't have been there."

My chin drops, ready to respond but I soon swallow down the words.

Instead, I nod at him and slip into the room.

He can say whatever he wants after the event, but something tells me that if I were to have said something to him back then, nothing would have changed.

He wouldn't have taken the chance on me telling the truth.

My stomach knots with that knowledge.

How he's behaving right now is because of the shock. Shock and pity for what I endured.

With a sigh, I reach into his shower and turn it on before stripping the clothes from my body.

The water is so hot it burns my skin and makes me wince when I first stand under it, but I don't make a move to turn it down.

I need it, anything to take the focus away from the pain in my chest from the loss.

Was I ready to be a mom? Absolutely not. I was living my dream life. I didn't want anything to change, but there was little I could do about it because I was not getting rid of my baby. Even if it was the spawn of the devil.

I knew I'd figure out a way, and hopefully, when I was brave enough to confess to my parents, they would have supported me and helped me do the right thing.

I just never got that far.

Looking down, I find my limited options of Kane's shower gel and one single bottle of shampoo.

"Okay then."

Without much choice, I reach out and grab the bottle.

The second I flip the lid, his scent engulfs me, and I immediately regret it. He's about to cover every inch of my skin and he isn't even touching me.

I make the most of my limited resources and turn the shower off once I'm done. With everything that's happened since I woke up here, I'd forgotten about the injury to my head until I shoved my fingers into my hair to wash it. I just about manage to hold in my cry of pain as my eyes fill with water.

Victor fucking Harris.

Thoughts of my dad have the tears returning. I need to know he's okay. I need to fucking talk to him. I need to know the truth.

Reaching out for the only towel on the rack, I attempt to wrap it around myself but it does very little to cover anything.

After finger brushing my teeth with Kane's toothpaste, I suck in a deep breath and pull the door open. I haven't heard him on the other side so I can only hope he's still downstairs and I can get some clothes on before he appears once more.

I'm grateful his room is empty. As promised, there's a shirt and a pair of what look like brand new boxers folded on top, but I don't make it all the way to the bed because the picture on the nightstand catches my eye.

Until I pulled it out of my little memory box to put inside the letter to Kane, I hadn't looked at it for months. It was easier to have it out of sight, although I never forgot. Not once.

Reaching out, I lift it from the side and stare at our baby as the pain of losing him washes through me once again. Everything that happened after hearing that devastating news will stay with me forever. I already know that I will never feel pain like that ever again. It was crippling.

I'm so lost in my memories that I don't hear him coming back up the stairs, and it isn't until he's closed the door behind him, his stare landing on my barely clad body that I realize he's even there.

"Sorry, I—"

"It's okay." Placing the scan back down, I turn to him. "Whoa, I thought you said you can't cook," I say, taking in the tray full of food in his hands.

Ripping his eyes from my legs, he clears his throat and finds my eyes.

"It's just pancakes."

"They look great, thank you."

"You're welcome."

An awkwardness fills the space between us as we both try to navigate this new truce between us.

I'm not naïve enough to think that it's going to last. He's just doing what he thinks is right given the situation, and I can't say it isn't welcome. The thought of being alone in my dorm room after everything that happened last night fills me with dread, especially because I know that everyone will bombard me with questions. I need to come up with a decent excuse for what happened. I can't exactly say that I was kidnapped and held prisoner by a gang boss, nor that I was in Kane's bed, will make anything any better.

Blowing out a long breath as I try to get my head together, I look to the clothes he left out once again.

"I-I can leave and let you—"

"Who are you and what have you done with Kane?" I ask.

"Princess," he breathes. "I'm just trying to do the right thing."

"It's weird," I admit.

"Would you rather I shout at you?"

"Maybe," I admit. At least it would feel normal. This right now is just... strange.

"I'll just give you—"

"It's okay. It's not like you haven't seen it all before."

"I know but—"

"Kane," I snap. "Stop trying to care, it doesn't suit you."

His lips part in shock at my outburst.

He looks like he wants to say something but I don't give him the chance. Instead, I snatch the clothes and turn my back on him, pulling the boxers up my legs under the towel. I slip the shirt over my head before tugging the towel away and using it to squeeze the water out of my hair.

"I don't suppose you have a hairbrush, do you?" I ask,

knowing just what kind of state my long mane must be in right now.

"Top drawer." He nods to his chest of drawers and I pull it open.

Inside, I find a comb, brush, wax, and a few other male hair products along with a massive box of condoms. Good to know he's intending on enjoying all the benefits of college life, although I do notice something.

"It doesn't look like you've been very busy," I mutter.

"Wha—oh, no."

"So you're trying to tell me that the infamous Kane Legend hasn't been sticking it into every jersey chaser who so much as looks at you?"

He looks up at me from where he's sitting resting back against the headboard with a plate on his lap.

He studies me for a second as he formulates his answer.

"Like Clara, you mean?"

"Was that her name?" I feign ignorance. The truth is, I still vividly remember how I felt when he called her princess.

He chuckles, shaking his head as he lifts a piece of bacon to his mouth and bites a bit off.

"You can't lie to me, Princess. I can practically taste your jealousy."

"Is that right?" I quirk my brow at him, irritated he can see what I'm so desperately trying to hide.

"Come and eat, Princess." There's no suggestion in his tone and his dominance sends a shiver skating down my spine.

My body moves of its own accord to his demand and

before I realize it, I'm climbing onto the bed beside him and he's placing a plate onto my lap.

"How's the head? I brought up more pills," he says, nodding to the bottle on the tray.

"Painful."

"Tell me what happened."

"Kane," I sigh, suspecting that me telling him the events of the night before will only anger him and change this thing we've got going on between us.

"Just tell me. Then I'll decide who to kill first."

"See, that's why I'm not telling you." A growl rips up his throat at my refusal.

"Tell me or I'll find the information elsewhere, but you won't like the results of you lying to me."

"I'm not lying, I'm—"

"Not telling me the truth. Why are you trying to protect me? You hate me."

A bitter laugh falls from my lips.

Yeah, that's why I'm sitting here in your bed eating breakfast, because I hate you that much.

"I have no idea who grabbed me," I say quietly. "After you... left, I decided that I couldn't go back to the party, so I took off through the forest."

The grip on Kane's fork tightens as I'm sure he remembers what I wasn't wearing.

"You decided to try to walk home... alone?" he seethes.

"Well, I wasn't walking back to the party and announcing to everyone that you'd just fucked me against the tree, was I?"

"You should have."

"Yeah, well, hindsight is a great thing. Facing Luca

and Leon after that would have been a hell of a lot easier than Victor, but it's a little late now, don't you think?" I spit, getting irritated that he chooses now to get all protective of me when he was the one to leave me in the woods to start with. What exactly did he expect me to do?

"What did he do?"

"Other than hitting me across the head and tying me to a chair, nothing, actually. Dad was in a bad way though. I need to help him, get him out of there."

"Princess, I admire you for wanting to try. But your dad is part of a gang. A very dangerous gang. You can't just turn up at his trailer, tell him you don't like it and expect him to be able to walk away. He's been doing this for years, it's his life."

"His family should be his life," I mutter.

"Sometimes we have to do bad things to protect those we love."

"Calm down, next you'll be showing me you have a heart."

His body tenses beside me, and I wonder if I just hit a nerve.

"You have no fucking idea. The shit I had to do to get Kyle back, I—" He shakes his head. "It doesn't matter."

"You can tell me," I offer, finally cutting into one of the pancakes sitting on my plate and popping a piece into my mouth.

"Nah, it's probably best I don't."

"Oh my God, this is really good," I moan.

He glances over, his blue eyes a shade darker than they were the last time I looked into them. They drop to my lips as I run my tongue along the bottom one collecting up the syrup that's on it.

"Hmm... yeah." The connection that's always between us cracks so loudly I can almost hear it. "T-tell me about it, a-about our..." He trails off.

"Baby?" I finish for him.

"Yeah. Fuck." He throws his now empty plate at the end of the bed and scrubs his hand down his face. "I can't get my head around the fact you were pregnant with my kid. It sounds so surreal."

"Trust me, it was all very real."

"Oh no, I didn't mean—"

"It's okay."

"No, it isn't." He twists so all his attention is focused on me. My skin heats as he looks over every inch of me.

"O-okay. I found out for sure about four weeks after the party. I knew I'd missed my period but I just thought —hoped it was stress or something. I've never been all that regular, so it wasn't unheard of. But as time went on, I just knew that I was putting off the inevitable.

"Up until that point, staring down at the small window that held my fate was the scariest thing I'd experienced. If only I knew what the future was going to hold, I might not have been so terrified."

"I hate that you couldn't tell me." The dejection in his voice threatens to slice me open but I know he understands.

"Me too. As time went on, I was so lonely. I can't tell you how many times I sat there with my cell in my hand and your contact staring back at me.

"I just knew you wouldn't accept it."

"I hate that you're probably right there too."

"It is what it is, Kane. There's no point beating yourself up about it now. It wouldn't have changed the outcome."

"But I could have been there."

I shrug. We both know that the chances are that he wouldn't have been. He wouldn't have accepted it.

"So what happened? Why did—"

"I don't know. They never found a reason. He just..."

"He?"

"Yeah. They told me after I delivered him."

"You had to... fuck, Scarlett."

13

KANE

Listening to her talk about having to deliver our never-to-be baby is the most heart-wrenching thing I've ever experienced. I've seen and done a lot of things that should have affected me over the years. But it all pales in comparison to hearing her talk so honestly about what she went through.

It sounds horrific and knowing that she went through the entire thing alone.

Fuck.

My fists clench in frustration. I want to help, I want to take the pain away, turn back time and be right beside her, holding her hand and wiping away her tears.

But I can't. The damage has been done, although I know the pain is going to stay with her forever.

"I wish you'd have told someone," I whisper after a few moments of silence after she bravely recalled the events which followed her scan.

"It doesn't matter now. Mom knows, I finally cracked

and left New York. I was in a bad place. I had been for months and I just couldn't take it any longer.

"I thought she was going to hate me for dropping out and ruining the best opportunity of my life, but she didn't. She just listened to me as I told her everything, held me, and told me everything was going to be okay, and most importantly, she got me some help.

"If she didn't do that, I'm not sure I'd be here right now."

"You mean at college, right?" I ask, the alternative doesn't even bear thinking about.

"I don't know," she whispers. "Things got bad, Kane. Really fucking bad."

I drop my head into my hands, not able to process all of this right now.

It's too much. Everything about Letty is too much, but this...

I never expected this.

I wanted to be mad at her that she had aborted my baby. I clung to that anger and didn't allow myself to consider any other possibility—that the reason our baby didn't exist wasn't that she'd chosen not to let it live.

"I should get back. Let everyone see for themselves that I'm okay."

"You don't have to go," I say. The words feel weird falling from my lips after all the times I pushed her away.

"I do, Kane. This," she says, gesturing between the two of us. "This isn't how we do things. I need to walk away and allow you to get your head around this and remember that you hate me."

A sad smile twitches at my lips. Unable to stop

myself, I reach out and take a lock of her now almost dry and curly hair between my fingers.

"I don't—"

"Don't," she snaps, jumping from the bed as if I just burned her. "Can I borrow—" She looks down at her legs. "Something. I'll wash it later and have it back to you in the morning."

"Sure, but keep it as long as you need." I find the smallest pair of sweats I own and pass them over, regretfully watching as she pulls them on, covering up her legs.

"Thanks. I'll just call an Uber and be out of your way."

"Letty, shut the fuck up. I'm taking you back."

"You really don't—" She cuts herself off when she finally looks up at me and sees the determination on my face. "Th-thank you."

"It'll give you a chance to tell me all about what happened to her, eh?"

She swallows almost nervously as if all the drama that's happened in the past few hours has made her forget all about her little car trick.

I quickly drag on some clothes while she gathers her things and together we head out of the room.

The guys are chatting in the living room when we hit the ground floor. The second she turns toward where the noise is coming from, I press my hand into the small of her back and encourage her to keep going but I soon realize that it's too late.

"Legend, you got some hot ass up there or something?" Footsteps approach faster than I can usher Letty from the house.

The second Devin appears in the doorway, his face contorts in anger.

"What the fuck?" he barks. "Coming back to try stitching us up again?"

"No, it isn't—"

"Leave it, Dev, yeah?"

"Leave it?" he asks, his eyes wide. "She tried fucking snitching on us to Vic. I'm not gonna fucking leave it."

"Well, you need to," I growl.

"Or fucking what?" He closes the space between us, clearly even more pissed than I thought he'd be about finding Letty in his house once again.

"Guys, please don't. I'm leaving, okay? I haven't done anything. I'm sorry for what happened. Your father gave me little choice."

Devin's eyes flicker with something, understanding, I think. He knows full well how hard it can be to do anything but his father's bidding at times.

"I failed, okay? He didn't get what he wanted from those cameras and I've been punished for it, my father too. So can we just let it go?"

Finally, Devin rips his angry eyes from mine and looks at Letty.

He might be my best friend, but the way he stares at her makes me want to pull her behind my body to protect her. It's easy to forget that Letty isn't like most girls. She grew up around some of the state's scariest men.

The Harris boys might not be their father, but his blood still runs through their veins and they can turn it on whenever they want.

"Get her the fuck out of here," he barks, his stare not

wavering from her.

"Bro," I say, slapping him in the chest. "She said her piece. Let it fucking go."

"Fuck me, Legend. She fucking slipped you something?"

"I fucking wish," I mutter, once again guiding Letty toward the front door. Anything would be easier to deal with than the blow she landed me with.

She's silent as I lead her toward my car. It's parked out front of the house at a funny angle, exactly how I left it when I pulled up after spending that short amount of time with her last night. I should have felt better about having her again, teaching her a lesson for thinking she could buy me off with fixing up my car. But deep down, mostly, I was just grateful to have my baby back.

"She looks as good as new, huh?" I ask, needing to know that she's okay after that run-in with Devin.

"She looks great."

I back out of the driveway and head toward campus while she fiddles with the ties on my sweats that are pulled tight around her middle in order to keep them up.

"Why did you do it?"

I notice her shrug out of the corner of my eye.

"After everything I've done to you, you got my car fixed up without a second thought for no reason."

"I know how much she means to you. And it was my fault you crashed her."

"I was the one driving, Princess. It was my fault."

She shakes her head.

"I should have told you about the cameras. Maybe we could have come up with something to pacify Victor.

That way I wouldn't have all the Harrises after my ass right now."

"They're not after you. Reid brought you to the house. He knows that you didn't have a choice."

"Then I let you run off thinking the worst of me," she continues, not stopping to consider what I just said about Reid.

But the truth is, if Reid is okay with her, which I can only assume he is. As he was the one to take her away from Victor and any danger by placing her with me, then the others will be fine too.

The younger Harris brothers might be okay with defying their cunt of a father, but Reid is an entirely different story.

"It wasn't your fault, Letty. I jumped to conclusions, let the past cloud my judgment."

"A past that you see completely differently to everyone else."

My grip on the wheel tightens as I picture Riley's face.

"Whatever, it doesn't matter now. We're all still alive and you've got your beloved car back."

"Yeah, everything is just fucking great," I mutter, my anger beginning to resurface.

It's the easiest thing to cling to when it feels like I'm losing a grip on everything around me. When the things I let fuel me all these years start morphing into something different.

I signal to turn into the parking lot closest to Letty's building and release the breath I've been holding as I pull into a space.

"Th-thank you," she stutters, releasing her belt and grabbing her purse ready to climb out.

She's got her fingers around the handle when I call her name.

"Yeah?"

"Do you want me to walk you up?" My fingers tighten once again around the wheel as I think about something happening to her in the short distance between her and her dorm room.

"I don't think that's a very good idea. No one up there likes you very much."

"I don't give a shit what they think."

"Well, yeah, but—"

"But nothing, Princess."

"Just leave it, yeah? Don't cause any more issues than you already have."

My jaw pops at her words.

"What are you going to tell them?" I manage to grit out.

"I haven't totally decided yet. It won't be the truth, that's for sure."

"Because I'm that bad to spend time with, right." I hate the dejection that wraps around me with each word I speak.

"Kane," she sighs, turning back to me. "I'm sorry I didn't tell you. Really, I am. But I know you understand why. I hope you won't hold it against me. I did everything I could for our baby, but it wasn't meant to be and I have to forever live with the memory of what happened."

"If... if things went differently... would you have told me before he was born?"

"I don't have an answer for that, Kane. I couldn't predict what the future held. If I could, everything might have been a little easier to take."

"Princess," I growl, not getting the answer I wanted.

"I hope that I would have. But..."

I glance at her for the first time as she tries to find the right words.

"But?" I prompt.

A smile twitches at her lips. "You can be really fucking scary when you want to be."

I laugh, my own smile pulling at my lips as she immediately shatters the tension that had descended around us.

"Yeah, it kinda comes with the job."

"I can't believe you still work for that asshole."

"You gotta do what you gotta do," I mutter, not all that impressed myself with the fact I'm still Victor's puppet. Even after all the years and all the promises I've fulfilled in order to make myself a better life.

She hesitates for a few seconds, making me dread what she's going to ask next. She isn't usually one to hold back, so the fact she is makes my stomach knot.

"What do you do for him?"

My lips part to respond but I quickly swallow down the words. "Nothing I want anyone knowing about."

"That bad, huh?"

"At times, but I've left most of it behind. Let's just say that my quest to get here involved more bloodshed than necessary."

"Fucking hell." She scrubs her hand down her face. "You're better than him, than them. You know that, right?"

"I'm a Creek kid, Letty. It doesn't get any better than this, you know that."

"No," she spits. "That's bullshit and you know it. You've got a one-way ticket to the NFL if you want it. If you don't squander this opportunity. You need to walk away from all that, focus on what's important."

"And what if I can't?" I ask, knowing that it's impossible to just walk away from Victor Harris and the Hawks, especially after being in as deep as I have been. I've been party to deals, battles, murders, and extortion that most members would never be because of my connection with the Harris kids. You don't get to walk away when you've got that kind of information.

She shrugs. "It's your life, not mine, Kane. I'm just telling you what I think."

When I don't respond, she reaches for the handle once more and this time, I don't stop her.

"I guess I'll see you around," she mutters. "Thank you for looking after me."

The door slams and she's gone before I get to respond.

"You're welcome," I mutter into the silence of my car as I watch her walk away.

My fingers tighten on the wheel with my need to go and watch her, and the second she disappears around the building, I lose my fight and climb out of the car.

I stay back, standing in the exact same place I did the night I watched her from her window as she disappears inside the building.

I know I should move and go back to my car. She's going to have some explaining to do to her roommates, so it isn't like she's going to appear in her room anytime soon.

But knowing all that still doesn't make me move and I stand exactly where I am, waiting. Waiting to know she's back in her room and that someone wasn't waiting for her on the stairs.

Pulling my cell from my pocket, I hit call on Reid's contact.

He doesn't answer right away, and when he does, his panting breaths are loud in my ear.

"You in the middle of fucking some ass?" I ask.

"Um... yeah, something like that," he mutters. "What do you need?"

"Is Victor done with Scarlett?"

"As far as I know, yeah."

"And what happened to her dad?"

"Sent back to work with a very painful warning."

"Okay good. If he touches her again, I'll—"

"He won't," Reid assures me and I instantly relax. If there's one person I trust completely in this world, it's him.

"Okay."

The line goes dead before I get to say anything else. I lower my hand and look up to her window.

My breath catches at the sight of her standing there like a fucking angel with the light of her room bright behind her.

Our gaze holds for a few seconds before she disappears, allowing me to walk away knowing that she's safe. For now, at least.

The second I push through the door everyone is on their feet and running at me.

"I'm fine. I'm fine," I argue as Ella runs her eyes all over me in a rush. Thankfully, my wild hair covers the sutures Kane put over my wound.

Happy with what she sees, she throws her arms around my shoulders.

"Do I need to go kill him in his sleep?" she whispers in my ear, making me wonder what she told the others if she's keeping her voice down.

"No, everything is fine. I promise."

"Okay." She gives me a little squeeze before she releases me.

"What the hell, Let?" Brax barks as he and West stand with their chests puffed out.

"I'm sorry, I didn't mean to worry any of you."

"Look, we get it, okay? But don't run off like that again, I don't care if you've seen the fucking Queen."

I glance at Ella who just smiles at me and winks.

"I'm really sorry. My cell died and... it was irresponsible of me."

"Seeing as you're safe, we'll let you off this time," West says. "But Luca and Leon have been going out of their minds. They might be a harder sell."

My stomach drops as I think of them. No matter what I'm going to tell them, whether it be lies or the truth, they're not going to be happy with me. I'm actually amazed they're not sitting here waiting.

As if he can read my mind, Micah pipes up. "They've been here all morning in the hope you'd appear. We sent them home knowing you were safe." He gives me a knowing smile which makes me think he knows exactly where I was too.

"I'll call them in a bit, I just really need to get into my own clothes." I look down at myself and wince when I notice that the hoodie he gave me is an MKU Panthers one.

So much for being discreet, Something tells me that if I were to look at the back, it's probably got his number on it too, to just really nail home that I'm lying to my friends.

"You hungry?" Violet asks, returning to her spot in the kitchen where I assume she's making dinner.

"Not right now, but I'd love something later."

"You got it. Enchiladas tonight."

"My favorite night of the week," West announces, rubbing his belly like a little kid.

"I can't wait," I say, moving toward my room, aware that Ella is hot on my heels.

I leave my door open, allowing her to walk in behind

me and lower my purse to my dresser as I walk toward the window.

I don't know why I do it, but I'm not in the least surprised when I find Kane down there staring up at me.

My breath catches despite my strong suspicion, and it doesn't go unnoticed by Ella.

"What's wrong?"

"N-nothing," I stutter, stepping away and turning to look at her. "Go on then, ask away," I say with a smirk.

"No questions. You can just tell me however much you're happy to."

With a sigh, I curl up on my bed, and she mimics my move at the other end.

It would be so easy to skim over everything, keep it all locked up inside, but there's something inside me begging me to just rip the Band-Aid off and let it out.

I've confessed to Kane now, and it was important that he was the first one to hear what had happened after Mom. Now it's time to say the words and attempt to properly move forward.

I take a deep breath, and just let the words flow.

"A little over eighteen months ago, I went to a party back home in Harrow Creek. I was assured he wasn't going to be there, but I should have known better.

"We ended up in the backyard and—"

"In the backyard?" she asks with a smirk.

"Yep, in a puddle to be precise, because it started lashing down with rain while we were out there."

She nods while amusement sparkles in her eyes.

"Anyway, he got me pregnant." She doesn't gasp or show any kind of shock, proving that I was right about how much she overheard of our argument. "But I miscarried at twenty weeks." Now comes the shock.

"Twenty fucking weeks. Oh my God, Let." She reaches for my hand as her own eyes fill with tears. I, however, feel remarkably stable.

"I never told him. I was too scared."

"He had no idea?" Her eyes go so wide I swear they're about to pop out.

"I didn't tell anyone. I didn't know how to. I knew that my mom would have been disappointed in me. I knew that Kane would hate me, that's if he even accepted I was telling the truth. I just... I freaked. And then it all came to an abrupt end, and I figured I could just move on, you know?"

She shakes her head. "No, not really. You don't just get over something like that alone, Letty."

A humorless laugh falls from my lips. "Don't I know it. I finally hit rock bottom at the end of May and I dragged my sorry ass home to confess to my mom. She helped so much and here I am."

"Shit, Letty. So last night?"

"Kane and I..." I trail off, how do I even begin to explain what Kane and I are. "Kane blames me for a lot of stuff that's happened to him. I'm pretty sure he's never really dealt with any of it and all those emotions have just festered within him and are unleashed as hate on me.

"As a kid, I dated his best friend, but he died. He blames me because the night I broke up with him, he got off his head drunk and drove his car into a tree."

"Jesus."

"The night of the party, his little brother got busted

for drugs and went to juvie for a year. Kane was with me while it was all going down. Again, my fault. It's just one thing after another."

"No wonder you didn't want to tell him about the baby."

"I know, but I was wrong. I should have at least tried. That argument you overheard, it's when I first told him. He assumed the worst and—"

"He thought you aborted it."

"Yeah."

"Another thing to hate you for."

"Then he went and damn near killed himself. My fault and..."

"You're aware that this would make a good book, right?"

"A book? It's a fucking disaster." And I haven't even mentioned the Hawks or Victor's involvement.

"There's always time for a happy ending." I stare at her in utter disbelief. "What? I'm a little bit of a romantic, sue me."

I can't help but laugh at the sappy look on her face.

"So? You hooked up with him for some hot and steamy hate sex last night?" she assumes.

"Uh... yeah, something like that."

"Guuurl, those Dunn boys are gonna be broken when they discover you've been banging the bad boy."

My heart drops. "I need to talk to them. They know I've been with him... after last time, they saw the evidence."

"I don't envy you, that conversation, but if they need

comforting, you know who to send them to." She wiggles her eyebrows and I burst out laughing.

"No hook up with Colt last night then?"

Her face drops, making me wish I didn't ask.

"No, last time I saw him, he had some redhead sucking his face off."

"Asshole."

"Right?"

"You deserve better than him."

"Maybe so, but right now I just kinda want him."

I smile sadly at her.

"I should leave you to it, maybe let you change into your own clothes." She stares down at my oversized outfit. "I mean, you're totally rocking it, but—"

"Yeah, I need to wear my own underwear."

"You really did run out of there in a rush last night, huh?"

I swallow nervously, as the memories of my departure from the party come back to me.

"Yeah," I whisper.

She climbs from my bed and walks toward the door.

"If you need anything, someone to go with you when you talk to the guys, just give me a shout."

"Thank you, Ella. I really appreciate your support."

"You got it." She smiles sweetly at me and disappears.

I fall back against my headboard and close my eyes for a few seconds, trying to drum up the courage to move and go see Luca and Leon.

I've got to do it today, I can't wait until class tomorrow. That's not fair to them.

It's almost two hours later when I finally emerge from

my room. The scent of Violet's enchiladas fills the dorm making my stomach growl but I know I can't stop to eat or I'll never do what I need to do.

"Ah, here she is. We thought you'd bailed on us," Brax says when I approach.

"Yeah, um..." All eyes turn on me and I swallow nervously. "I need to step out so don't worry about me."

"I'll plate you some up and you can have it later."

My lips part to argue but the firm look on Violet's face stops me.

"Thank you," I say, heading out the door before she convinces me to stay.

I'm a nervous wreck by the time I pull up out front of the Dunns' house. There are loads of cars out front and I dread them having people over and gate-crashing.

Blowing out a steeling breath, I climb from my car and head for the front door.

I stand there awkwardly after knocking when no one seems to be in a rush to answer.

In the end, I reach for the handle and push it open.

"Hello?" I call into the house, the low beat of music from the living room filtering down to me.

A familiar face walks out of the kitchen to see who it is, and Colt's eyes go wide the second they land on me.

"Oh shit, girl. You're brave."

His words hit me like a truck and it causes a wave of nerves to wash through me.

"W-where are they?"

"Follow me."

I do as I'm told and trail after him toward the living

room. But when he walks straight into the room, I hover in the doorway.

"Luc, Lee, you've got a visitor."

Oh God.

They both turn their eyes on me, and I swallow, trying to force down the lump that's suddenly appeared in my throat.

Their faces harden the moment they realize it's me and their eyes narrow. Their actions are almost simultaneous, and if I weren't so nervous, I might find it funny.

The room falls silent, clearly the team knows what happened last night and are as curious as the twins to hear the explanation. I take a step back when they stand and take a step toward me.

They approach me but barely look at me as they march into the hallway. I assume they want me to follow. I go down to another door which they walk through and drop down onto the two couches.

I look around at the den with the huge flat screen on the wall and multiple game consoles beneath.

I don't realize how much time has passed until Luca barks, "So?"

Standing with my back to the now closed door, I look him in the eyes. Although it's the last thing I want to do when I notice how furious they are.

"I'm sorry, I shouldn't have disappeared like that."

"Fucking right you shouldn't, Let. We were going out of our fucking minds. Then Ella calls with some bullshit about seeing an old friend. That's not you Letty, you don't just do that."

"I know, I'm sorry. I'd been drinking and—"

"It was him, wasn't it?" Luca spits, cutting me off.

My mouth waters as my hands begin to tremble. I knew coming here that I couldn't lie to them. I have zero intention of telling them about Victor, I knew I needed to confess about Kane.

My lips part to answer, but no words come out. Apparently, that's all Luca needs though because he stands, slamming his palm down on the unit beside him, making me squeak as I jump in fright.

"Luc, calm down," Lee pleads.

"She left, for him," Luc seethes. "For that fucking asshole. Jesus." He rubs his hand down his face, anger coming off him in waves. "What the fuck are you doing, Let?"

"It's complicated," I whisper.

"No, it's a fucking train wreck is what it is. He's a fucking cunt, yet you keep running back to him time and time again. Don't you remember how he treated you the last time?"

"Yeah, but I—"

"No. This is fucking ridiculous. I can't keep watching you do this to yourself."

"W-what?"

"Are you going to keep seeing him?"

"I... um... I don't know what happens next."

"I fucking do. It's me or him, Let. If you want him to continue treating you like shit, then I'm not going to sit around and watch when he fucking breaks you into a million pieces."

"You don't mean that," I whimper, already feeling like I'm about to shatter.

"Don't I?"

"Luc, please. It doesn't need to be like this."

"No, it really fucking doesn't," he barks before storming through the door. He slams it so hard behind him that I swear the entire house shakes.

A sob erupts and I cover my mouth with my hand trying to stop it but it's pointless.

My knees weaken and I begin to slide down the door.

It wasn't supposed to be like this.

But before I hit the floor, arms wrap around me and I'm lifted into a hard yet warm body.

My sobs get harder as I'm carried to the couch and lowered onto his lap.

"Shhh, Cupcake. It's okay."

Leon rubs his hand up and down my back as I try to get myself together.

"No, no, it isn't. He just..."

"I know," he soothes. "He's angry. He doesn't know what he's saying."

"He sounded pretty sure when he gave me that ultimatum."

"He doesn't mean it."

Leon's words don't make me feel any better.

"He sounded pretty sure," I whisper.

"Just give him some time. He's been freaking out that something happened to you, that Kane might have hurt you."

"I know how it looks, Lee. But... it's more complicated than that."

"I'm sure it is."

He lets me sit there while I pull myself together.

"I need to talk to him," I say, pushing from Leon's lap, but his grip only gets tighter.

"Let him cool off. Let him sleep on it. Maybe try tomorrow. He's stressed now the season has started, our dad is on his back. Things are piling on top of him, and you—"

"I didn't help."

"No."

"Shit," I say, dropping my head into my hands. "I'm so sorry. I never meant to—"

"I know, Let." He pulls my hands away from my face and cups my cheek, forcing me to look into his dark green eyes.

His concern bleeds through his own lingering anger and I almost sob again at the sight.

"I'm s-sorry." My voice cracks.

"I know." He gathers me into his arms once again and holds me tight, letting his support warm me.

I stay like that for another ten minutes before he allows me off him. I wipe my cheeks with the back of my hand and hold my head up high.

At no point does he ask me any questions, he just allows me to talk if I wish—which I don't right now. Telling Ella this afternoon was draining enough.

"I should go, let you get back to enjoying your night."

"You can stay as long as you need."

I shake my head at him. "I've got a ton of work to do. This weekend hasn't exactly gone as planned."

He stands as I make my way to the door, but his deep voice stops me before I get to pull it open.

"Let?"

I look back over my shoulder, my eyes locking with his.

"I'm right here. If you need to talk, about whatever, I'm all ears."

I smile at him. "I haven't forgotten our deal." I wink, remembering him telling me that he'd tell all if I did only a few short weeks ago.

Something akin to panic flashes through his eyes at my words telling me that whatever he's hiding, he's far from ready to talk about.

"Thank you," I say softly with a smile. "Can you check on Luc? I'm worried about him."

"He'll be fine, Let. Things are just intense right now."

Guilt threatens to swallow me whole. I don't want to put any more pressure on Luca's shoulders. I know he already carries enough weight with the team and insane expectations from his father.

I nod, pulling the door open.

"See you tomorrow."

"You got it."

Leon walks me to the door and drops a kiss to my forehead before I wave goodbye to him and head out to my car.

The second I'm in the driver's seat, I turn toward the house and look up to the third floor.

It's dark out now but with the light shining behind him, Luca's silhouette is clear to see in the window.

Everything inside me screams to go back into the

house and force him to talk, to shout, scream whatever it is he needs. But I know he doesn't want that.

I've known him long enough to know how he deals with stress, and this is it. He locks himself away and no matter what I do right now, his stubborn ass isn't going to accept it.

Leon is right. I just need to give him time.

We'll be okay. We always have been in the past.

I swallow down the little voice in my head that screams at me that things are different now because I don't want to accept that things are changing.

I start my car and regretfully rip my eyes from him.

I've got too much to do to sit here staring at the boy who seems to want me four years too late.

With a heavy heart, I drive away, knowing that I've got a plate of enchiladas and a paper to write ahead of me.

"**Y**ou shouldn't be here," a deep voice booms through the music playing in my ears.

Hitting the stop button on the treadmill, I pull one of my AirPods out and turn toward Coach.

"I know, sir. But I needed—"

"You're not playing Saturday. Doctor's orders."

"Can I train?" I ask, hoping he will trust me to know my limits.

"You will take it easy. If you miss more than two games of this season, we might just find a way to manage without you, Legend."

"You got it, sir." I nod, grateful he's allowing me this.

I fucking need it. Since the moment I walked away from Letty yesterday, my head has been a mess. I spent all night pacing my room, desperately trying to expel my pent-up energy and anger. By this morning when I woke in time for practice, I knew that I needed to do something. So here I am.

I was the first in the parking lot and the only one in the building.

But hitting the state-of-the-art gym gave me the release I was craving without hauling my ass into the ring and attempting to break some bones.

What Letty told me yesterday. What she confessed—

Fuck. I still can't get my mind around it.

Grabbing a towel from the rack, I scrub it over my face, wincing slightly when I hit the still healing bruise down the side of my face.

She lost our fucking baby and went through all of that alone.

My fists curl with my need to hit someone, something.

I've felt anger before. Daily, mostly.

But this right now. This hate, hopelessness. I have no fucking idea how to deal with it.

Knowing that Coach is waiting in the field house, I immediately head that way.

The second I step inside, silence washes through the team as they look up at me.

But it isn't until Luca steps forward, his face like fucking thunder, that I get any idea that things might be worse than usual.

"You fucking cunt. What did you do to her this time?" he barks, getting right in my face and slamming his palms down on my chest.

"Luc, chill the fuck out. Coach will be here any minute."

"I don't give a fuck. I want to know what he's done."

"I haven't done anything."

"She wouldn't just leave a party with us to be with a waste of space like you."

I stare at him for a beat, taking in the vein that's bulging in his forehead and the muscle that's pulsating in his neck.

He's really fucking pissed.

A smile twitches at my lips knowing that I'm leading him on and just waiting for him to try throwing his first punch. He's a fucking pussy who thinks he's all that. I've been waiting for years to take him down.

"Then you need to start reconsidering what you think. Because that's exactly what happened, Dunn."

"Luc," Leon says again, wrapping his hand around his brother's shoulder. "Just leave it."

Luca snarls at me, his fists clenching at his sides, building himself up for what's to come next, but sadly, he doesn't get the chance.

"Luca," Coach barks. "There are plenty of others who'd love to take your position if you can't take it seriously."

"Bro?" Leon breathes in his brother's ear, desperately tugging at his shoulder to force him to stand down.

"I'm fucking watching you, Legend. Hurt a fucking hair on her head and I'm going to fucking kill you."

A smile curls at my lips. "You're assuming she doesn't fucking love it when I hurt her." I know I shouldn't but I can't help myself.

"You fucking asshole."

"Luc. Dunn," Leon and Coach bark at the same time, forcing him to walk away. From the tense set of his shoulders as he puts some distance between us, it's clear it's the last thing he really wants to do.

I'm not sure if practice is more brutal than usual or it's just my healing body, but by the time we head for the lockers, I'm fucking beat. I can barely move one foot in front of the other. I feel weak and I fucking hate it.

I'm the last into the showers, which is probably a good thing because it gives Luca a chance to get in there first and get the fuck out of my way.

If he started something now, I fear I wouldn't have the strength to hold my own. And that is not how I want that situation to go. When it comes, I want to be in full form so I can take the motherfucker down. Show him why Letty chose my ass over his.

Most of the team have already left the locker room in favor of getting food, there are just a couple of guys lingering behind.

Standing under the hot spray of the shower, I tip my head up and let the water rain down on me. I allow my thoughts to drift back to yesterday and the revelations in Letty's letter, the devastation in her eyes as she told me everything she endured.

Before I know what I'm doing, I raise my arm and plow my fist into the tiles before me.

A guttural roar rips from my throat as I repeat the action again and again until the skin over my knuckles splits open and red blood coats the wall.

Emotion clogs my throat as I picture her alone in a hospital, tears in her eyes, and only that sonogram picture to hold on to.

"Fuck, fuck, fuuuuck," I roar, continuing to pound on the wall.

Exhausted, I rest my forearm on the wall and drop my head to it as my chest heaves and my body trembles with exertion and emotion.

It's not until I finally pull back and turn around that I realize I've got an audience.

Leon watches me with his brows drawn together and concern in his eyes.

"Stop it," I spit. "I don't need your fucking pity."

"Well, that's good because you're not fucking getting it."

"What the fuck did you want? Or were you intent on just standing there staring at my ass?"

"I wasn't—nah, actually, fuck you, Kane. I was going to ask if you were okay, seeing as you were beating the shit out of the wall. I was going to try to be a decent fucking person. But fuck you."

He spins and marches away from the showers.

Quickly, I turn the water off and grab a towel, wrapping it around my waist.

"Wait," I call, rushing after him. "Have you seen her?"

He turns and stares at me for a beat.

"Yeah, she came by last night. Why?"

My lips part but I swallow down the words that are on the tip of my tongue. I don't want them to think anything is wrong if she doesn't want them to know.

"N-no reason."

His brow quirks as he stands with his arms folded across his chest waiting for me to elaborate, only I never do.

"Do you actually like her? Are you actually going to turn into a decent fucking human being and treat her how she should be treated?"

Fuck, I want to say yes. And that thought in itself shakes me to my fucking core.

I want to be good enough. I clearly fucking wasn't a year ago when she needed me. She might blame herself because she was scared. But all that is on my head, not hers.

"Honestly, I have no idea. Shit between us... it's complicated. She told me some stuff over the weekend that changed things. Things she should have told me about a long time ago and fuck... I don't... I don't fucking know what to do with it." Lifting my hands, I run my fingers through my wet hair and tug until it hurts.

"It's all my fucking fault that she's here. That she had to give up Columbia. That she's been through so much fucking pain. I just—fuck." I breathe, noticing the shocked look on his face and realizing that I've said too much. "Fuck, forget I said anything."

An incredulous look appears on his face.

"Oh yeah, because that is going to happen. Letty is one of my best friends, Kane. She's been there for me when I needed her most, and I fully fucking intend on doing the same for her."

"So where were you last year?" I bark, knowing full well that she was alone. Where the fuck was he then? He doesn't even know what happened to her. Neither of them do.

He pales, his lips parting to respond, but I already know he doesn't have an argument.

"We all got sucked into our new lives."

"Yeah, well. She needed you, someone, any-fucking-one, and we were all too distracted by life."

"What happened?"

I shake my head. "Nice try, but you're going to have to talk to her if you want to know. I have no right to spill any of her secrets."

"Fair enough." He falls silent behind me as I clean up my knuckles and begin pulling on some clothes, ready to head to class. "Do you really want her?"

"Do you?"

"Uh..."

"All's fair in love and war, Dunn. May the best man win."

With one final look in his direction, I swipe my bag from the bench and throw it over my shoulder. My muscles ache with the movement but like fuck am I allowing him to see that. He's already seen more than I was willing to show, he isn't getting another ounce from me.

I jump in my car, wasting no time in turning the engine over and flooring it out of the lot. I've got someone I need to see.

Glancing down at the clock, I notice that I've got a bit of time before class. Hopefully, she'll still be there and Luca fucking Dunn won't have beat me to it.

Campus is still relatively quiet as I pull into the parking lot, run my hand through my still wet and messy hair, and climb from the car.

The jog up the stairs makes my legs burn after my long morning but I don't let it stop me, I just have to take a moment to catch my breath when I get to the top like a fucking pussy.

It's easy to forget about the accident and my short hospital stay when I'm so focused on getting back to normal life.

Once I've caught my breath, I march for the main door and walk inside as if I live here.

The brunette girl is in the kitchen cooking something that makes my mouth water as I approach. It isn't just her because every single set of eyes, aside from the pair I want, turn to stare back at me.

Much like when I showed up to practice this morning, the room falls silent as a million and one unspoken question fills the air.

"Is Letty still here?"

Both of the guys who've now experienced this shock twice this morning, push to stand.

Their protectiveness makes me smile, not that I allow them to see it.

They might have pissed me off in the past by never allowing me to get anywhere near her and always being attached to her hip, but right now, I'm glad she has these guys.

"It's okay," Ella soothes, her southern accent thicker than I remember from the brief phone call we had.

She takes a step toward me, holding my stare as if she isn't barely five-foot and that I could snap her like a twig if I so desired.

"Does she know you're coming?" Her eyes narrow in warning.

"No. Does that matter?"

Her eyes drop from mine in favor of checking me out. It isn't done in a way that makes me think she wants to fuck me, more trying to figure out how best to kill me when I inevitably fuck this up.

She shakes her head, her eyes lifting once more.

"Hurt her again and we're coming for you, asshole," she hisses. If it weren't for the deadly serious face, I might laugh but I've got a feeling she really believes those words.

"Okay, sweetheart. I'll do my best."

I take a step to move around her but her tiny hand lands on my forearm, stopping me.

"I'm serious, Kane. She's been through enough heartache," she whispers, ensuring no one else hears her words.

Our eyes hold for a beat, silent understanding passing between us.

She knows.

"She's in her room. Think she overslept."

That's hardly a surprise after everything she went through this weekend.

I nod at Ella and make my way over as Brax and West start voicing their disapproval for allowing me in.

Ignoring them bickering behind me, I rap on her door with my non-busted knuckles.

"Yeah," she calls, her soft voice sending a shiver down my spine.

I have no idea how she's going to take to me showing up like this. When she walked away from me yesterday she made it quite clear that she was expecting us to go back to how things were before.

But I don't want that.

Twisting the handle, I push the door open and step inside, only the room is empty.

Her makeup and hairbrush are out on the desk and the scent of her perfume permeates the air. My mouth waters, my cock swelling at the memory of how her body smells up close.

"I'll be right there," she calls from the bathroom. "You can go without me if you want."

Assuming she thinks she's talking to Ella or one of the others, I take a seat on the end of her bed and wait.

In only a few seconds, the light turns off and she appears in the doorway.

My breath catches at the sight of her. She looks fucking perfect. Her skirt sits high on her thighs showing off insane legs. Her shirt hugs her torso accentuating her small waist and round tits. Her face is flawless and shows no signs of the events of Saturday night.

She was lucky to get away as lightly as she did. A shudder rips through me knowing what Victor is capable of and how much worse it could have been.

"K-Kane?" she stutters, straightening her spine as if she's preparing to fight. "What are you doing here?"

Resting forward, placing my elbows on my knees, I make a show of looking her up and down once more before I find her narrowed, suspicious eyes.

"Come to take you to class."

"Umm... why?"

I laugh at her, pushing from the bed and closing the space between us.

I don't stop until I'm right in front of her.

"How's your head?" Lifting her hair, I expose the cut that runs into her hairline. She gasps the second I reach out and touch her, even if it is only the briefest graze of my fingertips against her temple.

"I-it's okay."

Happy that it looks to be healing, I lower her hair back down and focus on her eyes instead.

She tries to take a step back but with the angle she's now standing at, all she achieves is bumping into the doorframe.

Reaching out once more, I cup her jaw with my hand, rubbing my thumb over her cheek.

"K-Kane?"

Her eyes search mine, confusion filling hers as she bites down on her bottom lip, trying to figure out what the hell I'm playing at.

Not able to vocalize exactly why I'm here. Hell, I can't even admit it to myself, let alone her, I lean forward intending on being the one who's biting her lip.

"No," she says, quickly placing her fingers in the space between our lips.

"Princess," I breathe, my lips brushing against the soft skin before my tongue sneaks out to get a taste of her.

"W-we're not doing this."

"And what is it that you think we're doing?"

"I'm not allowing you to suddenly be all nice and pretend that you care because I finally told you the hell I've been through. I don't want your fucking pity, Kane. That isn't why I told you."

A bitter laugh falls from my lips. "This isn't pity, Princess."

"Well, whatever it is, I don't want it."

Her words hit me like a fucking bullet.

"You don't..." Taking a step back from her, I keep my eyes firmly on hers. "You don't want it?" I shake my head, running my eyes down her body. Her flush travels from her cheeks down onto her chest, her nipples are hard behind her shirt and her thighs are squeezed tightly together. "Then you'd better tell your body."

She pushes from the wall and turns her back on me.

My anger kicks up a notch that she can just dismiss me like that. I move faster than her and in a beat, my front is pressed to her back. I've got one arm around her waist, pinning her to me and the other around her throat.

Her pulse thunders against my fingers, giving away exactly how she's feeling right now.

"You can't run from me, Princess."

"Ah, there he is," she jokes. "The Kane Legend I know and hate."

My fingers tighten at her comment.

"You don't want me to be nice, do you, Princess. You want me wicked."

The entire length of her body trembles against me.

"You're a dirty little whore, Scarlett."

Her tremble is accompanied by a whimper this time and I can't fight my smile knowing that she can't see me.

We stand like that for long seconds, her increased breaths the only sound in the room.

It's not until I move my hand, splaying it across her stomach so that I can press myself harder against her, that she moves.

"Kane," she gasps, "What did you do?"

Her hands drop to mine and she lifts it, inspecting my busted knuckles.

"It doesn't matter," I mutter.

"Who did you hit? Did you have a job last night? My dad—" She panics. "Is my dad okay?"

"As far as I know, he's fine, Princess."

She relaxes a little in my hold. "He didn't answer his cell when I called him last night."

"He was probably just busy."

"I need to see him."

"No," I bark.

She uses my moment of distraction to remove herself from my hold and turns back to face me.

"No? I'm not allowed to go and see my dad? You need to leave," she says, throwing her arm out and pointing in the general direction of the door.

"Promise me something," I say, taking another step toward her and ignoring the 'leave me alone' vibes coming off her.

She keeps her arms wrapped around herself as I stare down at her.

"Promise you something? That's meant to be a joke, right? I owe you nothing, Kane. Nothing."

Ignoring her words, I continue. "Do not go to the Creek," I warn, my voice low and I hope it holds the seriousness in which I intend it to.

"It's my home, Kane. Why wouldn't I go there?"

"Because you know the truth now. Victor might have let you go, but he isn't going to forget that you're aware of what your father does, and he has no reason to trust you. You want to stay off his radar, then you stay the fuck here. You want to see your father, I'll sort it out."

She shakes her head at me as if I'm talking nonsense.

"You go there and you could end up never leaving."

Her nervous swallow tells me that she's at least hearing my words.

"Now, are you ready to go to class?"

Her chin drops in shock.

"I'm not walking to class with you. I don't need a fucking bodyguard."

"You're safe here, and that's not why I was offering."

"Just leave, Kane. I don't want or need you to walk me to class. And—" she adds quickly. "If I find out your fists look like that because Luca or Leon were at the other end then—"

"Then what, Princess?" Closing the space between us once more.

"Then... then..." she stutters.

Reaching out, I grip her chin and force her to look up at me.

"They don't deserve you, Letty."

"And you do?" she whispers, already cracking under my hold.

"Hell no, but I'll fight fucking harder."

My lips slam down on hers before she has a chance to move.

I'm desperate to deepen it, to force her to submit to me, but if that happens then we'll both miss class, and I can't afford to do that. So instead, I pull back long before I'm ready to and release her.

"I'll see you later. Don't do anything stupid."

16

LETTY

The second my door slams shut, I breathe for what feels like the first time since I found Kane sitting on my bed.

I don't need to ask to know who let him in here. It has Little Miss Romantic Ella's name written all over it. Hell knows the guys never would have let him in here without a fight. A fight I already know he would win, damn it.

He's right about what he just said, he does fight harder, dirtier too.

My body flushes hot as I think about the dirty side. And fuck if I didn't want to say to hell to it all when he grabbed me and pinned me against him.

But I can't. I can't lose myself to him and his wicked mouth and rough touch because of what... his pity and guilt about me losing our baby.

No, not happening.

We are not happening.

I'm glad he listened to me. I'm glad he believed me. At no point did he question how sure I was that it was his baby. He didn't revert to his usual insult of calling me a whore or suggest that I'd slept with half of the guys at Columbia in the lead up to being with him. He just took my words as what they were, the truth.

Hell, I even believe him when he said he'd have been there. Right now, learning about it a year later, I really believe that he thinks he would have been there to support me. I think the reality might have been very different but it's a little too late to worry about that now.

A crash at the door startles me and when I look up, I find Ella stumbling through like a whirlwind.

"Are you okay?" she asks in a rush.

Putting on a brave face, I stuff everything with Kane back into the box it belongs in and turn to her.

"Yep, I'm fine. Ready to head to class?" I ask, glancing at the time.

"You're sure?" she asks curiously.

"I really am."

She falls silent as I gather up my stuff and together we head out of the building.

"What did he want?"

"Honestly, I think he's just trying to placate his guilt by being nice."

"He was nice?" she asks as if it's the most absurd thing she's ever heard.

"He wanted to walk me to class."

"Whoa, was he going to hold your books too?"

I can't help laughing with her, and after the weekend I've had, it feels so freaking good.

The sun is shining, the early morning warmth hits my skin and the scent of late summer fills my nose. Despite everything. I'm feeling good. No matter how painful it's been going back there, knowing that I'm no longer keeping a secret from Kane is like a massive weight lifted. Add to that Ella knowing the truth as well, and each step I take just feels a little easier.

Although, that all comes crashing down a little when we approach the building and I find only one Dunn waiting for me.

The events of last night come rushing back and the hurt and anger on Luca's face.

I never meant to hurt him, but I also wasn't going to lie to him either.

"'Morning," he says with a forced smile.

"Where's the other bodyguard this morning?" Ella asks innocently.

"Er..." Leon hesitates, his eyes finding mine.

"I told them both the truth about where I was Saturday night. Luca didn't take it very well," I say to Ella. "How is he?" I ask, turning to Leon.

"He's... you remember how he used to get during the high school season?"

"Yeah," I whisper, remembering all too well the pressure he put on himself, let alone the pressure he felt from their father.

"Well, being in college, the stakes are higher, and the pressure is worse."

"Jesus. Maybe I shouldn't have..."

"No, Letty. You did the right thing. He'd hate it even more if you were lying to him."

"Ugh, I know. I just..."

"You can't protect him, Let. Just give him the time he needs, he'll come around."

"Once the season is over?" I ask dryly.

"Nah, he'll get over it before then."

At that, something over my shoulder catches his eye. I don't need to look to know it's the man in question. I can read it on Leon's face.

The tension becomes heavy as he steps up to us.

"We're going to be late," he says coldly, his eyes never meeting mine.

Before any of us get a chance to say anything, he spins on his heels and marches into the building.

"So I guess we're going in then," Ella mutters, taking off after him.

"Maybe you should talk to him, offer to cheer him up," Leon says lightly to Ella before she's too far away.

"Oh I'd love to, but I don't think I'm the one he wants."

My heart drops into my stomach at her words and my chest aches.

I don't want to hurt him.

The three of us trail behind him as we make our way inside.

Ella says her goodbyes and disappears toward her class while Leon and I turn into ours.

Luca is already seated by the time we walk in, but by some miracle, he has left our two usual seats beside him.

Maybe he isn't that pissed then.

As we walk across the front of the lecture hall, a different set of angry eyes burn into me.

My heart races as I continue to put one foot in front of the other

I take my usual seat next to Luca, but unlike usual, he's tense beside me.

I look over at him, wanting to say something but not able to find the words I need to say. He's aware of my attention because his jaw tics as I stare at his profile but he makes no effort to turn to me.

My lips part to apologize but the words die on my tongue before I even get the first one out.

Our professor beginning our lecture eventually drags my attention from Luca to what I should be concentrating on.

Feeling Leon's eyes on me, I glance over at him and he smiles, although it nowhere near meets his eyes.

I hate this. I hate that Luca is pissed at me and causing a rift between them.

I hate that Kane is pissed at me, although I really shouldn't give two shits about what he thinks.

Professor Whitman talks for the entire class. I focus on bits but I soon find myself drifting in and out, worrying about the guys sitting on either side of me along with my dad back in the Creek.

By the time class comes to an end and I look down at my notes, I realize that I didn't manage much more than the title and the date.

Transferring here was meant to be a shot at a fresh start but I can't help but feel like I'm just fucking everything up all over again.

The second he can escape, Luca is out of his seat and leaving the lecture hall without looking back.

I watch his every move with a heavy heart.

I wait for Leon to pack up before moving out and to

the stairs.

"Coffee?" I ask, wishing it could be like my last few Mondays and the three of us could go together.

"You got it. I've been craving one of those cupcakes since I woke this morning."

"It's the sprinkles. They're addictive," I joke, trying to drag myself from my dark mood.

I'm at the door when I feel his presence behind me.

"Trouble in paradise, Princess?" he whispers in my ear, sending shivers racing down my spine.

Keeping my head held high, I continue walking, not wanting to alert Leon who's a little ahead of me talking to Colt.

"So you're going to ignore me now, is that the game plan?"

"I don't have a fucking game plan," I bark, spinning on my heels and pinning him with a furious look.

All he does is smirk at me and I curse myself for reacting to him.

"If you're trying to appear unaffected by me, you're doing a really shitty job."

"I'm not trying to do anything, I am unaffected by you." It's a bare-faced lie and we both know it. But I'm not prepared to accept how I really feel with him standing right in front of me.

"So Dunn's pissed because you spent the night in my bed again," he announces a little too loudly for my liking.

"This has nothing to do with you," I mutter. My eyes pleading with him to keep his voice down.

"Oh, Princess. When your fine ass spends the night in my bed, it means it's everything to do with me."

"I didn't even fuck you," I blurt, right as Leon appears at my side to see what's going on.

My cheeks burn as Kane considers my comment.

"In my bed, no. I'll give you that." He leans in, his lips brushing the shell of my ear. "But I know for a fact that you've still got scratches on your back from the tree."

I can't stop the needy whimper that erupts from my lips at the memories his words drag up.

"Let it go. We're done."

He chuckles as Leon's fingers twist with mine and he pulls me away.

"Sure thing, Princess. You keep believing that."

I can't help myself and I flip him off over my shoulder as we leave the room.

***

Ella finds us still in the coffee shop after her morning class, making us a table of three like we're used to, but Luca's absence is obvious. I have no idea where he disappeared to. I asked Leon if he thought we should go and find him, he shot me down, so I keep my mouth shut about him from then on out. I know Leon is worried as well and keeping on about it isn't going to help anyone.

Thankfully, without the distraction of either Luca or Kane in my afternoon psych class with Ella, I actually manage to focus. I get some decent notes down which will help with the paper I've got to write.

"Any plans for tonight?" Ella asks as we make our way toward our dorm building.

"Yeah, actually. I'm heading home to see my dad."

The image of him beaten and bloody in the chair next to me on Sunday turns my blood cold.

Kane has assured me that he's fine. Until I can see that with my own eyes, I'm not going to be able to get that final image of him. The blood dripping from his wrists and Victor with a pair of pliers out of my mind.

"You?" I ask.

"Oh you know, hot date with an economics paper. I think he might be the one," she jokes.

"Wild."

"I know, right. I thought college was meant to be all about parties and doing crazy shit."

We laugh together as we make our way up to our dorm before she disappears into her room, wishing me a nice night with my dad.

I smile sweetly at her, but I have a feeling that tonight is going to be anything but nice.

Now I know the truth, I want to know everything. And I'm not intending on leaving that trailer until he's told me everything I need to know.

I drop my books to my desk and I run a brush through my hair and spritz myself with some perfume before heading back out.

My stomach twists with nerves during the entire journey to the Creek. All the questions I have for my dad spin around my mind like a whirlwind. By the time I get there, the number of things I need to know has only doubled.

The lights are off in the trailer when I pull up and it's the first time I consider the possibility that he might not be home.

He's always home, hence why I just assumed he wasn't actually working anymore.

The curtains twitch as I pull up beside his beat-up old car and I cut the engine, my hand trembling as I reach for the off button.

As I climb from my car, I look out at the trailer opposite, Kane's gran's trailer, and let out a sigh.

I want to say that I wish I could go back and do things differently where he's concerned, but the truth is, I didn't do anything to deserve the way he's treated me over the years.

Once upon a time, we were friends, sure. There was even a time when we were younger when I thought it could have been us. But then Riley asked me to a winter dance, and I said yes, and that was that. I became his.

It was then that Kane changed. But I never did anything to him. Not in all the ways he's always blamed me for.

Ripping my eyes away, I shove that part of my life aside and focus on the reason I'm here. Spinning around, I head toward the front door. But unlike the many other times I've visited since we all left, he isn't there greeting me with a wide smile.

I knock, despite knowing that he's aware I'm here before giving the swollen door a good shove and stepping inside.

"Dad," I call. "It's just me."

He remains quiet as I walk through the kitchen and turn into the living area.

He's sitting in his usual seat on the couch but unlike normal, he barely even looks like my father. The bruising and swelling from his beating is even worse than I was anticipating.

"Oh my God," I cry, racing over to sit next to him.

"I'm okay," he forces out.

"No, you're really not. Have you even seen a doctor?"

"I'm fine."

"Dad, come on," I argue. "You're not fine. You need to make sure nothing is broken."

"I can't, sweetheart. Doctors call the authorities and..." He trails off because he knows I know exactly what he means.

"This is Harrow Creek, Dad. There must be at least one dodgy doctor hanging around who you can call."

"Letty, it's okay. I'll be fine. It's nothing I haven't dealt with before."

Anger surges within me that this has been Dad's life and none of us knew about it.

"No, that's bullshit," I bark, much to his surprise. "I'm not leaving you to sit there in pain. Something might be broken."

"It's not," he says firmly.

"Right... well..."

I stand and march from the room before he even has a chance to say anything.

"Scarlett, please. I'm... I'm s-sorry." His voice cracks and my footsteps falter on my way to the bathroom.

Shaking my head at the fact he thought I was leaving because of his stubborn ass. I continue forward and root around for the first aid kit that always used to be in the cupboard under the sink.

His eyes are full of unshed tears when I return with

the box in hand.

"I'm so sorry," he whispers.

"Not now."

I crawl onto the couch on my knees and pop open the box so I can grab what I need.

As gently as I can, I set to work cleaning up all the dried blood on his face. It looks like he's tried to clean up since getting home but he hasn't been very successful.

He's silent as I work but he keeps his eyes on me. It's almost as if they're begging me not to ask the questions that he knows is coming but he's got little chance of getting away with the inevitable.

I clean him up, cover some of his worse cuts with sutures before tending to his wrists which look horrendous with lacerations the whole way around. I hate that they're like it because of me, because he was trying to protect me.

"I'm so sorry, Dad." The words fall out without my knowledge, and he looks at me in disbelief.

"Oh, sweetheart. This is so not your fault. The reason I was there was entirely my fault. Victor was punishing me. He thought I was going against him and he used you as leverage into scaring me into confessing."

"No," I say, shaking my head. "I was there because I failed at a job he gave me." I can't look him in the eyes as I say the words, yet I feel his disappointment coming off him in waves.

"Scarlett, no. Why? Why would you do that?"

My eyes snap up to his. "Because of you. Because of all of you. He was going to hurt you if I didn't do it."

"Well—" he starts but I cut him off.

"Clearly, I had no idea you worked for him at the time. I had no reason to believe you had anything to do with the freaking gang lord, Dad. What the hell were you thinking?"

"The exact same thing you were. I had to protect my family."

"There had to have been another way."

He opens his mouth to respond but only a rush of air comes out before he shakes his head.

"I was about to lose everything, Letty. The business, the house, everything I'd worked years for because of that accident."

"I-I know, but Victor Harris? Surely you could have got a loan from somewhere else, found another buyer."

"I tried. No one was interested in a garage that barely got by. But he made me an offer I couldn't refuse."

"To become his fucking puppet?" I snap.

Dad's lips twist in frustration at my language but I don't apologize for it. We're far past the point of that happening right now.

"I couldn't see another way. Your mom had her dream to get out of here and I wanted it, Let. I wanted it so fucking bad for all of you. I figured I could do a few years, make a bit of money, and then we could all leave together. Get the family life we always wanted."

"But we left without you," I whisper, remembering all too well the day we waved goodbye to him and drove away to begin our new lives in Rosewood.

Leaving him behind was one of the hardest things I've ever done. As a kid, I had the happiest parents. They never fought, and I was always one-hundred percent convinced that they'd go the distance. But then the arguments started not long after Dad's accident and everything began to change for us. It's all making so much sense now.

"Did Mom know?"

"At the beginning, no. But it didn't take her long to learn the truth." A sad smile curls at his lips, the love I remember all too well for my mother appearing in his eyes. "She was so mad. I literally thought she was going to kill me."

"Jesus, Dad," I mutter, pushing the first aid box away and looking at his broken face.

"I'm so sorry. I just wanted you all to have the world and—"

"I get it. I know your intentions were good. Good but stupid," I quickly add. "What happened? Why couldn't you come with us? Start over as a family like you planned?"

"I naïvely overlooked something. You don't just walk away from Victor Harris and the Hawks. Especially not when you have all the knowledge about their shipments and their supply chain. I signed my own death certificate by selling my soul to the devil. So I had to let you all go and pay for my mistake."

"You still love her, don't you? The fighting, the harsh words, it was all—"

"I'll love your mother until the day I die, Scarlett. She's the most incredible woman I've ever met. She's so clever, so strong, so..." He trails off thinking about her. "You're just like her, you know." He reaches for my hand, wincing in pain as he squeezes it. "You have the same strength, the same determination. You're going to do something really incredible with your life, I just know it."

His words have a ball of emotion forming in my throat that becomes harder and harder to swallow around.

"I ended up in the exact same place as you, are you really sure about that?"

"What did he ask of you?"

I tell him about the cameras and setting them up in the Harris house. "I have no idea what he was trying to find out really but he thinks they're lying to him, clearly."

"I do," he states.

"Y-you do?"

"Sweetheart, I know more than I ever wanted to. I've ended up in deeper than I ever expected. D-did, Reid look after you?"

"W-what?" I stutter, getting whiplash from his sudden topic change.

"Reid, after he took you out, did he look after you?"

"Uh... y-yeah, he did."

"Okay good. Scarlett, I need you to promise me something, okay?"

"Um... s-sure," I whisper, not liking the harsh tone of his voice.

The rumble of an engine fills the silence around us as I wait for what he's about to hit me with but neither of us pay it any mind as it comes to a stop and a door slams.

"I need you to stay away from him. Away from the Harrises and anyone connected with them."

My lips part to respond when the trailer door crashes back against the wall and a cold, angry voice booms, making every hair on my body stand on end.

17

KANE

I showed up for practice after class with the best intentions despite the fact my body was still screaming at me from this morning's session. I'm desperate to get back to normal, to get out on the field and feel that leather beneath my fingertips. But Coach took one look at me and firmly sent me away, much to Luca's relief if his smug as fuck smirk over Coach's shoulder told me anything. I flipped him off before I left, but it didn't really sate my need for what I really wanted to do to him.

I saw the way he blanked Letty in class this morning. The way he refused to so much as look at her when she clearly so desperately wanted to talk to him, and then the way he all but ran from the auditorium the second Whitman had finished.

When Letty explained to me that she'd told them the truth about where she'd been, I knew they'd both be pissed. But for Luca to blank her. That I was not expecting. I thought he was too infatuated with her to even consider that. Interesting.

Knowing she isn't going to be expecting me, I head to her dorm. I warned her that I'd fight to prove that she's wrong and that may as well start now seeing as I'm not wanted elsewhere.

"Oh look, he's back for another round," Ella mutters, barely glancing up from her notebook on the dining table when I storm into their dorm for the second time in the day.

"She in her room?" I ask, marching that way before she's even answered.

"Nope."

That one word stops me in my tracks.

"Okay, so where is she?"

Slowly, she drags her eyes from what she's doing as if I'm seriously inconveniencing her right now.

"Why would I tell you that?"

"Because you're not fucking stupid."

"You keep hurting her, Kane. Over and over." My teeth grind and my fist curls at her words.

"And this is anything to do with you because..."

"Because she's my friend and she's hurting. She doesn't want you here. She doesn't want you near her."

"Are those her words or yours because I happen to know that she loves it when I'm near her."

"Ugh, you are such a pig."

Her chair legs screech across the tiled floor as she stands.

"Huh, weird because I thought you had a thing for dirty players. That should make me your perfect type."

"Assholes don't do it for me," she snarls, looking me up and down.

"Ah, is that why Colt binned you off for a better model Saturday night?" I ask, making her chin drop.

"H-how'd you know that?" she stutters, unable to cover her hurt.

I take a step toward her. "Because..." I lower my voice, knowing that it'll terrify her and make her squirm like a little mouse. "I know everything."

In truth, I'm only guessing from what I've heard the guys talk about over the past couple of weeks and what I've seen on social media. She doesn't need to know that because I know that I've hit right on the mark.

"Does it hurt being cast aside like the jersey chaser that you really are?"

"Fuck you, Kane. Fuck. You."

Swiping her notebook from the side, she storms past me before slamming her bedroom door so hard the entire dorm rattles with her anger.

I, on the other hand, can't help but smile.

"Hey, man. What's... uh... what's going on?" The quiet guy of the group asks. I've seen him with Ellis a few times, so I know they're friends.

"Nothing. She's just being a little over-emotional."

"Ella?" he confirms. "Yeah, she has her days." He shakes his head, a soft smile playing on his lips as he thinks of her before walking toward the refrigerator to grab a bottle of water.

"Do you happen to know where Letty is?" I ask on the off-chance.

"Yeah, she's headed home to see her dad," he replies innocently.

My blood turns to lava at his words.

I glance at her door for the briefest moment as our conversation plays out in my mind from earlier this morning.

"Promise me something. Do not go to the Creek."

Motherfucker.

Plastering on a smile that I really, really don't fucking feel, I thank the guy before heading back out to my car.

My grip on the wheel is too tight as I floor it toward our shithole of a home. My knuckles splitting open once more, but I don't let it stop me because the thought of her walking straight into Victor fucking Harris on arrival in Harrow Creek scares the fuck out of me.

She got off lightly Saturday night but there's nothing to say that won't happen again when he finds her snooping around in his patch.

The trailer park looks exactly the same as it has done for my entire life. It's dark, damp and one of the most depressing places I've ever had the joy of spending time in. There are beat-up cars lining the potholed track, broken furniture, toys, and all sorts of other shit everywhere.

I fucking hate it.

How my parents managed to get themselves stuck here fuck only knows. I've wondered more than once over the years, if them losing their lives in that collision that day was actually the best thing for them. It sure beats rotting to hell in this place.

I bring the car to a stop behind Letty's and jump out.

I don't bother knocking, I already know she's inside.

"Scarlett?" I shout the second the door is open. I march inside the dated trailer, more grateful than ever that I've got a decent fucking house to live in and go in search of her.

"What the hell, Kane?" she snaps, jumping from the couch as if she intends to physically remove me from her dad's house.

Lowering my voice, I keep my eyes trained on her. "I told you not to come here."

"And I told you to fuck off."

My teeth grind to the point I wonder if I'm about to crack one.

"It's like you enjoy pissing me off, Princess," I growl, ignoring the fact that William Hunter's death glare is burning holes into my skull.

Her lips part, I'm sure to spit more abuse at me that's going to make me want to punish her, but it isn't her voice that fills the space around us.

"You need to leave," William barks, sitting forward on the couch despite the fact he looks like he can barely fucking move.

"No problem, but I'm taking your daughter with me."

"Like fuck you are. I'm not some rag doll you get to drag around, Kane."

"You'll be whatever I want you to be when you defy me on purpose and put yourself in danger."

"She isn't in danger," William spits.

Ripping my eyes from Letty, I turn my attention to her father.

"Are you sure about that?" He pales slightly, giving me the answer I need. "Exactly. You fucked up, old man. She now knows the truth, which means she's in fucking danger."

"Victor wouldn't risk touching her."

An unamused chuckle falls from my lips.

"Victor doesn't give a shit about anyone. He'd wipe out his own flesh and blood if it benefited him. Gray hasn't been seen for fucking months. Do we see Victor walking around like he gives two shits about where his youngest son is or if he's still alive?"

"He nearly killed my daughter," William growls.

"Even more reason to protect this one, don't you think?" I ask, raising a brow.

His eyes hold mine for a beat longer, a silent warning within them. He doesn't want me anywhere near Scarlett, that much is obvious, but he also knows that I'm right.

"But you're one of them. Why would I trust you with her?"

"Because you have no other choice. You knew all of this, yet you didn't seem to be in a rush to send her back to where she's safe."

"You think she's safe in Maddison?"

"Safer than she is here in this shithole."

"But the Harris brothers—"

"Are not a fucking threat to her. I am not a threat to her," I interrupt. "But Victor Harris, he's a fucking threat."

William nods his head, conceding to me.

"He's right, sweetheart. You should leave."

"What?" Letty screeches at her dad. "No. No, you can't be serious. I'm not leaving you like this. Have you even eaten since you got back?"

"I'm fine, Scarlett. I can look after myself perfectly fine."

Letty fumes, her lips pursed in frustration and her little fists curled in anger.

"Great, shall we?" I ask, gesturing toward the exit. I think it's fairly polite seeing as what I really want to do is throw her over my shoulder and march her out of this place.

"I'm not going anywhere with you," she spits, much to her dad's delight.

"See, just like your mother," he mutters while she stands with her hands on her hips and a petulant expression on her face.

"You two are unbelievable."

"Please, Let. Just go back to college and stay out of harm's way. You can call me, video call me. I promise I'm fine."

"You work for the devil, you're not freaking fine."

"Letty, this is my life," he says with a defeated sigh. "It's been my life for years. Please, just let me continue."

"No, I'm not leaving until I've made you dinner and sorted this place out."

As father and daughter stare each other down, both of their stubborn streaks too strong to concede, my patience snaps.

"Kane, what the fuck are you doing?" she screams as I do exactly as I should have done the second I got here and throw her over my shoulder.

"We're leaving."

"No, he needs—"

"Dinner, I heard. We'll order him a pizza on the way back."

"I'm not going with you." Her fists slam down on my

ass as I walk us out of her dad's trailer. "Dad, help me," she screams, kicking her legs in the hope it'll make me put her down.

It won't work.

I spin, looking at her father before I walk out of his home.

His features are hard, his eyes narrowed at me.

"I hope you know that I'd just warned her to stay away from the likes of you, Legend."

"Yeah, well. Sometimes it isn't that easy."

"If you put her in harm's way, I'll kill you myself."

"You can trust me, sir. Nothing will happen to her. I'm not the bad guy here."

Letty scoffs at my words.

"No, you're the fucking devil," she spits.

"Now, now, we all know that title is reserved for Victor," I growl at her. "I'll call someone to help you clean this place up a little, while you recover."

I nod at him before swinging the door open and marching through, Letty still flailing about in my arms.

"Put me down," she screams, starting up with the kicking and punching once again. A couple of teenagers who are kicking a ball down the track look up. Pretty much like everything that happens here, they don't bat an eyelid at the fact I'm manhandling a woman. That pretty much sums up this place.

I open my passenger door and lower her inside.

"I'm not coming with you." She fights, clawing at my forearm when I pin her in place with my hand around her neck.

Leaning in until my nose is almost touching hers, I stare into her dark, angry eyes.

"You totally ignored my orders, Princess."

She scoffs. "I don't take fucking orders from you, Kane. In fact, I don't actually take orders from anyone. I wanted to make sure my dad was okay. I don't give a shit about Victor or any of the fucking Hawks. You're all a bunch of fucked-up, psychotic criminals as far as I'm concerned."

"You should fucking care. How many times do I need to say it? He will kill you."

"So then fucking let him," she cries, her shoulders lifting in a shrug as if she really doesn't care.

My fingers tighten around her throat but she doesn't so much as flinch.

"Go on, be a good little minion and do his dirty work for him. That's what you do isn't it, Kane? You kill people for that cunt."

My jaw pops, my teeth grinding so hard they actually hurt. My heart races and I have to fight to stop my hand from trembling against her.

"Princess," I force out through the red haze of anger that's descended over me.

She stares at me as if she has no cares in the world. Unfortunately for her, I can feel her pulse thundering under my touch.

"Don't fucking move or your father is going to witness something he really fucking doesn't want to."

Her lips part to respond but when her eyes rip from mine and look over my shoulder, I know that he is indeed watching us.

She swallows nervously before lowering her head and looking down at her lap.

It's good to know that she can follow orders when her family is involved.

With a warning squeeze of her throat, I throw her purse onto her lap and slam the door closed before jogging around to the driver's seat.

I start the engine and without looking up at where I know William is standing watching us. I back away from his trailer and floor it from the place I'd quite happily never set foot inside again.

"Kane, I—"

"Don't," I bark, my grip on the wheel so tight it's painful and causes my fingers to cramp up.

She blows out a breath and twists away from me, resting her head on the window.

Leaning my own back against the headrest, I drag in a couple of deep breaths, willing my anger at her fucking stupid decisions to cool off.

It works for a second but then I glance over at her. The image of her bound to a chair like Reid explained to me after she only gave me the very basics of what happened pops into my mind.

"What the fuck are you doing?" she cries, startled when I take a sharp left, cutting off the car that was approaching on the other side of the road.

I grit my teeth and swallow down my response as we continue forward for a few miles before the car begins to bounce around as the terrain changes. We soon find ourselves under the cover of trees and totally alone.

"Oh good, you've brought me to the middle of nowhere to kill me."

"Don't fucking tempt me, Princess," I growl, reaching over and sliding my fingers into the hair at the nape of her neck and dragging her toward me.

Her lips part in shock but she doesn't say anything as I smash her lips against mine. I plunge my tongue into her mouth as her hands attack my arms and chest—anything she can—in her attempt to push me away.

She fights my every movement, every swipe of my tongue trying to force her to submit. It isn't until I once again take her by the throat that her hands let up their attack and her body begins to relax under my hold.

"Give in, Princess."

"Fuck you, Kane."

"Now there's a fucking idea."

Still refusing to kiss me, our lips remain pressed together unmoving as our increased breaths mingle. Her eyes hold mine but with each passing second, I see her resolve begin to weaken.

Reaching down, I pop open the fly of my pants and awkwardly push the fabric down over my ass.

Slipping my hand back into her hair, I pull her back from me and her eyes immediately dart down to where I'm now slowly working my hard length.

Desire darkens her eyes, the gold flecks damn near glittering.

"Kane?"

"You owe me, Princess."

"Uh—"

"You disobeyed me. Forced me to the Creek to get you."

"I didn't—" Not interested in her argument, I push her head lower until she's hovering right over my length.

"Suck me, Princess. Make all of this worth my while."

My heart thunders and my temperature soars as his fingers tighten in my hair, forcing me toward his length.

I'm so fucking mad at him right now, my body trembles with my restraint. The desire to reach out and bite the thing off as revenge for his alpha caveman act in front of my dad is strong. But not as strong as my desire for him.

My clit throbs as I pause here, suspended over the center console like a cheap whore.

But I guess that's what this is.

He thinks I owe him, and what better way to make me pay.

"Princess," he growls, his deep low voice sending a violent shiver through my body. "I don't have all fuckin—fuck," he barks as I close the space between us and suck him deep into my mouth.

His taste explodes on my tongue, making my mouth water for more.

His tight grip on my hair as he pulls me back up his length bites but the pain only adds to the intensity between my legs.

"Fuck, Princess, your mouth is..." His words trail off as he pushes me down again, taking total control of my rhythm.

Each time he lowers me down, he forces his cock farther back into my throat until he starts to make me gag around him.

"Fuck. So fucking good, Princess," he groans as he continues using me for his own pleasure.

By the time he begins to harden even more in my mouth showing that he's close, my panties are ruined and my core clenches to feel him inside me once again.

"Kane," I moan when he pulls me off, making me release him.

"You're not calling the fucking shots right now, Princess," he growls, the roughness of his voice not helping my situation.

Before I know what's happening, his giant hands are around my waist and I'm being lifted over to his side of the car.

"You wore a skirt. It's almost like you knew this was going to happen," he murmurs, pushing the fabric up around my waist and wrapping his fingers around the side of my panties, the sound of ripping lace mixing with that of our heaving breaths.

Anger surges through me at his words. How can he even suggest that? There is no part of me that thought he'd come chasing after me and force his cock down my throat for the privilege.

My hand flies out without instruction from my brain but he's faster than me and his fingers encircle mine in a tight grip long before I make any kind of contact with him.

"You want to make this worse, Princess?"

His grip on both my wrists and my hip tighten until the point of pain, enough to ensure both will be bruised tomorrow.

"Then don't insinuate I fucking planned this," I hiss.

"Then don't pretend you don't want this."

Moving my hand so it wraps around his neck, he lowers his own to my core.

"You're fucking dripping," he states, dipping two fingers inside me and making my muscles tighten to pull him deeper. "Dirty little whore."

As always, his words send a bolt of heat to my pussy, flooding his hand even more, something he doesn't miss.

"Fuck, Princess."

I almost cry out at the loss of his fingers but I soon forget about it when he runs the head of his cock through my wetness.

"Kane," I moan, trying to force myself down on him when he gets to my entrance. My hand tightens around his neck as I fight to take control.

"That isn't how this works," he forces out, reaching up to grab my throat once more, pushing me back against the steering wheel.

The second I'm where he wants me, his hips surge up, his cock filling me in one quick thrust.

"Kane," I cry as the burn from his intrusion gives way to the pleasure.

"Missed me, Princess?"

The smugness in his voice and the smirk on his face makes me want to try to slap him again, but I know it's pointless because he can read the thought in my eyes, I'm sure.

My arms flail around trying to find something to hold on to as he begins pistoning inside me, pulling my hips down to meet every one of his brutal thrusts.

My palm lands on the window, the cold glass cooling my heated skin for the briefest of moments as it slides down.

"When will you learn to do as you're fucking told?" he spits as he continues fucking me.

His hair has fallen over his brow and his skin is flushed with exertion, his lips twisted as if he's in pain.

"Shit," I say in the rush, trying to grapple onto the edges of reality that are quickly slipping away while he's inside me. "Are you okay? You shouldn't be—"

"Shut up, Princess," he growls and my lips immediately slam closed.

I stare at him with my brows raised.

You know what, I hope it really fucking hurts.

His smirk tells me that he knows exactly what I'm thinking.

His fingers tighten and I'm pulled down lower onto him ensuring that his cock hits that magical deep spot inside me every time he surges up.

My body burns, my nerve endings tingling, ready for the release that's just in touching distance.

He knows I'm close. We've played this game long enough now for him to know my tells. Reaching up under my shirt, he drags the cup of my bra down and squeezes my nipple until it burns with pain.

"I've got a million reasons why I shouldn't let you come, Princess," he warns. "How about you tell me why I should?"

I stare at him. The muscles running down his neck strain with tension. My eyes run over his chest and abs. I wish like hell that he didn't have a shirt on so I could take in the muscles clenching there too as he thrusts inside me.

I find his eyes once more. The blue has almost been entirely swallowed by the darkness of his anger and desire. The knowledge that I'm the one to cause that reaction in his makes me feel like a fucking goddess.

"B-because you want to?"

"Fuck, Letty. Fuck." His palm slams against the window with such force I let out a startled cry before he grips my hips to move me exactly where he wants me as he ups the ante.

"Come, Princess. Come all over my fucking cock."

He slams up into me once more and my head falls back as pleasure engulfs me. My body convulses as wave after wave of pleasure hits me over and over.

Kane's brutal movements, or grip on my body, don't falter until his cock swells even more, stretching me that bit wider as he falls over the edge. The sight of him and the feeling of his cock jerking inside me forces me into a second release almost before the first had subsided.

Unable to hold myself up, I fall forward into his chest as I fight to regain control of my breathing.

His cock softens inside me but it's not enough to slip out when I push from his body and sit up.

A groan rips from his throat at my movement and when I find his eyes, I find his eyelids squeezed tight.

"I should bend you over the hood of the car and treat you like you deserve," he grits out.

"Because fucking me in the front seat wasn't enough?" I ask, amusement lacing my tone.

"It's never e-fucking-nough," he mutters but his breath catches as if he didn't actually mean to say the words out loud.

Not willing to even acknowledge what he means by that statement, I shift, more than ready to climb off him..

His hands slip down my thighs, his fingers clenching for a few seconds, stopping me. But he eventually releases me and allows me to fall down into the passenger seat.

"We should get back." My voice is flat, void of any emotion as I climb back to my own seat and attempt to fix my clothing. My thighs ache and the evidence that he just came inside me without a fucking condom makes itself known.

My heart continues to race but I refuse to let thoughts of the past into my head.

Feeling naked with a short skirt and no panties, I reluctantly glance over at him as he puts himself back together but I don't miss the flash of red lace that's poking out of his pocket.

"Are you for real?" I blurt, my eyes still at his waist.

He chuckles darkly but doesn't say anything as he sits straight and lowers the window a little, letting some fresh woodland air mix with the scent of sex that's filling the car.

My skin burns as I remember what just went down in here.

Lifting my hands, I run my fingers through my hair to smooth it down and try to find some calm in all this chaos.

Kane's angry stare burns the side of my face but he makes no attempt to take us away from here.

"Can we go, please?"

"Always wanting to get away from me, Princess."

"And you're surprised?" I mutter, more than ready to put this whole evening behind me.

"Here," he says, passing his cell over. "Order your dad some dinner."

I stare down at the phone and frown.

"I can do it myself," I snap, reaching forward for my purse, hoping like hell there's also a freaking tissue in there too because... yuck.

"Order his food, Princess," he growls, his voice rough and deep, sending shivers racing through me as he throws his cell into my lap.

"O-okay."

I pick it up with shaking hands and find he's left an app open for me.

I scroll until I find something I know Dad loves and then tap in his address.

"Done. Here." I throw it back at him, much like he did me and I can't fight my smirk when I obviously hit him in the balls and he jolts in shock.

He glances over as we turn back onto the main road but he doesn't say anything.

I curl up once more and keep my eyes trained on the

passing buildings before the scenery changes as we make our way out of town.

"MKU is that way," I say, pointing to a turn he missed to finally take us away from Harrow Creek.

"I'm aware, Princess."

"But—"

He shoots me a look that expertly cuts off any argument that might have been about to fall from my lips.

I have no idea what's out here, we're now mostly surrounded by forest, but I have a feeling that whatever it is, isn't good.

I swallow nervously and watch as he keeps driving. Only a few minutes later, a sign comes into view.

"Kane?"

"What? I'm hungry," he says as if this was the plan all along.

"Y-you're taking me to Hallie's?"

"Yeah. Problem?"

I shake my head as he pulls into the lot.

I haven't been here for years. I remember Mom and Dad bringing us for pancakes when we were kids once. I think it was for Zayn's birthday or something as a special treat. We didn't have the kind of money that meant we could eat out a lot, even at a diner.

It's not until I stand from the car that I remember what I'm missing. The cool air surrounds my swollen core and I gasp.

"Problem?" Kane asks again, now around the hood and approaching me with a dark expression on his face.

"Yeah, you've got my fucking panties," I hiss, feeling

naked without them despite the fact no one would know right now.

"Oh these?" he asks, a smirk tugging at his lips as he pulls them from his pocket.

My teeth grind as he holds them up.

"They're no use to you now. They're ruined. Much like your cunt, Princess. Because in case you hadn't realized—" He takes a step forward, forcing me against the car. The length of his body presses against mine, his still hard cock against my stomach as he lowers his lip to my ear. "I fucking own you."

His hand slips between us and he finds the bottom of my skirt.

Oh my God.

I squeeze my eyes closed in an attempt to block out where we really are as his fingertips part me and graze my still very sensitive clit.

"So fucking wet for me, Princess," he growls, slipping farther back and spearing his finger inside me.

"K-Kane, we're in a parking lot," I breathe, desperately wanting him to stop and turn up the heat all at the same time.

I've never met anyone who's made my head and body war in a way that Kane does.

I hate him, I want him.

I want him to leave, I want him to stay.

I want it to end, I want more.

One thing I do know is that he makes me fucking crazy.

"An empty parking lot," he corrects. "No one would see if I fucked you right here."

"Kane," I whimper as he curls his fingers and starts rubbing at the perfect spot. "Oh shit."

"But do you know what?" he whispers, his hot breath causing goose bumps to erupt over my entire body.

I shake my head, but the movement is so slight I'm surprised he even notices.

I gasp as he swiftly removes his fingers from me.

"I won't."

He moves back, runs his eyes down my body before lifting his fingers to his mouth and sucks on them.

A rush of heat floods my core as his eyes shutter as he tastes me.

Why the hell does he look so fucking dangerous doing that?

Because he knows full well how much it's turning you on right now.

"Come on then," he says abruptly, reaching for my hand and pulling me from the car to make our way to the diner entrance.

The parking lot might have been deserted, but inside the diner isn't and the second I see eyes on us my cheeks burn red hot knowing that they were probably watching.

I hang back slightly, hiding behind Kane.

"Hey," he snaps, pulling me beside him. "They're just jealous." His smirk shows just how proud he is of the fact they know exactly what he was doing to me against his car.

Asshole.

"I don't give a fuck if they are." I don't want them staring at me like that, like they're stripping me naked with their eyes.

The thought turns my stomach.

"Don't worry, Princess. They'll die before getting anywhere near you. I can promise you that."

"Kane, my boy," a soft female voice says as an older woman heads our way with a huge smile on her face.

She looks like the grandmother I always wished I had. The one who'll teach you to bake, make clothes for your dolls and let you get away with all the naughty things you never would with your parents. And she's looking at Kane like he is literally the light of her life.

Glancing at him, I see a similar fondness in his eyes and a soft smile that doesn't appear very often playing on his lips. The sight of it has something flitting inside my stomach and the desire for him to look at me like that is suddenly impossible to ignore.

"Oh, oh, oh." She stops dead in her tracks when she spots me beside Kane. "Scarlett Hunter, well, I never!"

My breath catches that she knows my name. I left the Creek years ago, why would she have any reason to know who I am?

"Uh... H-hi," I stutter. "H-have we met before?" I ask, totally confused by all of this.

"A couple of times, but you were young," she says softly.

"I'm Hallie." She smiles. "Usual table, young man?"

"You got it, H."

She smiles at Kane again in a way I'm sure she would to a sweet young boy. Not like she would to a vicious gang member who could probably squeeze the life out of her with one hand and without breaking a sweat.

With Kane's hand on the small of my back, we're led

to a booth right in the back of the diner, cutting us off from all the other customers. I take a seat and expect him to slide in opposite me but to my shock, he drops down beside me.

My stomach flips but I'm not sure if it's with excitement or dread as his hot palm lands on my bare thigh.

"Drinks?" Hallie asks, either not seeing where Kane's hand is or just ignoring his actions. I'm inclined to say it's the latter.

"S-soda, please." I try to push his hand off, or at least lower, but he's having none of it.

"Same," Kane adds.

"And your usual?"

"Yep, for both of us."

"Coming right up. You kids enjoy yourselves." She beams at Kane and my heart melts. It's nice that he's got some kind of family aside from the Harrises after losing his parents when he was younger and then his gran less than a year ago.

"I don't get a say in what I eat?" I ask as he watches Hallie retreat to the kitchen.

"Nope."

"What if I don't like it?"

"You will," he states, full of confidence. He leans toward me, pushing my hair away from my ear with his nose. "I know exactly what you need, Princess."

My breathing falters at his words, his deep voice and the silent promise of what's to come sending a shiver down my spine.

His hand squeezes my thigh before he shifts a little

higher.

"Kane," I warn, my eyes scanning the space around us for spectators.

"No one can see you and no one would dare walk up to this table unless they're bringing food or drinks."

"Th-that's enough. Hallie seems too sweet for the likes of you."

He chuckles at my words. "Don't let her sweet smile fool you. That woman knows everything."

"Yeah, apparently so. How exactly did she know who I was?"

He thinks for a moment.

"Because I've talked to her about you," he admits, although he doesn't look at me when he does.

"Why? What have you said?"

He shrugs as a younger waitress walks over with our sodas and places them down in front of him. Her eyes don't waver from him, and if it weren't for the fact she just delivered two glasses then I'd have no doubt that she's no clue that I was even sitting here.

Kane, however, doesn't even look at her, not even when he mutters a thank you.

"What have you told her about me, Kane?"

"It doesn't matter."

"It does to me." I don't know why I say it or even think that he might take pity on me.

He stills before slowly twisting in his seat so he can look at me.

"She knows everything," he confesses. His eyes holding mine so I can see the truth in them.

"E-everything?"

"Well, not the recent developments. Or the sex in the library. She'd probably get a kick out of that though. So—" He turns and lifts his arm. "Hal—"

"No," I squeal, reaching to grab his arm. "Don't you dare."

When he looks back at me, I swear to God I stop breathing because he's got the most breathtaking smile on his face.

"I was joking. But it's good to know how you feel about sharing."

"She's an old woman, Kane. Old enough to be your grandmother."

He shrugs as two plates with the biggest burgers I have ever seen piled on the top appear before us.

"I am never going to eat that all," I mutter, taking in the sheer amount of food.

Hallie smiles softly at me as I stare at the food in horror.

"Just do your best, sweetie. This one will finish up what you can't manage."

"Thank you."

"Scarlett," she says as if she can't really believe I'm here. "You are more than welcome." The way she studies me makes me wonder what exactly she knows about me. If what Kane is saying is true and that she knows everything, then why doesn't she hate me like he does? There's no way he's painted me in a good light.

"Eat," he says after a few seconds once Hallie has left us to it and I'm still sitting there lost in my own thoughts.

"Why doesn't she hate me?"

Kane's got the giant burger in front of his face when I

look up at him but I don't miss the way his eyes wrinkle with his smile.

"Why would she?"

"Because you do."

"Hallie is more clever than me," is all he says before stuffing the food in his mouth and cutting off any more conversation.

"I'm so full," I complain from Kane's passenger seat with my hands on my bloated belly as he finally drives us back toward Maddison. "I haven't been this fat in a long time."

"You're not fat, Princess."

"Don't I know it. I lost so much weight after everything."

The mood in the car darkens at my mention of the past and what we lost.

"You should have looked after yourself better."

"Easier said than done when you can't see the point in life."

"Jesus." He rubs at his jaw before running his fingers through his hair in frustration. "I keep fucking this up. I don't even know what to say to make it any better."

My chin drops at the vulnerability in his tone. He's trying, I know he is. But I'm not sure he'll ever truly understand how it felt to lose our baby the way I did.

"You're not fucking anything up. There is no right thing to say, no way to magically fix what's broken."

"You're not broken, Let," he says, briefly glancing over at me before taking a turn.

"I wasn't actually talking about me but I'm glad you don't think I am." Shame I don't feel the same way. I've lived for the past year with the feeling that I could shatter into a million pieces at any second. Granted, it's getting better but it's still there, under the surface.

Silence falls around us once more as he takes the final turn into the parking lot for my dorm.

"What about my car?" I ask, not forgetting that it's sitting outside Dad's trailer.

"I'll get a couple of the guys to deliver it back to you."

"No, it's okay. I'll get one of the guys to help me tomorrow." It's impossible not to notice how tight his fingers grip the wheel.

"*They* don't need to get involved."

For a second, I've no clue what he's talking about but then it hits me.

"I wasn't actually talking about Luca or Leon, Kane. You need to let that shit go with them. They're good guys."

"Luca is blanking you because you were with me Saturday night. That's not a good guy."

"He just wants the best for me and you've never given him a reason to make him think that you're it."

"No, he wants you for him, not the best."

I shake my head. "He doesn't matter. That ship's sailed."

"So you have fucked him?" he asks, turning his narrowed eyes on me.

"Luca? No, never." He nods, but his eyes flash with anger as he registers my unspoken words. That knowledge doesn't seem to piss him off as much as assuming something has happened with Luca though.

"Go pack a bag," he demands.

"Uh... what?"

"Go and pack a bag," he repeats as if I'm an idiot. "You're not staying here."

"This is where I live."

"Maybe so, but it's not where you're sleeping tonight."

"Uh..."

His eyes drop down my body and stop where my thighs are pressed tightly together. "Do I need to remind you why it would be in your favor to do as you're told?"

"N-no," I stutter as tingles erupt in my lower belly.

"Good. You've got ten minutes or I'm coming to find you. And you won't like what will happen if I have to do that." His threat has a pool of heat surging between my legs.

"Uh... okay," I agree, knowing that I don't really have a choice, not that I really want one.

His blue eyes sparkle with wicked intent as I unbuckle myself and reach for my purse.

"Be quick."

"Feeling impatient?"

"I've spent the past almost two hours with you sitting beside me with no panties on. I'm beyond fucking impatient, Princess."

Feeling bare but accomplished, I climb from his car, careful not to flash anyone who might be loitering around the lot and hurry toward my dorm.

I shouldn't be this excited about spending the night with the devil. Although, with his little touches and teases the past few hours, plus seeing how sweet he was with Hallie, something inside me has softened. Well, that or I'm just really fucking horny. It's probably better that I don't think about it too much and just go with the flow. Go with what feels right.

The dorm is empty as I make my way to my room. I'm grateful because the last thing I want to do is explain where I've been or where I'm now going with a packed overnight bag.

I rush into my room, mentally listing all the things I'm going to need for my impromptu sleepover but the second I push the door open I come to a grinding halt.

Reaching down, I tug at my pants, trying to make some space for my cock as I watch her ass sway as she walks away from me.

Part of me wants to go with her to ensure she does as she's fucking told, packs a bag and comes back. But the other part wants to see if she'll actually do it. That part is also secretly hoping that she doesn't because I'd really like to go up there in ten minutes and spank her ass for not following orders.

My fist clenches at the thought alone, my semi threatening to go full mast as the image of my handprint on her round ass fills my mind.

Beautiful. Fucking beautiful.

I grip the wheel in the hope it'll help keep me seated instead of giving in to my need to follow her.

Thankfully, my cell rings in my pocket, it's the perfect distraction.

Or at least it should be.

I answer the call, knowing that it's the only way I'll get rid of him.

"Legend," Victor barks the second the call connects. "Wednesday night. Alana. No excuses, and the whole night this time. No pussying out."

"No, Vic. I'm done, remember."

"And I can get you kicked off that team faster than Alana can make you come. Do the right thing."

The tone that fills my ear tells me that he's already hung up.

"Motherfucker," I snap, slamming my palm down on the wheel. "Fuck. Fuck."

Resting my head back, I try to get my breathing under control.

I knew this was going to happen. I knew he was never going to keep to his end of the deal, but what choice did I have? I either did what he wanted of me or I kissed goodbye to getting guardianship of Kyle and my dream of playing college football.

"Fuck."

When my eyes find the clock again, I notice how long Letty has been gone and anger blooms, sending red hot fury through my veins.

I'd have been mad that she ignored me before, but after that very brief conversation with Victor, it's even worse.

Jumping from the car, I all but run toward the building and take the stairs up to her floor three at a time.

The communal area is deserted as I storm through toward Letty's closed door.

I don't stop to think about what might be happening

inside other than her hiding from me. I'm expecting the door to be locked in a pathetic attempt to keep me away. I'm surprised when I push the handle down and the door swings open but what I'm even more shocked by is the scene unfolding before my eyes.

My teeth grind and my fists curl, ready to finally get the punch in that I'm more than desperate for.

Standing in the middle of her room is Letty whose face is being cupped by a frustrated-looking Luca.

Only, he's no longer staring down at her but shooting his death stares in my direction.

"Get your fucking hands off her," I seethe, my blood at boiling point from his innocent touch alone.

His lips curl up in a smirk.

"Fuck off, Legend. She doesn't want you here." He releases her and pulls her behind him.

"Me?" I ask incredulously. "She doesn't want me here? I'm not the one who blanked her all day. I'm the one who's treated her right, made her scream and took her for dinner."

Luca's chin drops as Letty hisses, "Kane."

"You've been with him tonight?" Luca asks Letty, clearly not believing a word that comes out of my mouth.

"Yes," she whispers.

"And you fucked him, again?"

"Luca, please. Do we have to do this?" She looks up at him through her lashes, begging him to leave it.

His shoulders drop in defeat as he stares back at her.

I might not like the prick, but right now, I can't help feeling a little sorry for him.

He likes her, that much is obvious, but he's getting

nowhere and his reaction only solidifies what Letty told me earlier about them having never slept together. He's clutching at straws right now although I'm pretty sure deep down he knows he's already lost.

"Do you really want him?"

I stop breathing the second the question falls from his lips.

"Uh..." Letty glances over at me briefly.

"Go on, Princess. Answer his question."

"I... um..." She looks between the two of us, panic filling her eyes. To her, there is no right answer here, she's going to hurt at least one of us no matter what she says.

"Let," he pleads, dragging her eyes back to him once more.

"You should just leave," I suggest, giving Letty an out seeing as we both already know the answer to his question.

She came up here to pack a bag to spend the night with me. Me, not him.

The reason she's standing there with no panties on is because of me. And it was my name she was screaming only a few hours ago while her pussy was stretched around my cock.

He blows out a breath and I immediately suck one in, my chest rising knowing from his reaction that I've won.

He spins on his heels and closes the space between us.

"If you fucking hurt her again, I will kill you." His finger pokes me in the chest as his eyes hold mine.

The fire that was in them when I first burst in is gone. He just looks... defeated.

Unlike usual, I don't smirk in his face or spit back some insult to rub salt into the wound.

"Deal."

His eyes widen a little in surprise but he doesn't say anymore, instead, he nods once and then walks out of the room, swinging the door close behind him.

"Luca," Letty cries in a panic as she races forward as if she's going to chase him but my arm shoots out, stopping her in her tracks. "No, I need to go—"

"No, Princess. You don't. He's a big boy, he can look after himself."

"I don't want to hurt him, Kane."

I pull her into my body and wrap my arms around her waist, taking in the tears that are filling her eyes and the slight tremble to her bottom lip.

"He isn't your responsibility."

"He's my best friend," she whispers, unable to look into my eyes any longer.

"So he should support you, not make you feel like this."

Her head snaps up, her eyes narrowing in anger. "Don't turn this around on him," she snaps. "He hasn't done anything wrong."

"And you have?"

Her lips part to answer but she can't find any words.

Spinning us around, I back her up against the wall.

"Exactly. You're not in the wrong either."

"I've been lying to him."

"So? That's your prerogative. Just because he's your friend—" I damn near spit that word at her. "It doesn't mean he has to know everything about your life."

"I've been lying to him for years," she admits. "I never told him we had a history."

"Well, I guess that explains a lot."

"Your rivalry was already bad enough. I didn't want to make it worse by telling him how much you hated me."

"Hmm..." I murmur.

"I never thought we'd all end up in the same fucking place." She sighs, looking exhausted with the whole situation.

"Well, fate had other ideas because here we are, and I fully intend on showing you just how good that can be."

"Why, Kane? Why are you being so... so decent all of a sudden?" Her body tenses under my hold and I've no doubt that if I weren't holding her in place right now then she'd have bolted.

Cupping her jaw, I rub my thumb over her cheek, holding her eyes captive.

"Fuck going to my place. We'll stay here."

She gasps as I lift her, pinning her into place with my hips. Her legs automatically wrap around my waist and her lips part for me.

Plunging my tongue to her mouth, she eagerly sucks on it. I've forgotten the question she asked. It gives me just a little longer to figure out the answer because right now, all I know is that there isn't anywhere else in the world I'd rather be.

"Y-you need to leave," she forces out when I rip my lips from hers in favor of her neck.

"Fuck that, Princess. I'm not going anywhere."

Wrapping my fingers around the hem of her shirt, I

pull it up her body. She resists for the briefest of seconds before lifting her arms to allow it to happen.

"Feel free to keep fighting me though, you know how much I love that."

"You're an asshole," she pants as I kiss over her swollen breast, pulling the lace away to expose her stiff nipple beneath.

"I know."

Wrapping my lips around her peak, I suck it deep into my mouth making her arch from the wall and for her head to fall back in pleasure.

"Oh God, Kane."

"Want me to leave now, baby?"

I switch to the other side, giving it the same rough treatment. Her hips grind against me as she tries to find the friction she needs.

Moving her from the wall, I unhook her bra as I walk her toward her bed.

I lower her down, undo the button on her skirt and pull her remaining piece of clothing from her body, knocking her Vans off her feet as I do so.

The sight of her laid out before me makes my chest ache.

She shouldn't want this after everything. She shouldn't allow me this after what I've put her through. But as I drop to my knees and part her thighs, I know without a doubt that right now, she also wouldn't be anywhere else—with anyone else.

Parting her, I lean forward and run my tongue up the length of her pussy, collecting up her sweet juices and making them mine.

"Kane," she cries, loud enough to alert the entire dorm. Not that I give a shit. She can scream my name until she's hoarse for all I care.

Her hips lift from the bed as I suck her clit into my mouth and drag my teeth along it, biting hard enough to cause a sting of pain that I know she loves.

Others might think she's all sweet and innocent, but I know the truth. And my girl loves a bit of rough.

Reaching my arm out, I skate my hand up her stomach, holding her in place until I find her breasts once more.

Rolling her nipple between my thumb and forefinger, I tease her entrance with my other hand making her writhe and beg for more.

"Getting a little impatient, Princess?" I growl against her, ensuring she feels every vibration of my deep voice.

Her fingers thread through my hair, dragging me closer until it starts to burn. It drives me fucking wild.

"Come for me, Princess." I bend my fingers, finding the spot that makes her scream and suck harder on her clit until she's no choice but to shatter beneath me.

"Kane," she cries. "Fuck. Fuck. Fuck," she chants as she rides out the pleasure.

The second she's done, I stand, wiping my mouth with the back of my hand. Dragging my shirt over my head, I drop my pants to the floor, kicking off my sneakers and I dive for her. I capture her mouth in a dirty and wet kiss as I take myself in hand and line up with her entrance.

"C-condom," she mutters, breaking our kiss.

"I don't have one, Princess."

I pull back slightly just in time to see fear pass through her eyes.

My heart aches for the pain she was forced to endure because of me. Because I was such a fucking cunt that she didn't feel like she could tell me the truth.

"We can stop," I say, even though it fucking pains me to do so.

I expect her to agree so when her lips curl up into a smile and she barks out a laugh, my brows pull together in confusion.

"You'd really do that? You'd stop right now?"

Every single inch of me screams no, demands that I tell her that one time was really bad luck and that it won't happen again and take what I need. It's what I'd usually do. It's what I'm sure she's used to. But I can't, not this time.

"Y-yes," I force out, knowing it's the right thing to do.

The most beautiful smile appears on her lips.

"Kane," she sighs, reaching up to cup my cheek. "Who are you?" Her eyes search mine for a few seconds. I fear she's seeing more than I'm willing to show her but unable to look away all at the same time.

I don't answer, I can't. I've no clue what's going on right now, all I know is that I don't want it to stop.

"Top drawer."

"Uh..." I hesitate, my brain not following for a few seconds.

"Condoms. Top drawer."

"Oh... y-yeah."

Leaning over, I pull it open and find the box but

before I can take one out, Letty rips it from my fingers and opens it.

I sit back on my heels and watch as she pulls it from the packet and reaches for me.

The second she touches me, an electric bolt shoots through my body.

Noticing it, she looks up at me through her lashes, a seductive smile playing on her lips.

"You're playing with fire, Princess."

"Good. I want to get burned." She rolls the rubber down my length then sits back on her palms, her legs spread wide and every inch of her on show for me. "Fuck me, Kane. Don't hold back."

"Fuck," I growl, wrapping my arm around her waist and dragging her into my body, immediately positioning her so I can thrust straight inside her.

She cries out, her nails sinking into my back as I stretch her wide.

Sliding my hands into her hair, I force her head back and slam my lips down on hers, sucking her bottom lip into my mouth and biting until the taste of copper fills both of our mouths.

"Mine," I grunt, sitting forward and forcing her onto her back so I can fuck her exactly as she needs it.

Pushing her thighs wide, I pull all the way out slowly as her pussy ripples around me before slamming back in so hard the bed rattles against the wall.

With one hand around her hip holding her in place, I reach up and wrap the other around her throat, immediately feeling her thundering pulse beneath my fingertips.

"You want me to fuck you? You got it, Princess."

A smirk curls at her lips before I thrust once more and wipe it straight from her face.

"Oh fuck," she screams.

By the time I collapse beside her, we're both panting, our skin covered in a sheen of sweat, red and raw with scratches, hickeys, and bite marks.

Exactly as it fucking should be.

By some miracle, no one knocks on her door to make sure I'm not actually trying to kill her because I could only imagine how it sounded to her roommates.

When I finally pass out, my body aches in the most delicious way and it's with her plastered against me, our limbs twisted together and her scent filling my nose.

I know I need to leave, but right in this moment, I can't bring myself to do it.

I stretch my legs out as I begin to come around and the ache in my thighs forces me awake quicker as memories of why they hurt slam into me like a truck.

"Kane?" I whisper, twisting to look at the other side of my small bed. I don't know why I bother, I already know what I'm going to find.

"Fuck," I breathe, finding it empty and drop my face into the pillow.

Did I fuck up yesterday?

Should I have fought harder and pushed him away?

"Fuck. Fuck."

A knock on my door startles me and I pull the covers up to hide my naked body on instinct.

"Y-yeah?" I call.

"It's me and Vi. Can we come in?" an amused sounding Ella says.

"Um..."

"No point hiding, Let. We heard it all," Violet adds.

"Fucking hell," I mutter, dropping my head into my hands. No wonder he wanted to go back to his place. "Hang on a second."

I hop out of bed, my body screaming at me for moving so fast as I tug on a pair of shorts and a shirt. I tidy up the empty condom packets littering the floor and the nightstand before opening the door for the nosey bitches.

"Holy fuck," Ella gasps the second she steps into my room and gets a look at me.

I probably should have looked in the mirror first.

"Okay, where can I get me one of those men? Does he have any hot friends because damn girl," Violet says, an impressed smile on her face as she looks me up and down.

"He has friends but I wouldn't want to introduce them to any of mine," I mutter, walking toward the bathroom to check out the damage that they seem so impressed by.

"Fucking hell," I whisper to myself. Although, I don't know why I'm so surprised. Not only can I feel everything he inflicted on me last night, but it's also not my first roll around the sack with Kane. I knew exactly how it was going to go when I demanded he fuck me. I knew exactly what I was doing and what I was asking for.

A smile curls at my lips because despite the fact I look like I've been mauled by a bear once again, I can't regret a second of it.

The instant he touches me, he brings out something within me that I didn't know existed until him.

I thought it was the hate, the fact he loathed me as much as I did him.

But last night wasn't about that.

Okay, so in his car, it might have been. He was mad.

So fucking mad that I'd ignored his demands and gone to the Creek to see my dad regardless. But when we got back here, the way he kissed me, the way he touched me, although brutal, it was different. Everything about him was different.

And as good as that might be, it's also terrifying.

Grabbing a hair tie from the side, I twist my matted mane up into a messy bun then brush my teeth and clean my face.

I still look like I've been attacked but at least I don't have smeared makeup all over my face.

"So," Ella says, holding out a coffee cup that I didn't notice she was carrying when she walked in. I eagerly take it from her as I wait for what's about to come out of her mouth.

"We're assuming your night was as hot as it sounded."

I can't help but snort a laugh as my face burns bright red.

"Um... it was something."

"I bet Luca thought all his Christmases came at once. What about—"

"It wasn't Luca," I blurt, cutting her off.

"B-but I let him in. He came to talk things out with you and—"

"He was here when I came back, but he left." They both stare at me, waiting for more information.

With a sigh, I drop into my chair and tell him the basic events of the night before ending up back here to pack a bag and finding Luca waiting for me.

"He apologized, tried explaining to me why he kicked

off the way he did but then Kane marched into the room, clearly too impatient to wait for me and—"

"Who threw the first punch?" Violet asks.

"No one, actually. It was... almost calm."

"You broke his heart, didn't you?"

I suck in a breath, trying to figure out a way to explain things about Luca.

"Luc doesn't want me, not really."

"He told you that?" Ella asks. "Because it certainly doesn't look that way every time he so much as glances at you."

"It's complicated but I know Luca almost better than I do myself. I know he's just trying to make something of what once might have been there a few years ago. He's got the pressure on him and he's trying to deflect to an easier time."

"He said that?" Ella asks again.

"No, he probably has no idea." I shake my head, my concern for my best friend getting stronger.

"But what if you're wrong?"

I consider her question for a few moments. "I'm not," I state confidently. "He just needs to figure it out."

"So he just left. Just like that?" Violet asks, looking confused.

"After threatening to kill him, yeah."

"That sounds more like it." She laughs.

"So, Kane? You two a thing now then?" Ella asks.

"Fuck knows what's going on. One minute he hates me and the next, well..." I share a look with Ella, silently adding in the middle part of that sentence about him finding out the truth.

"He's banging your fucking brains out and making you scream like a banshee?"

"Yeah. I don't know. He's probably woken up this morning, remembers that he hates me and regrets the whole thing," I mutter.

They both stare at me like I've suddenly grown a second head.

"Do you regret it?" Ella asks, her head tilting to the side like a puppy.

"I should," I answer honestly.

"But you don't?"

"Ugh," I moan, standing from the chair and starting to pace the room. "I know you think I'm crazy, that I shouldn't be anywhere near him after what he's done. I just—"

"Whoa," Ella says, standing in front of me and forcing me to stop. "I'm not thinking anything. You are the only one in the middle of the situation, you're the only one who knows everything. I told you before. I don't judge. I just want to make sure you make the right decision and don't end up hurt."

"But I'm going to though, aren't I? There is no happily ever after with a guy like Kane."

I think of the Hawks and all the widowed women still living in the Creek because becoming a member of that fucking gang is a death sentence. I think of Hallie yesterday and Kane telling me how she'd lost her husband in a gang war.

I don't know what I would do if something happens with Kane. If by some fucking miracle we figure out a way to overcome everything that's gone before, how the hell could I be with him knowing the kind of work he does. The kind of people he's involved with, and ultimately, that he's probably going to die.

"There's always a chance," Ella says softly, her inner romantic coming out.

"Maybe," I whisper, not wanting to get into my real concerns where Kane is concerned. I don't want them to know that I have any connection with the Hawks. The less they know the safer they are.

"Last night was fun," I say, laughing at the looks on their faces. "And maybe that's all it's meant to be. Us finally expelling all the tension that's built up over the years. Maybe it'll happen again and maybe it won't. Whatever. It's not like I actually have time for anything serious and he's got football. There are more important things right now."

My chest aches as I say the words, but I school my features to ensure they can't see just how much suggesting that it won't happen again actually pains me.

"I should get ready. See if I can find something to wear that covers all this up."

"The jersey chasers are going to hate you," Violet says, looking smug.

"Even more reason to cover up," I mutter, heading inside my small closet to find something to wear.

"Right, we'll leave you with that. Ready to go in thirty?"

"You got it," I say as they head to the door.

I think they've both gone when the door closes, so Ella's voice startles me.

Glancing over at her, I see her sappy romantic face and internally groan.

"It's okay to want more with him, Let. I know you think it will end in disaster, but there's always the chance it might not. All that you went through, it could have happened as a way to finally bring the two of you together."

My lips part but I find that I don't have any words.

She smiles at me and finally disappears, leaving me to consider her theory.

Up until that twenty-week ultrasound, I believed that everything happened for a reason, or at least I wanted to. But hearing that my baby was no more shattered everything I thought I knew about life.

I pull an oversized sweater from my closet and a pair of leggings. The neck is slashed and is never going to cover all the marks around my throat and collarbone but it's the best I've got.

After a quick shower and swiping on minimal makeup, I head out to grab breakfast and then to walk to class with the girls.

Only, it's not just the girls because all the guys have descended on the kitchen and I'm now something akin to the star attraction at the zoo.

I roll my eyes as I walk toward them all, fighting my need to run back to my room and hide.

"Good night, Miss Scarlett?" West asks with a similar amused smirk to both Brax and even Micah. I thought at least he might be able to cover his enjoyment as I squirm under their watch.

"Yes, thank you. You?" I realize my mistake the second the question rolls off my tongue.

"Oh yeah, hell. It was like a real-life fucking porno. My hand hasn't had that kind of a workout in—ow," he complains as Violet slaps him around the back of his head. "What was that for?" He sulks.

"We don't want to hear about it."

"Oh but it's okay for all of us to hear that?" He waves his hand in my general direction and I pray that the ground will just swallow me up.

"Ugh, you're a dog," she complains, getting up and dumping her plate in the sink.

"Hey, I wasn't the one getting railed last night so loud that it kept us all up."

"I'm leaving," I say, marching toward the door, foregoing breakfast. I don't think I could stomach it anyway.

"Letty, wait," Brax calls before I manage to escape.

"Yes," I hiss, reluctantly turning back toward him.

"Kane looks about as beat up as you do this morning. Good work, girl. You should be proud."

Lifting my hand, I flip both him and West off and all but run from the dorm.

I race down the stairs, my heart thundering in my chest as the realization hits me that Kane showed up to practice looking like he got attacked by a bitch in heat and that Luca will have seen it.

"Argh," I scream as I crash through the main entrance and suck in lungfuls of late summer air.

I hate this feeling that I'm being ripped in two by two completely different guys. I roll my eyes, three if you add

Leon in, although he seems to be able to see what's happening in a way that Luca can't. He's able to take a step away and look at the situation with an open mind.

I don't want to hurt Luca, he's been the best friend I could have asked for over the years, but at the same time, I can't be the person he thinks he needs me to be right now. He's deflecting and it's not going to help him in the long run.

Then Kane... I don't even know what to think about what's going on there.

I have no idea if the girls are coming or not, but I don't hang around. The prospect of a silent walk to class to clear my head actually seems like a better option right now anyway.

I keep my eyes down while my head spins with thoughts of Luca and Kane and everything that's happened since I started here.

I've only made it a few steps when a familiar voice calling my name makes my steps falter.

When I hear it again, I stop and turn around.

The sight before me is one I never thought I'd ever see but I can't help my lips curl up in a smile that almost matches his as Kane runs to catch up with me.

"Hey, are you trying to run away?" he asks, stepping right into my body and sweeping me up into his arms.

"Um... yeah, something like that."

His brows pull together in concern. "I left you a note telling you to wait for me."

"You did? I didn't see it. I kinda got ambushed by the girls wanting the details of last night," I say, quirking my brow in accusation.

"Hey, don't blame me. I wanted to take you to my place."

"Well, it seems they enjoyed it. Made use of the... live sound effects."

A satisfied smirk curls at his lips as his eyes sparkle with excitement.

"You don't need to look so pleased with yourself," I mutter, slapping his chest in mock frustration. I'm finding it harder and harder to actually get mad around him these days. That smirk that I used to think was wicked now just does weird things to my insides.

"Princess, if you saw my back, you'd know why I was so fucking pleased with myself."

"Oh my God."

"But then again," he says, reaching out to lift my hair from my neck. "You are looking pretty fine right now." His stare burns my skin as he admires his handiwork.

"Oh yeah? Why am I not surprised that you're more than happy for me to walk around looking like this?"

His hand wraps around the length of my hair and he pulls, forcing me to look up at him.

"I fucking love it. It just needs my signature one day."

"What do—" I don't get to ask what he means by that because his lips crash against mine and all previous thoughts fall from my head as his tongue pushes its way into my mouth.

"Alright playboy, put our girl down," Ella shouts the second they emerge from the building and find Kane manhandling me.

I try to pull away, but Kane grasps my chin and forces me to stay exactly where I am as they both join us.

"You're both just jealous," he says, his lips brushing mine, his hot, minty breath fanning my face.

"Hell yeah I am," Violet announces, much to Kane's amusement. "I'm not sure I've ever had a night quite like that before."

"Are you two coming or are you intending on going another round on the sidewalk," Ella mutters.

"We're coming," I tell her. "Aren't we?" I pin Kane with a look that hopefully means he has no option but to agree.

He grinds his hips ensuring that I'm able to feel his length pressing against my stomach. "If we have to. Although I could think of a much better way of spending my morning." Another grind.

"We've got class."

"Hmm, so we do. You reckon I might get lucky in the back row?" he asks, wiggling his brows.

"I'd say your chances are slim, playboy."

He throws his head back and barks out a laugh at my use of Ella's nickname.

"Come on," I say, making the most of his distraction. I step back from his body, but he doesn't let me get very far because he threads his fingers through mine and side by side we set off following Ella and Violet.

21

KANE

I had no idea what to expect when I showed up to practice this morning. Part of me thought Luca would fly straight at me after what went down in Letty's dorm last night. He'd had hours to dwell on it, to imagine what might have happened after he walked out. I could only imagine that he was ready to take me to the fucking floor.

What I really wasn't expecting was for him to totally ignore me.

He didn't look up from his place at the bench when I walked in. The only reaction he had to the other guys ribbing me about the state of my mauled back was for his muscles to tense.

I've no reason to think that he suddenly doesn't care though because he does. Part of me is grateful that Letty has a friend who would probably do anything for her should she ask but the other part of me doesn't want her to have anyone else to turn to. Selfishly, now I've got her, I want her all to myself.

Training passed without any drama, which wasn't only a shock to me but also Leon who spent almost the whole time looking between his brother and me as if we were a ticking time bomb. I guess we are.

At some point the tension between us is going to boil over. I think even Coach knows that it's inevitable, he's probably just praying it doesn't happen on the field.

I was just about to leave so I could go to pick her up and walk her to class when a shadow fell over me, only when I looked it wasn't the person I was expecting. Instead, it was Zayn.

"I appreciate that you haven't once mentioned her name while the guys were ribbing you about those." He lifts his chin to the bite marks on my neck. "But don't think I'm naïve about who it was." His eyes narrow in warning as I stand staring back at him. "If you hurt her—"

"Let me save you the speech, Hunter. How about you just go and stand behind our captain so you can have a pop after he has when I fuck this up."

"When you fuck this up?"

Yeah, when, I think to myself. I think we all know that it's going to happen no matter how hard I try.

"Was there anything else?"

"She's been through so much, Kane. You don't—"

"I know," I say, lowering my voice. "She's told me everything."

"E-everything?" he asks, stunned.

"Yeah. We've talked. Sorted shit out, hence." I gesture to my body.

"You've talked. Really?" He smirks.

"A bit," I admit because hell knows we could have

done a lot more talking. We've got enough years to make up for.

"Right, well can I suggest you do some more instead of just using her for whatever sick and twisted game you're playing."

"I'm not pl—"

"I know you, Kane. I know guys like you. Don't forget that." He takes a step back as if he wants those to be his final words but there's no way I'm letting him have it.

"You don't know fuck all about *guys like me*," I spit. "Just because you were born in the Creek, it doesn't mean you know anything about what it's like to really live there, to survive there."

He shakes his head, his eyes darkening with contempt.

"I know that the only reason you're here right now is because of your connections. Connections to some people I want my sister nowhere near."

I can't help the chuckle that falls from my lips.

"I'm not the one you need to be worrying about. I'd die before I let anything happen to her."

"I'll believe it when I see it, Legend."

"Whatever." I tug my hoodie over my head and sweep my hair back from my face, feeling his stare on me the whole time. "What happens between me and your sister is none of your business. Just like what happens between your little sister and my little brother is none of mine. Excuse me." I push past him, long past listening to his little lecture. If he really cared that much about Letty or was as close to her as he's making out, then maybe she wouldn't have been alone last year.

We spent the day together in a way we never have before. I kept her hand locked in mine when we walked into our sociology class. We sat together at the back like I warned we would, although I didn't get to fulfill the next part of my fantasy. That's something to work toward, I guess.

"I'm taking you out tonight," I tell her after we follow West and Brax out of statistics at the end of the day.

She immediately stops causing the students trying to escape behind us to crash right into her.

"Hey, watch where you're going," a high-pitched voice whines.

I only just about manage to hold in my groan of frustration when I look over Letty's shoulder to find Clara staring at her with her lip curled in disgust as if Letty is below her.

"Sorry," Letty mutters, moving aside to let everyone pass.

"Oh, Kane," she breathes the second she realizes that I'm there. Her expression instantly transforms. Her resting bitch face is long gone as she bats her eyelashes and pouts her already swollen lips at me. "Long time no see," she purrs, taking a step forward and lifting her hand as if she's about to reach out and place it on my chest.

Tugging on Letty's hand, which is still locked in mine, I pull her into my chest and wrap my arm around her waist.

"I'm great. Been busy." Ripping my eyes from her, I look down at Letty. "Ready to go, Princess."

"Uh?" Clara starts but the second I turn my death

stare on her she soon shuts her mouth. If she dares say anything about Letty then I have no issue with teaching her a lesson about respect.

Turning Letty away from her, I guide her out of the building.

"She's a slut," Letty mutters once we're out of Clara's earshot.

"Jealous, Princess?"

"Of her? Puh-lease."

"Not of her, but because she wants me."

She glances up at me with an incredulous look on her face. "Really?" she spits before turning away from me and attempting to walk away.

"What? She isn't exactly making a secret of it," I say, jogging after her.

"Yeah, and chances are that you've already fucked her."

"W-what?" I ask.

"Oh, don't look so shocked. You're a player and you know it."

I open my mouth to argue but I can't really. "I've had my moments."

She rolls her eyes and tries walking off again.

Catching up to her, I wrap my hand around the side of her neck and hold her close.

"Princess, I haven't been with anyone but you since starting here." I stare down into her eyes so she can see the truth in them.

She looks away briefly as she sighs before coming back to me.

"It's been like four weeks, Kane. That's not all that impressive."

"Not really if you knew how many offers I've had." Her lips part to rip me a new one. "I'm kidding, I'm kidding." *I'm really not.*

"Yeah well, I haven't been with anyone other than you since *that* night so..."

"Princess," I say, resting my head down against hers. "I don't want Clara. I don't want any jersey chaser or any other girl."

I don't think she knew she needed to hear that but the second the words are out of my mouth, her entire body relaxes.

"What is this, Kane?" she asks, vulnerability oozing from her. "I keep expecting you to pull the rug out from under me and tell me that this was all one sick joke."

My fingers tighten and I pull her even closer, leaving no question to anyone around us about how I feel, even if she's fucking clueless.

"It's not a joke, Let. It's... I don't know. New. Exciting. The beginning of something?"

"Exciting until you remember you hate me and you change your mind?" I can see the defeat and hurt already in her eyes and I'm not the one who's even saying the words.

"No. Exciting because I'm discovering things, I was too fucking stupid too for all these years."

She nods, accepting what I'm saying, for now at least.

A shadow falls over us forcing me to release her although what I really want to do is throw her in my car once more and take her home.

"As cute as this is, we've got practice, Legend," West says, as he and Brax watch us.

It looks like her bodyguards trust me as much as she does.

"I know, I'm coming." Turning back to Letty, I drop a kiss on her forehead.

"Come on," I say, taking her hand and turning her toward the direction of her dorm building, seeing as my car is in the lot.

West and Brax follow behind us but I block them out as we talk about the assignment Letty is starting while I'm at practice.

"I'll pick you up at seven," I tell her when we come to a stop outside her building. "Be ready and wear something nice."

"You don't need to take me somewhere fancy."

"Shh." I press my fingers over her lips. "Nowhere fancy, just not a diner."

"Okay," she breathes, pulling my hand away from her lips so she can reach up and brush them against mine.

"And pack a bag. You're sleeping in my bed tonight."

A seductive smile curls at her lips making my cock swell at just the thought alone.

She watches me from the edge of the parking lot as I climb in my car and drive away. I can still sense her confusion over what's happening, but I'm determined to prove to her that I'm not playing games.

My cell pings as I'm driving and it's not until I pull up at the training facility that I pull it from my pocket.

My stomach drops when I see the name lighting up my screen.

> Alana: Can't wait to see you tomorrow, sweetie. x

"Fucking hell," I mutter, scrubbing my hand down my face.

I need to get out of tomorrow night, but I'm not sure anything will work aside from my own death.

I look up at the imposing building before me. This has always been my dream, what I literally used to dream about as a little boy. College football, a chance at the NFL. And despite all the odds, I'm here, I made it. But at what cost?

Is it worth remaining under Victor's control to continue? Kids from the Creek don't get these kinds of opportunities, was it always meant to be an unreachable dream?

I lose myself in my thoughts until someone drums on my car window, scaring the living shit out of me.

"You coming in?" Zayn shouts, pointing at the door.

Nodding, I kill the engine and climb out.

"Don't tell me you fucked it up already," he starts before I've even closed the door.

"I'm taking her out tonight, if you must know."

"On a date?" he asks as if I've just told her that I'm taking her to the fucking moon.

"Yes, on a date."

"Wow, you must be serious," he mutters as we walk through the main doors.

"I am."

"Did she hit you in the head when she told you everything?"

"It fucking felt like it, man. How's your girl?" I ask after a couple of seconds of silence.

"She's good. Fed up of being stuck at school while I'm here."

"That must suck."

"You have no fucking idea."

"She'll be here before you know it."

We push through the locker room door and every set of eyes turns to us. Luca looks at me then Zayn beside me and his face damn near turns purple as he looks back to me.

"Hunter?" he barks.

Ignoring all of them, I head to my locker and tug the door open. I'm not interested in forcing anyone to choose sides. This isn't a fucking high school cheer squad. We're supposed to be fucking professionals now.

***

"Which ho has daddy dearest got you servicing tonight then?" Devin asks when I stop in the doorway to the living room dressed in a white button-down and black dress pants.

My fingernails dig into the wooden doorframe at his suggestion.

"None of them. I'm taking Letty out."

Devin damn near spits out the beer he'd just taken a sip of.

"Letty? You're taking Letty out?"

"Yes," I hiss, irritated that he still seems to think she's

the bad guy here. The only one trying to ruin our lives is his cunt of a father. "Problem?"

He raises his brows, telling me without words that he indeed has a fucking problem.

"You need to get over it. Victor left her little choice."

"She still went behind our backs. And, in case you've forgotten, you hate her."

"Yeah, well. Things change, Dev."

"Yeah, like you getting inside her fucking pussy. Is it really that magical?"

My teeth grind in irritation.

"I'm bringing her back here. Be nice."

He lifts his hands up in defeat. "When am I anything but nice?" I stare at him, really not wanting to remind him how he spoke to her the last time she was here.

"Whatever."

"I heard they made quite the porno," Ezra mutters, walking into the room with a steaming bowl of something in his hand.

"How the fuck would you know that?"

"I heard some rumors from last night."

A smirk twitches at my lips.

"The walls in dorms are thin as fuck apparently. I've got my lube ready for later."

"There's something fucking wrong with you, Ez. But if knocking one out while thinking of me gets you off, then who am I to comment."

"Wha—no... that's not what—"

"I'm out. Later." I flip them both off before heading for the door but not before I hear them discussing how I've been pussy-whipped. Whether I'm willingly taking a girl out on a date and not just bang her. Assholes.

I don't get nervous. Victor has sent me into the most fucked up situations over the years. I haven't batted an eyelid once, but as I drive toward Letty's dorm building something I'm not used to flutters in my stomach.

I tell myself it's just excitement for what tonight holds, but deep down, I know it's more than that.

I invite myself into their dorm and this time when I walk inside everyone looks at me as if I belong there as much as they do.

"Evening," West mutters as he nods. "You don't scrub up too bad."

"I know it's been a while, man, but really. Checking out teammates is a little desperate," Brax deadpans.

"Fuck you," West spits, slapping Brax around the back of the head.

"Right. Is she ready?"

"Almost," Ella says, slipping from Letty's room right on cue. "Looking good, Legend. You'd better have something good lined up for our girl."

"I think you all already know that I know how to treat her right." I wink at Ella and she flushes bright red and West and Brax simultaneously bark, "Hell yeah."

"You're going to need to find your own entertainment tonight though, she's staying with me."

"Spoilsport."

"Well, we wouldn't want to waste your subscription to the Hub, would we?"

West's chin drops ready to rip me a new one but he soon closes it. It only confirms to everyone in the room that he does indeed spend too much time watching others fucking instead of getting some action himself.

"Whatever. It's not like you can all try to tell me you've never watched it," he mutters.

We're all still laughing when Letty's door opens once again.

I watch as her shadow fills the space before she emerges.

"Holy shit," I breathe, taking a step forward.

A shy smile plays on her lips as every set of eyes turn on her. The urge to force her back into the room so that no one else can look at her is strong. But I promised her a night out and I fully intend on seeing it through.

Walking up to her, I wrap my hand around the back of her neck and pull her body flush against mine.

"That dress—" I whisper in her ear.

"Is it too much?" she asks nervously.

"No, Princess. It's fucking perfect. It looks like—"

"The one from that night," she finishes for me.

"Yeah. You look fucking hot."

"I thought that maybe we should have a do-over." My heart thunders as she takes a step back from me, her eyes trailing down my body. "Not too bad yourself, Legend."

My body heats, my clothes suddenly feeling a few sizes too small as my need to rip them off and forego going out only gets stronger.

22

LETTY

I was going to spend a couple of hours working like I told Kane. But the second Ella heard about my impromptu date tonight, she immediately dragged me toward my closet and demanded to know what I was going to wear.

Unable to agree, she threw my purse at me and dragged me out of the building and to the closest mall.

We didn't even get into a shop. I saw the little black dress in the window and immediately slowed to a stop.

It wasn't the same as the one I wore to Skye's party, but it was similar enough.

I didn't bother looking at anything else. We just found the rack with the dresses on it, grabbed the right size and went straight for the register.

It was probably a little too much for whatever Kane was planning. He told me that it wouldn't be anything fancy, but I knew the second my eyes landed on it that it was fate. It was the only dress that I'd be able to wear tonight.

There's a huge part of me that wants to forget about that night. For a long time I thought that absolutely nothing good came from it, but Ella's words from earlier in the day won't stop repeating in my head. Maybe, just maybe, she has a point.

Were we always meant to end up here now?

I smile as Kane opens his passenger door for me to climb in.

"You know, I'd have put money on you having no redeemable features, but it seems you might just be able to pull the gentleman thing out of the bag."

"Princess," he growls, taking my chin in his harsh grip. "I think you already know that I can deliver everything you need."

My knees get a little weak at his words. I nod, as much as his grip allows as my muscles clench, aching and reminding me exactly how he delivers.

"Keep looking at me like that and we'll have to christen the back seat of my car this time."

Liquid lust fills my veins as I vividly remember just how good both the hood and the front seat of his car was. I've no doubt the back will be equally as mind-blowing.

"You know," I say, running my fingertip down his neck and onto his chest that's exposed by his open collar. "You never finished me off on the hood. You still owe me that."

His eyes flash with desire.

He steps closer, forcing me to bump against the car, his large hand landing in his favorite spot around my neck. The move sends tingles shooting around my body. The only thing better is when it's around my throat. "Is that right?" he asks, staring right into my eyes.

"Uh-huh."

"Anyone would think you don't want to go for dinner, Princess."

"I have no idea what gave you that idea," I say innocently, although the roughness to my voice gives me away.

His hand slips down, his finger tucking into the low neckline and pulling it from my body. His eyes drop from mine to look inside.

"Princess," he growls, finding my bare breasts staring back at him.

His cock that was already growing against my belly, hardens even more.

"Tell me you're wearing panties."

"Hmm... I don't remember. I guess you'll have to find out."

His eyes hold mine for long, agonizing seconds as both our chests heave with desire.

"Get in the fucking car, Princess," he growls, his voice so deep that it's almost a warning.

His eyes darken further until they're terrifyingly black causing my insides to flip.

I knew I was playing with fire when I bought this dress, but fuck is it going to be worth it later.

Slipping from between him and the car, I drop down into the passenger seat, careful not to expose what I might or might not be wearing beneath.

After a couple of seconds, he lets out a long, pained sigh and slams the door on me, cutting off our connection. It allows my body to cool off, even if it is only for a few seconds while he stalks around the hood toward the driver's side.

He doesn't say a word as he starts the engine and backs out of the space.

"Where are we going?" I ask as the campus disappears into the distance behind us.

His grip on the wheel tightens before he glances over at me. My breath catches as I notice that wicked look is still in his eyes.

"Wait and see."

Reaching over, he places his hand on my thigh, his fingertips sneaking under the hem to caress my skin.

I fight to keep control of my breathing as he continues to torment me as we drive through town.

When he finally stops, it's on a street that's littered with restaurants of every kind you could possibly imagine. I look up and down, trying to guess which one he's taking me to.

Assuming he wants me to wait, I linger in my seat until he pulls the door open and holds his hand out to help me.

"Thank you, sir," I say seductively as I stand to my full height. He's so close that my breasts graze his chest making me gasp.

He doesn't miss my reaction to the innocent touch.

"Tonight is going to be fun, Princess," he promises.

With my hand clamped in his, he leads me toward a Greek restaurant. The scent of the food cooking inside hits me before he even opens the door and my stomach growls in anticipation.

"Good evening, Mr. Legend. Madame," the maître d' says when we stop at his station.

I glance at Kane after hearing the man greet him by name but he doesn't return my attention, instead, he's too busy saying hello like he's just bumped into a long-lost friend.

"Adrian, this is Scarlett."

"Hi," I say awkwardly, wondering how Kane knows someone here quite so well when he's spent almost all his life in the Creek.

"I hope you're hungry," he says with a smile. "We serve the best food this side of Greece."

"I can't wait," I say, hoping that I sound eager but mostly I'm just confused.

He leads us to a table in the back corner of the restaurant where we're mostly out of view from the other diners that are littered around the room. We get more than a few looks from the other tables, probably because I'm way too overdressed but I ignore all of them as we pass.

The restaurant is stunning, everything is light, the walls are exposed brick and there are lush green plants everywhere. It almost feels like we're on holiday, not in the center of Maddison.

Adrian leaves us with some olives in the middle of the table and some kind of shot that Kane knocks back before the guy has barely stepped away from the table.

"Come here often?" I ask, something just not feeling right about the place.

"A few times, yeah. The food is insane."

I glance back over to where Adrian is now welcoming another couple inside and try to force my concerns down.

"What's wrong, Let?" He reaches over the table and I

can't help my pull to him and lift my own hand so he can take it. His brows pull together as he looks at me.

"I-I—" I blow out a breath, feeling ridiculous for being so weird about all of this. "It's nothing. This is just... unexpected. I'm struggling to get my head around it."

He smiles at me and I'm relieved to see that he understands.

He wraps his other hand around the base of my chair and tugs me closer.

Tucking a lock of my hair behind my ear, his nose runs around the shell and sends shivers skating down my spine.

"Stop overthinking it, Princess. Just do what feels right," he whispers.

"What has always felt right was to run as far away from you as possible."

He chuckles. "Things change, Letty. People change."

"Do they?" I ask, turning to him and holding his eyes. I'm desperate to see something that confirms that he's telling me the truth. That this really is something, that he isn't just stringing me along and waiting for the perfect time to drop me from a great height.

His hand finds the side of my neck, his thumb stroking my cheek. My body wants to lean into his touch but I'm so terrified of what's going to happen if I let my guard down too much with him.

I stare into his heated blue eyes, my heart steadily racing in my chest and I accept for the first time just how quickly everything has changed for me.

Or has it? Has there always been something between us? Was it just veiled by the hate and the need to hurt?

"They do," he confirms after a long pause. It takes a few seconds to remember that I even asked him a question. My thoughts spinning at a million miles a minute inside my head making me lose my grip on reality.

"Whatever this is, Princess. It feels so fucking good, don't you think?"

I nod because I already know I can't lie to him. He's proved to me before that he can read me like a book.

He leans in a little closer. "And I don't think I can stop, even if I wanted to." He takes my hand in his, lifting it to his head. "You've been in here for fucking years, Let." He taps my fingertips against his temple. "Nothing I've done has got you out. And I fear that somewhere along the way, you've nestled your way in here too." He lowers his hand to his chest, right above his heart and my breath catches.

It races as fast as mine under my palm as his eyes hold mine and for the first time in my life, I really believe that I'm staring at the real Kane. Not the football player, the Hawk, the boy trying to prove himself in the Creek. Just Kane. The man who's been hurt over and over. The man who wants a better life than the one he was handed. The Kane who would do anything for his family—for his brother. The Kane that, dare I say it, just wants a normal life, love, a future.

I nod at him, the ball of emotion growing so huge in my throat that I've no chance of saying anything.

"Are you ready to order?" The heavy Greek accent startles me and when I look over I find a young lady with a notebook poised and staring right at Kane.

Rolling my eyes, I look back at him but instead of looking at the waitress, his eyes are still firmly on me.

"Oh, I haven't even had a chance to look," I confess.

"Can I?" Kane asks, glancing at the menu.

Knowing he's been here before, I agree and listen as he rattles off our order forcing the waitress to depart much to her disappointment.

Kane waits until she's gone until he leans into me once more.

"I'm sorry, Letty."

An incredulous laugh falls from my lips. "That you're so hot she couldn't help but ogle you in front of me," I blurt, instantly regretting the words when I see the cocky smirk on his face.

"Well, no, but it's good to know you think I'm hot."

"Would you think I'd be sitting here if it hurts to look at you?" I ask.

He shakes his head and goes back to what he was saying. "No, Let. I'm sorry for everything, for the past, for all the things I blamed you for. For everything I put you through. For allowing you to think I hated you so much that you couldn't even tell me about—" In a rush, I lift my fingers to his lips to cut his words off.

"Not tonight. Okay? I've spent the past year thinking about that. Not tonight."

"Okay," he says against my fingers before tilting his head and capturing my fingertips between his lips and sucking.

"Oh," I breathe, my eyes locked on his lips. My teeth sink into my bottom one as I watch his tongue sneak out as he caresses them. "Kane." I wanted it to be a warning but it comes out as anything but.

"I want you," he states, releasing my hand and lacing our fingers together once more. "I've always wanted you."

My lips part to respond but I've got no words.

"Letting Riley have you was the biggest mistake of my life."

All the air rushes from my lungs at his confession.

"But—" He mimics my previous action, cutting off my words.

"No more of the past. Not tonight. Tonight we forget about the bullshit that's behind us and we... we just be us. Right now. In this moment. Just two people who can't wait to get out of here so we can get naked."

I burst out laughing. "You did not just say that."

"Deny it, Princess. I know for a fact that if you are indeed wearing panties then they're fucking soaking."

Damn him.

"Exactly," he says around a smile when I don't respond.

"**I**'ve really got to go," I say into her kiss.

In reality, dragging on some clothes and going to work out with a bunch of sweaty dudes is the last thing I want to do right now while I've got a naked Letty in my bed. I made the decision at practice yesterday that I was going to prove to Coach that I'm back to full health and that I can play on Saturday.

I did everything for that cunt to get myself here, I'm not missing fucking games because my body aches a bit. Fuck that.

Plus, I've still not decided how the fuck I'm going to deal with Alana later. Depending on how that goes, Saturday might be my first and last chance to play a game as a Panther if Victor gets word that I'm done being his little bitch boy.

"No, ten more minutes," Letty pleads in her deep and raspy morning voice.

She reaches for my cock and wraps her fingers around the steel length.

"Again?" she asks, her brow rising, knowing that she only just made me come.

"You're in my bed, Princess. It's a side effect you're just going to have to deal with."

"Hmm... I'm sure I can cope."

"Good, because it's not changing anytime soon." I manage to twist out of her hold and reluctantly climb from bed. "Go back to sleep, I'll be back to pick you up when we're done."

I watch as she snuggles into my pillow, breathing in my scent, and my chest aches.

I think I'm already becoming a little bit too obsessed with seeing her there.

I drag on some clothes and throw my bag over my shoulder.

"Sweet dreams," I whisper, assuming she's already fallen back asleep seeing as she isn't watching me. I drop a kiss to her head and make my way to the door.

"Kane?" she whispers before I pull the door open.

"Yeah, baby?"

"Go easy on Luc. He's struggling with more than just the shit with you."

I stare at her for a beat. She's here. She's in my bed. And she'll be waiting for me to come back. I've got exactly what he wants. Maybe it is time to let shit lie.

"Anything you want, Princess."

"Well, I'd like you to be friends, but one step at a time, yeah?"

"Probably for the best."

I slip out of the room, allowing her to rest. Hell knows

we didn't get a lot of sleep when we finally got back here last night.

Part of me wanted to pull over down a dark road to take care of her request. For me to fuck her on the hood of my car again and ensure she screamed my fucking name this time but I decided against it. I needed her in a bed. Again and again after the way she teased me all night with that tiny black dress and the possibility of nothing being under it. I discovered that there actually were a pair of panties beneath, although they were so small it was debatable if they counted.

Unsurprisingly, I'm the last to enter the locker room after not being able to rip myself away from Letty.

Both Luca and Leon look straight over at me when I rush through the door but neither say anything, instead they take off in the opposite direction to begin warming up.

"Good night?" Zayn asks.

"Yeah, thanks, man. You?"

"Drinks with the guys."

I rip my hoodie off, change my sneakers, and follow the others toward the gym.

"Legend, a word," Coach barks as I pass his office.

"Yes, sir," I say, slipping into the room and dropping into the chair in front of his desk.

"How are you feeling?"

"Great, actually. I was hoping to talk to you about Saturday."

"You're not playing. Doctor's orders."

"Coach," I say, scrubbing my hand down my face. "I'm fine. Honestly."

"I need you in top form, Legend. I know what you can do, and I want one-hundred percent."

"You'll get it."

"Next week."

"No, come on, Coach. Please. I've worked too fucking hard to be benched." I try to argue but I can tell from the hard set of his face that it's not going to work.

"Get your ass out there and prove it to me then."

I'm up before he's finished talking and at the door.

I put everything I have into our session trying to prove that I'm back on form, even if I know on the inside that I'm not. Like fuck am I letting anyone else see that.

By the time I get back to the house, just one look at the stairs makes my muscles ache.

"Hey, I'm in here," a familiar soft voice says from the living room.

Turning back on myself, I walk in to find her sitting with the guys at the dining table with coffees.

"Hey, I thought you were going to wait in my room," I say, my eyes trained on Devin who looks less than impressed by my guest.

"I know, but Ellis knocked. Made me coffee."

I smile at Ellis for accepting her after what went down and he nods back at me.

"Well, I bought bagels, so if anyone wants to make me a coffee."

"I'll go, you sit," Letty says, hopping up and going to race around me.

Throwing my arm out, I pull her into my body.

"Hey," she says, smiling up at me.

"Missed you," I whisper, although it's not quiet

enough because Devin makes a puking sound and I flip him off behind her back.

Dropping my lips to hers, I make a show of showing her just how much I missed her, mostly to irritate Devin but also because she looks hot as fuck and she's all mine.

I smack her ass as she heads for the kitchen before dropping into the seat she vacated with a satisfied smirk on my face.

"Oh fuck off," Devin mutters.

"Jealous, Dev?" I ask, stretching my legs out. "Been a while, hasn't it?"

"You're a fucking asshole, Legend. She know what you do for a fucking living yet?"

"What I did?" I correct, although seeing as I've got a 'date' with Alana tonight, I guess it's a lie.

"Oh yeah. Is Vic aware of that because rumor has it that—"

He stops talking when footsteps head back our way.

We both watch Letty as she walks toward us with a mug in her hand before passing it to me.

"Be careful with this one, Letty. He bites."

"Oh." She chuckles. "I'm more than aware. Thanks."

She holds Devin's hard stare for a beat before turning to me and taking a seat on my lap when I gesture for her to do so.

Forty-five minutes later and we're sitting in my car looking at the Anderson building where Letty's psych class is waiting for Ella to appear.

"Are we doing anything tonight?" Letty asks and my stomach drops into my feet.

"I can't tonight, Princess. I've got shit to do with the guys." The lie tastes bitter on my tongue but I can hardly tell her the truth. And I'm still trying to figure out how I'm going to get out of what's going to be expected of me. I don't even want to see Alana, let alone have to touch her.

She looks at me with disappointment in her eyes.

"You've got a job?"

"Nothing official. I don't work for him anymore."

"You are though, aren't you?"

I blow out a long breath. "We had a deal but—"

"Let me guess, he hasn't stuck to it. Shocker. It's almost like he isn't trustworthy."

I want to laugh at her comment but the reality is that it's anything but funny.

"You need to find a way to walk away, Kane."

"Trust me, Princess. You don't need to tell me that. I thought I had."

"If you really want this. College, football..." *Me.* I hear her unspoken word loud and clear. "Then you need to find a way to get out once and for all, or you may as well give up on this and just walk back into that life."

"I want this," I promise her, reaching over and taking her hand. I bring her knuckles to my lips and pepper kisses over them. "I want you."

Her eyes shutter as she hears the words. Slowly she nods but I don't see a lot of hope in her eyes.

"I won't be connected to that world, Kane. I won't. Whether it's my dad, or you. I'm going nowhere near it. And if that means I have to cut ties with Dad and we have to put this behind us, then I will. I got out of that place, I refuse to be dragged back into it."

"I don't want that life for you, Let. You deserve so much better."

"I know," she states and her confidence and strength to do the right thing makes my chest swell with pride. It also solidifies my knowledge that I need to figure a way out of this. I have got to find something that will force Victor to set me free.

I fall back into my seat with a sigh.

"I'll figure out a way. I'm not walking away from all of this now that I've got it."

She smiles at me. "Ella's over there. I should go."

"What are you going to do tonight?"

"Work, seeing as you've monopolized all my time the past two nights."

"Oh, like you were complaining about it."

"Maybe not, but I'm behind."

"I'll see you tomorrow then?" I ask, tugging on her arm and forcing her to lean over the center console so I can kiss her.

I'm desperate to tell her that I'll see her after I'm done tonight, but I can't. I can't do that to her.

"Pick me up for statistics?"

"You got it, Princess."

Gripping the back of her head, I bring her lips to mine and give her a kiss that she isn't likely to forget by tomorrow morning.

After long minutes, she pulls back and wipes her lips.

"Tomorrow. Please, try to stay safe."

"As long as you're waiting for me."

She smiles, her eyes dropping from mine and to my lips again like she's really trying to convince herself not to just stay here and make out instead of going to class.

"Okay. I really need to go."

I hold my hands up. "I'm not stopping you."

"Maybe not. You're still guilty though, aren't you?"

She climbs from the car and pulls her bag from the back.

More than you know, Princess.

My stomach is in knots knowing that Kane is somewhere doing something for Victor. I know it's crazy. He's worked for the guy for years and anything could have happened to him before now and I wouldn't really have given it a second thought. But after the past few weeks, after last night, I'd be lying if I said I wasn't scared for him.

The Creek is littered with widowed Hawk wives, and I know we're nowhere near that level. I don't want to know what it feels like to lose someone I'm beginning to care for because of some stupid gang.

Ugh, who the hell am I kidding—beginning to care for. I roll my eyes at myself. I more than care for him. And I think that after what he told me in the restaurant last night that he might just more than care for me too.

I hated how I felt when we first showed up in that place, the feeling that he might have taken others there, that everything might be a joke to him. But what he said to me about how he feels. It meant everything to me. I know I should be more cautious, I know it's crazy because it's Kane Legend I'm talking about. The boy who has hated me for as long as I can remember and blamed every bad thing that's happened to him over the years on me, but staring into his eyes as he told me I've wormed my way into his heart. Fuck. It gives me tingles now just thinking about it. I could tell by his eyes that he was telling me the truth.

My heart pounds as I stare aimlessly across the quiet library. I should be working, that's why I came here. I tried to focus in my room but the guys were there with music playing and enjoying themselves, plus every time I looked at my bed I remember Kane being there and I just needed to get out. I needed somewhere quiet where I could clear my head and focus. Only, I can't because I'm worrying about him.

I'm still zoned out imagining all the dangerous and illegal things he could be doing right now, so I don't notice someone approaching me until she perches her ass on my table.

Turning to see who it is, I find a smug-looking Clara staring back at me.

I just about manage to hold in my groan of frustration as I wait for her to say something. "What do you want?" I eventually snap when she seems more than happy to just sit there staring at me.

"No *boyfriend* tonight?"

"We're not attached at the hip, if that's what you mean," I mutter, looking down at my computer which has gone to sleep stopping me from pretending I was actually doing something before she came over.

"So where is he?"

"With friends," I snap, really not interested in getting dragged into this bullshit.

"Are you sure about that?"

"Yes, are you about done?"

"You think you're so special, don't you?"

I shake my head in surprise. "No, not really," I answer honestly.

"Have you even looked at his social media? You think he's yours—" She laughs like a lunatic. "You have no idea, sweetie." She reaches out and smoothes my hair down as if she's consoling me and I slap it away.

"If I wanted your opinion on my life, I'd have asked for it. Now, would you kindly leave me alone?"

"Sure. But a bit of friendly advice," she says, finally standing to her feet once more. I don't say anything to encourage her for fear my true feelings about her might accidentally slip out. I'd like to come out of this as the bigger person and not stoop to her level. "Leave guys like Kane Legend to girls who know how to handle them."

My teeth grind and my fists curl under the desk. I'm a Creek girl, I could take her down and finish her off down to her pretty blonde extensions if I wanted to, but I won't because I'm better than that.

"Great, thanks, have a good night."

I watch her as she walks off, anger swirling around me like a storm but I refuse to allow her words to fester. It's not like it's news to me that Kane's been with his fair share of women. He'd already been with a few before I left the Creek, I can only imagine the number of notches on his bedpost now.

I force my jealousy down. They might have been there once, but I was the one in his bed last night. It was my palm he held against his chest and told me I was worming my way inside.

Me. Not Clara or any of the other jersey chasing bitches, or the girls from his past. Me.

And I have no reason to think he's anywhere right now other than what he told me. If he was going to lie about anything, he'd have covered up that he was working for the Hawks tonight. But he didn't, he openly told me that knowing I wouldn't like it.

I force her comments down about his social media and focus on what I really came here for, my lit paper, not to stalk Kane on every platform I can find him on.

That being said though, by the time I get back to my dorm later that evening and pull my cell out to find that I have no messages or anything from him, my curiosity gets the better of me.

Opening Instagram, I search for him and then look at his tagged photos and videos.

There are a few from the guys from practice and a couple that Ezra has tagged him in of them all hanging out at the house. But the one that stands out contains a certain blonde I had the displeasure of seeing tonight.

Knowing that I shouldn't, I try to force myself to shut the app down and forget about it. Clara is a slut, I know her type. I remember them all hanging off Luca and Leon during high school. It's all games to try to snag the players. But even knowing that, I don't close the app and instead, I hit play.

My lips curl in disgust as I'm forced to watch her

touch him, walking her fingers up his bicep like she owns him.

But that's nothing compared to the way he looks at her and turns into her body.

"Holy shit," I gasp, my hand covering my mouth as he leans down to her.

Finally, a minute or two too late. I close the app.

I tell myself over and over that it won't have been how it looked. I remember how sincere he'd been when he said he'd not been with anyone else since starting here, and I believe him. Plus, we're not actually together, are we? I have no right to be pissed at anything he does. He might have said all the right things to make me melt last night, but really this thing between us has barely started.

But none of that matters because the image of her with him, of the way he leaned into her, is now burned into my mind. It's feeding my insecurities about what he's doing with me and my suspicions that he's playing me for the fun of it.

Sitting on the edge of my bed with my cell still in my hand, I open our previous conversation and shoot him a message asking him how his night went.

I sit there for ten minutes but it doesn't show as read and finally, I get a grip on myself, put it down and head for the shower.

I had no message waiting for me when I got back to check my cell last night, and the first thing I did this morning when I woke up was to check again. But still, nothing, and still, the message hadn't even been read.

As I lay staring at the ceiling, my concerns about what might have happened continue to flood my mind.

What if something went wrong last night. Would anyone even know where he is?

My heart races as I remain there imagining all the worst possibilities. In the end, I cave and I hit call on his number.

It rings and it rings and eventually goes to his voicemail.

I hang up. He'll see that I've called, he doesn't need to hear me freaking out. Assuming he's still alive.

I shouldn't care, I tell myself for the millionth time.

But I do. I care more than I want to admit and I'm terrified that this might be over before it's even really started because finally, out of all the shit, things were starting to look up.

Finally, focusing on the time, I realize that he'll be at practice. He was probably just out late last night then up early this morning. He probably hasn't checked his cell.

I get ready for class telling myself that he'll be here like he promised. I eventually emerge from the building a little over an hour later, and I'm filled with hope that I certainly wasn't feeling earlier, but the second I look around, I find no one.

My heart sinks once more, the fear I felt when I woke returns and causes a lump to clog my throat.

"Hey, I thought Kane was meeting you," Ella says when she follows me out of the building not long later to find me sitting on the wall that leads down to the sidewalk in the hope he'd appear.

"Yeah, me too," I mutter sadly.

"Well, the guys haven't come back yet so maybe they got held up at practice," she says, hope glittering in her eyes. She really wants to believe this thing with Kane could be real, that there could be a magical happily ever after for us. Right now, I'm not feeling the positivity.

"Yeah, maybe. Come on, let's go."

I find West and Brax hanging out by our morning class.

"Scarlett," Brax calls when he spots me and opens his arms as if he's going to give me an over-the-top hug.

"What happened to you two this morning?" I say, swerving his overexcitement.

"Ugh, Coach would not stop talking about Saturday's game. Literally think my ears are still bleeding."

So Ella was right then.

"Come on, you've still got a day of lectures to listen to," I joke, threading my arms through theirs and dragging them into the room.

"What about your boy?" West asks.

"What about him? I'm sure he's big enough to get himself to class," I say with a smile as if the words don't make my chest ache.

The three of us find a seat together and as much as I fight it, I can't help but look to the back of the room where Kane and I sat the last time.

The other students file in behind us, quickly filling up the seats before Professor Richman appears and kicks off the lecture.

"Kane was at practice?" I ask West.

"Yeah, looked like fucking shit though. Maybe he's sick and went back to bed."

I discreetly pull my cell from my purse to see if he's replied yet. Still nothing.

Dread sits heavy in my stomach and it only gets worse with each passing minute. I'm desperate to get out of class and call him, to find out what's going on.

But the second I do, the call once again goes to voicemail.

Motherfucker.

The day drags, and it only gets worse when I run into Devin on my way out of the library where I was hiding from the world.

"Shit, I'm so sorry," I say as he all but tips coffee over himself.

A surefire way to get him to like me, well done, Scarlett.

"No problem," he mutters, clearly pissed with me.

"Um... Dev?" I ask when he takes a step around me, obviously not wanting to stand and have a chat.

"Yeah?"

"W-where's Kane? He missed class and—"

"He's with Reid."

Well, I can only assume that he's alive.

"Why?"

"Fuck knows." He shrugs. "Trying to sort his shitshow of a life out, I think." His tone as he says this makes it very obvious that all of this is my fault.

"I never asked him to change, Devin." *No, you just told*

him to choose a side, is that any better? "Trust me when I tell you that I'm as shocked by all of this as you."

"I'm not shocked, Letty. Kane has wanted you for a long time. I was on your side, told him to stay away from you and let you lead your own life, but then you went behind our backs."

"Not out of choice. Victor threatened my family."

"It's fine, I get it. Just watch your back because you've made it more than clear that we need to watch ours."

I blow out a frustrated breath and he uses the opportunity to turn away from me and disappear inside the library.

Not feeling any better about the situation as I head toward our lit class, I keep my head up and smile when I approach Leon, who's loitering outside the lecture hall.

"Hey, you waiting for someone?" I ask, looking over my shoulder.

"Yeah, you."

I look up at him and open my lips to say something but he beats me to it.

"Are you okay?"

Tears fill my eyes as he looks at me with concern in his.

"Yeah, everything is fine."

His brows rise in suspicion.

"Do I need to kick his ass already?" he asks with a smirk.

"No. You don't need to get involved. How's Luc?"

A sad smile pulls at Leon's lips and it's all the answer I need.

"He'll be fine. You coming in?"

I look over my shoulder on the off-chance that he's about to walk through the door and sweep me into his arms. I already know he isn't going to be there, but still, a disappointed sigh falls from my lips.

"Come on, Cupcake," Leon says, wrapping his arm around my shoulder and turning me toward the door.

He takes me to our usual seats but instead of sitting in between the twins, Leon takes my usual seat, separating me from Luca.

I look over at him, but despite the fact I know he's aware of my presence, he doesn't look at me. It's like Monday all over again and I hate it.

"Anything?" Ella asks me when I find her loitering outside my lit class ready to head back to dorms.

"Nope." Her expression drops until movement over my shoulder catches her eye.

"We should go," she says, coming to stand beside me and threading her arm through mine.

Glancing over my shoulder, I find Leon, Luca, and Colt walking out of the lecture hall.

"Anything I need to know about?" I ask as we step into the late afternoon sun.

"Absolutely not. So the guys have practice, you're stressing over Kane. Let's go relax."

"El, I've got a ton of work to do."

"It'll still be there when we get back. Come on." She tugs on my arm harder, making me move faster.

"Where are we going?"

"Surprise. Pack a bag, grab a swimsuit and put your troubles behind you."

I wish I could say that the excitement twinkling in her eyes was infectious but still, all I can feel in my belly is the heavyweight of my dread for what's to come with Kane.

Something is off, I might not be able to put my finger on what, but I know it's not going to be good.

I'm in the bathroom trying to do something with my hair when my cell finally rings. My brush clatters to the counter before dropping to the floor as I run from the room.

I let out the breath I wasn't aware I was holding when I see Kane's name.

"Hello," I say in the rush long before I've even got my cell to my ear. "Is everything okay? Are you okay?"

He doesn't speak for a second and my head starts to spin as my heart races in my chest.

But when his voice finally does come down the line, it doesn't make me feel any better about the situation.

"Y-yeah. Everything is fine." Every hair on my body stands on end at the distant tone of his voice. It's cold and like he isn't really here with me right now.

"You're lying," I spit, not wanting to beat around the bush. We've done enough of that over the years.

"No, I'm not. I've just got a few things I need to sort out."

"With Reid?"

"Uh—"

"I ran into Devin," I say, filling in the gaps for him.

"Right, yeah. I'm with him, we're just sorting some shit out."

"Okay, well. Will you be in class tomorrow?"

"I don't know. Listen, I need to go. I just... I'm sorry, Letty. The second all this is done, I'll be right there with you. I promise."

I hesitate, not knowing what to say back, in the end, what I say is probably the wrong thing. "I meant what I said in the car yesterday morning, Kane. I'm not going to live that life, so if you are, then you need to tell me now."

"Princess," he sighs, and I picture him running his hand through his hair in frustration. "I need you to trust me. Can you do that?"

I bite down on my bottom lip. My jerk reaction is yes, but that's crazy. He's proved to me time and time again over the years that I shouldn't, and I'm still not convinced that he isn't playing me.

"Okay, fair enough," he says sadly when I don't respond. "But I'm going to prove to you that you can."

"Okay. So..."

"I'll see you soon, Let. I promise."

"And what do you expect me to do in the meantime, just sit here and wait like a loser?"

"What? No. I don't expect that of you. Enjoy yourself, you're at college. I'll be there before you know it."

"Right, okay, fine." There's a soft knock on my door. "I've got to go." I hang up before he can say anything back and I school my features before calling out for Elle to come in.

"You ready?" she asks but I've got my head in my

closet pretending to search for a swimsuit when really, I'm just fighting my tears.

Trust him, he says. Yeah, as if it's that easy.

Ella took us to a spa on the other side of town. Apparently, she had vouchers for her birthday earlier in the year and hadn't had a chance to use them.

The place was incredible, and it should have been relaxing. If it weren't for the fact I spent the whole time repeating my brief conversation with Kane over and over in my head as if there was a clue in his words somewhere as to what's really going on.

I tried to get involved with the conversation with Ella and Vi but every time they looked at me, I saw my own sadness reflected back at me in their eyes, I knew I was failing.

Friday is much like the day before. Kane isn't there to walk me to class, and aside from knowing that he was at practice because Brax let it slip over breakfast once they came back. But I don't see or hear from him all day.

I sit on my own in our sociology class, trying to focus on what the professor is saying but barely hearing a word of it as I worry about where the man is who should be sitting beside me.

I think back to Tuesday's class when he spent the entire time trying to feel me up while we were hidden in the shadows, and I can't help wishing that we could go back to that.

Needing some caffeine, I head toward the coffee shop

and order myself a skinny vanilla latte with an extra shot and a cupcake with sprinkles. It's not the same as having them with Luca and Leon but I guess it'll have to do before I spend the afternoon trying to distract myself with assignments.

The place is packed but lucky for me a couple get up right in front of me and I quickly snag their table.

I haven't even had a chance to pull the wrapper off the cupcake when someone helps themselves to the chair beside me.

"Do you mind?" a blonde woman whispers, pausing the conversation she was having with someone on her cell and pointing at the chair she's already decided she's sitting in.

"Sure," I say and watch as she finally lowers her ass into it.

"I know," she says, "I'm going to have to tell him soon. He's going to start noticing."

I focus on my cake but I can't help eavesdropping on her conversation, seeing as she's basically invited me into it.

"Thirteen weeks. I had my first scan last Wednesday."

The person on the other end speaks as my heart aches for the incredible experience this woman's just had seeing her baby for the first time. I remember that moment well.

"Yeah, it's definitely not my husband's."

My eyes widen at her confession.

"It's been like... six months at least, but why would I care when I've got a college guy taking care of me instead."

Silence.

"Oh yeah, I'll totally leave him. I just need to tell the dad first, make sure I've got somewhere to live."

They chat for a few more minutes about this woman's plans and I do my best to stop listening but in the end, I give up even trying, it's better than watching the TV.

I'm just finishing my cupcake when she finally ends her call and lowers her cell to the table.

"I'm so sorry, I just really needed to get off my feet."

Realizing she's talking to me, I look up into her light blue eyes and take in her flawless face for the first time. She's breathtakingly beautiful and I can't help wondering what's wrong with her husband for not touching her for all those months.

"O-oh, it's okay. I wasn't waiting for anyone or anything."

"Great. I'm just struggling with the worst morning sickness." She pulls a bottle of water from her bag and takes a sip. "It's exhausting."

"Well... um, congratulations."

She smiles at me, her head tilting to the side as if she actually cares about my words. "Thank you. I'm really excited about it."

I bet others aren't going to be, I think to myself.

"I should really get going. Thank you so much for the seat."

"You're... welcome," I mutter when I realize that she's already gone.

"Hey," Ella says, bounding toward me. "New friend?" she asks, watching the woman disappear through the doors.

"Nope."

"Ugh, I've just been given the most insane assignment. It's going to take like all weekend," she complains, dumping her bags on the floor. "You want another?" she asks, nodding at my coffee.

"Y-yeah, sure."

She bounces off to join the queue to get us both a drink and in only minutes she's back once more.

"So no party tonight then?" I ask, sounding a little too hopeful about it if her raised brow is anything to go by.

"Ha, nice try. We are going out tonight and you are going to enjoy yourself. Fuck Kane fucking Legend. We are going to get drunk and dance the night away."

As promised, a few hours later, that's exactly where I found myself with a very strong vodka in hand watching Ella and Vi grind it up on the dance floor.

"Not going to join them?" a familiar voice says from behind me.

Micah comes to stand next to me as we watch the pair of them dance and joke about.

"You like her, huh?" I ask, the vodka loosening my tongue.

Micah tenses a little before he recovers from his shock at my question.

"That obvious?"

"I see things."

"It doesn't matter. She isn't interested in a guy like me."

"Micah, you're a great guy," I say, ripping my gaze from the girl and turning to look at him.

"Not a football player though, am I?"

"That's just a fantasy."

"Is it?"

"Sometimes we just don't see what's right under our noses. Maybe she needs a little push in the right direction," I say, bumping my shoulder against his.

"I can't. If I screwed up our dorm dynamics, I'd never forgive myself."

My lips part to say more, but I decide against it. I can barely get a handle on my own love life right now, the last thing I should be doing is giving anyone else advice.

As if he can read my mind, Micah steps in front of me, ensuring my attention is firmly on him. "Everything's going to be okay, you know."

I narrow my eyes at him. I've still no idea how deep his connection with Ellis goes, but as time goes on, I'm starting to wonder if it's more than I initially thought.

"What do you know?"

He holds his hands up innocently.

"Letty, I—"

Leaning toward him, I ask a question that's been nagging at me for a while. "Micah, are you a Hawk?"

His entire body freezes as that last word rolls off my tongue.

"No," he states. "I'm not one of them but—"

"You're connected," I guess.

"Something like that."

"You need to be careful. They're—"

"You don't need to warn me about anything, Let. I

know the kind of men they are. But sometimes, you've got to dance with the devil to get the things you want."

"What the hell is that meant to mean?" I bark.

He stares at me, his eyes saying everything his lips aren't.

"Kane's going to be okay, Let. Just give him some time to figure all this out."

My lips part but my cell buzzing in my pants pocket distracts me from what I was going to say.

Pulling it out, the name staring back at me makes my heart begin to race.

> Kane: Don't make plans for after the game tomorrow.

LETTY

There wasn't a question as to whether I was going to be watching the game. Since I first became friends with Luca and Leon, I never missed a game—well, unless they were playing the Harriers, but I have my reasons for that.

I pull on my purple Panthers jersey and stand in front of my mirror, looking at my reflection.

The majority of the marks from my night with Kane have faded, but even in his absence, the memories haven't. And in the past two days, my frustration has only grown.

I know I said that I don't want any details about the Hawks or what he's doing for them. I'm aware of what I told him. But that still doesn't mean that I'm not desperate to get a hold of him and force him to tell me everything he's done in the past three days.

He's shown up to practice with the guys, so he's been here. If he's fine like he told me on the phone the other night, then why couldn't he come and see me. What has he been doing that forces him to hide from me?

Clara's little visit to my table on Wednesday night flickers through my mind, but I once again shoot it down. He has not been with someone else. I trusted him when he told me he'd only been with me, and I really want to hold on to that. Kane is a lot of things, a lot of bad things, but what he told me Tuesday in that restaurant, I believe.

"Ugh," I groan, getting frustrated with myself. I've been over this time and time again in the past forty-eight hours, and I'm fed up with going round and round in circles.

What I need is him. Him standing in front of me and telling me the truth.

I straighten my hair, apply some light makeup before spritzing myself with my favorite perfume, and head out to meet the others.

Ella, Vi, Micah, and I all head to the stadium together. I'm a nervous wreck long before we pull up to a parking space but it's not for seeing Kane later, it's for Luca and Leon.

It's always been the same. While they were as cool as cucumbers before a game, I was a jittery wreck.

Ella glances over at me and must be able to read the expression on my face. "You know they're gonna smash it," she says with a wide smile.

"I'm sure they will."

We find our seats and watch as the cheerleaders flip and twist across the field getting the crowd in the mood. But no matter how many people cheer around me, I can't find it in myself to get excited.

I'm nervous for the guys and now I'm here, I'm

assuming where Kane is, I'm getting more and more anxious for what he might have to tell me.

I scan the stadium as we wait for the teams to appear, taking in the black and orange of the Missouri fans who have traveled for the game. From what I've heard over the breakfast table, the Panthers smashed the Tigers last year so they've shown up with something to prove and their fans sure seem fired up.

I hold my breath as the teams emerge and get ready for the whistle.

My eyes immediately land on Luca and Leon as I send up a silent prayer for them. I know how much they both want this, how much pressure Luca especially puts on himself. I really want it all to pay off and for him to go all the way.

Ella and Vi scream beside me, getting swept up in the excitement.

I search the team, looking for the others, I find West, Brax, and Zayn. My heart swells seeing my brother down there making his own dreams come true. But I don't see Kane.

Please don't tell me he's missing this game too.

I know he shouldn't be playing but I still expected him to be here. He told me how he's begged Coach to let him out on the field this week after missing the last game. I didn't think he'd give up this easily.

But then the sea of purple parts and all the air rushes out of my lungs as he appears.

I haven't seen him on a football field for... a lot of years. I tried to avoid going to Harrow Creek High games but it wasn't always that easy with Zayn playing. But seeing him down there now does weird things to me, not to mention it quadruples my previous nerves.

The minutes fly by as Coach talks to them and they get ready but my heart drops when Kane heads for the bench, the second-string wide receiver starting in his place.

The guys get into position, the whistle blows and the crowd around me goes wild but I remain in my seat watching. Even after all these years supporting Luca and Leon, I still don't entirely understand why everyone around me shouts and hollers at the times they do, unless of course we score, which sadly doesn't seem to happen all that often.

As I watch Luca bark instructions at his offense, I can see his frustration getting the better of him, especially at whoever the other wide receiver is who seemingly keeps fucking up the plays.

At one point, Leon ends up dragging Luca away from him after he fumbles a pass.

"Calm the fuck down," I mutter, worried that if he carries on he's going to get himself kicked out of the game for fighting with his own freaking team.

The whistle blows for the end of the third quarter and we're down by twenty.

The excitement of those around me is beginning to wane as reality sets in that this isn't going to happen for them today.

"What the fuck happened to them?" I hear someone say behind me. "They fucking killed it last year."

A few others mutter similar comments as I will Luca to get his shit together.

Guilt weighs down on my shoulders that I haven't helped with all the pressure he's been feeling this week. I hate that I might have something to do with this potential loss so early in their season.

"Holy shit," Ella gasps, her hand wrapping around my forearm, dragging my eyes up from my lap.

"What?"

"Kane's playing."

My eyes immediately find him pulling his helmet on and getting ready to play the final quarter.

"Shit. I hope he's ready for this."

"He isn't stupid, Let. If he wasn't then he wouldn't play. But they need a fucking miracle right now, so I hope he's on form."

I watch Luca as Kane hits the field but he doesn't look as happy as I thought he would at having a replacement on his offense.

Leon, on the other hand, slaps Kane on the shoulder as he heads for his starting position and the two of them share a nod before focusing on the task at hand.

The whistle blows once more and everyone inches forward to the edges of their seats to see if we're able to pull it off at the last minute.

The difference in the team is almost immediately noticeable, even to a football-phobe like me.

Luca might not be happy about his replacement, but I'm beginning to really understand why Kane was gifted the position of starting wide receiver from the beginning because he is really fucking good.

I smile to myself as I watch him run down the field, glad that those who might have been doubting him, thinking that his appearance on the team was purely due to his connections with Victor and the Hawks might just be proven wrong.

Pride swells within me as I watch my three favorite men work together like there might actually be a way for them to co-exist for the next few years without killing each other.

I'm watching but I'm not paying attention to what's actually happening before me when an almighty roar erupts from around me as we make a touchdown.

I stand with the crowd, not wanting to look like the only one not getting excited and clap as Luca rallies the team once more in the hope that there's still time to pull this thing off.

The final few minutes of the game are tense, every single move one of the guys makes causes a gasp or an ooh or an aah to ripple around the stadium.

<hr>

"Holy fucking shit, that was tight," Ella exclaims as we make our way out of the stadium once the game is over and the guys have headed off the field.

"Yeah, it was," I agree, my head still lost in my own thoughts.

"I can't believe that after all these years supporting the Dunns you have no fucking clue what you just watched," Micah shouts, sounding utterly astounded.

"I've tried, it's just not my thing. I'm sure they'd be the same if I forced them to the ballet or something every weekend."

He laughs at me as we pour out toward the parking lot.

Spotting Kane's car, I tell the others that I'll meet them at the party later and head over to wait for him.

I rest my ass on the hood of his baby and watch as everyone else leaves and the whole place slowly becomes deserted.

Eventually, the team emerges from the back entrance of the stadium.

There's a pretty huge crowd waiting for them, most of whom seem to be female. I roll my eyes, almost able to taste the desperation of the jersey chasers from here.

I see Luca and Leon emerge before they get sucked into the crowd. I'm too far away for them to spot me. I'm pretty sure I'm the last person Luca wants to see right now anyway.

We'll talk soon, I'm sure. I just want to let him come to grips with all of this in his own time. Football is the most important thing for him to be focusing on right now.

The moment I spot Kane emerging from the building, my entire body tenses and I push myself from the car as he scans the lot and finds me.

A smile curls at his lips as he picks up the pace to get to me faster. His movements aren't as smooth as usual and I wonder how much damage he did to himself by playing that last fifteen minutes when we all know he shouldn't have.

He's almost at me when I sense someone approaching me from behind. But I don't turn around, I'm too lost in Kane to even care who it might be.

That is until he notices whoever it is and his whole

expression changes from one of excitement to one of pure horror.

I'm forcefully pushed aside as whoever it is passes me. If it weren't for Kane's car then I'm sure I'd have ended up on the ground from the strength behind the shove.

"Kane, oh my God, you were incredible. I told you that Coach should have let you start." Her sickly sweet voice makes me wince but a weird sense of familiarity washes through me.

Righting myself, I turn to find a blonde curling herself into Kane's side.

But not just any blonde. The blonde from the coffee shop yesterday.

An angry growl fills my ears and it's not until she turns her blue eyes on me that I realize it came from me.

"Oh I'm sorry, sweetie. I didn't mean to shove you, I was just so excited to get to my man here."

"N-no, Letty. Listen—"

"You," I growl, ignoring Kane's attempt to say something.

She has the audacity to smile sweetly at me. "Oh, you're the girl from the coffee shop." She pretends to look confused but I see through it. She planned it. All of it.

I stand tall as I stare at her, my fists curling at my sides as my stomach churns at the memory of what I overheard of her phone call comes back to me.

She's pregnant, and not by her husband. By a college student.

No.

My eyes shoot to Kane who's trying to push the woman away from him.

"Letty, no. It isn't what it looks like. We're not—"

I stare into his eyes, allowing him to watch my heart shatter into a million pieces.

"No, Kane. It's exactly what it looks like. We're done. So fucking done."

I spin on my heels and run as fast as I can, but it isn't fast enough because soon I hear feet pounding behind me before his warm hand wraps around my upper arm.

He spins me to him and gasps when he sees the tears streaming down my cheeks.

"Letty, please. Let me—"

"She's fucking pregnant," I scream, my voice cracking with emotion. "She's fucking pregnant with your baby."

He stills, his eyes wide as my words register in his head.

"Surprise, sweetie," she says, appearing at his side and confirming my worst nightmare.

This time when I run, no one stops me. And when I finally fall into a pair of arms I know that they'll always hold me up.

Want more? Keep reading for a sneak peek at, *The Betrayal You Serve*, book #3 in the Maddison Kings University series!

Or alternatively you can grab your copy here.

Chapter 1
Kane

"She's fucking pregnant," Letty screams, her voice cracking with emotion as tears cascade down her cheeks. "She's fucking pregnant with your baby."

My world begins to spin, confusion fogging my brain as I stare back at her.

What the hell is she—

"Surprise, sweetie," Alana breathes as she wraps her hands around my upper arm, her presence startling me yet her voice turning my blood to lava.

Ripping my eyes from a shattering Letty, I stare down at her in disbelief.

My heartbeat pounds in my ears as I try to gain a grip on reality.

"I'm sorry, that wasn't how I intended on telling you. I wanted to surprise you with it on Wednesday night, but you know how things went," she says, lowering her voice and wiggling her brows.

My stomach churns at the reminder of the other night, threatening to expel its contents right here in the parking lot.

Looking away from her vindictive eyes for a beat, I find that Letty is gone. My body screams at me to run, to chase her, to tell her this is all one big joke and to pull her into my arms. But I have no idea if any of that would be true, because I have no fucking clue what is going on right now.

I turn back to Alana, the accomplished smirk on her face causes something to explode inside me.

Red hot fury replaces everything else as I grab her by the throat and pin her back against the side of my car.

A terrified gasp rips from her lips before I crowd her, staring down into her now tear-filled eyes.

"You're lying," I say, although, I want to scream it in her face. I don't need her to see how fast I'm losing control right now.

"N-no, I'm n-not," she stutters, her entire body trembling against my rough hold.

I stare down into her eyes, needing to know the truth.

I already know she's a lying, vindictive cunt. I have zero reason to trust a single word that comes out of her mouth.

The fact that Letty was the one to spill her supposed secret has alarm bells screaming in my head.

Why would Letty know first? How does Letty even know Alana?

I only have one answer.
Alana.

Letty and Kane's story concludes in The Betrayal You Serve.

ABOUT THE AUTHOR

Tracy Lorraine is a *USA Today* and *Wall Street Journal* bestselling new adult and contemporary romance author. Tracy has recently turned thirty and lives in a cute Cotswold village in England with her husband, baby girl and lovable but slightly crazy dog. Having always been a bookaholic with her head stuck in her Kindle, Tracy decided to try her hand at a story idea she dreamt up and hasn't looked back since.

Be the first to find out about new releases and offers. Sign up to my newsletter here.

If you want to know what I'm up to and see teasers and snippets of what I'm working on, then you need to be in my Facebook group. Join Tracy's Angels here.

Keep up to date with Tracy's books at
www.tracylorraine.com

<u>Hate You</u> #1

<u>Trick You</u> #2

<u>Defy You</u> #3

<u>Play You</u> #4

<u>Inked</u> (A Rebel Ink/Driven Crossover)

<u>Rosewood High Series</u>

<u>Thorn</u> #1

<u>Paine</u> #2

<u>Savage</u> #3

<u>Fierce</u> #4

<u>Hunter</u> #5

Faze (#6 Prequel)

<u>Fury</u> #6

<u>Legend</u> #7

<u>Maddison Kings University Series</u>

<u>TMYM: Prequel</u>

<u>TRYS #1</u>

<u>TDYW</u> #2

<u>TBYS</u> #3

<u>TVYC</u> #4

<u>TDYD</u> #5

<u>TDYR</u> #6

<u>TRYD</u> #7

<u>**Knight's Ridge Empire Series**</u>

<u>Wicked Summer Knight</u>: Prequel (Stella & Seb)

<u>Wicked Knight</u> #1 (Stella & Seb)

<u>Wicked Princess #2</u> (Stella & Seb)

<u>Wicked Empire</u> #3 (Stella & Seb)

<u>Deviant Knight</u> #4 (Emmie & Theo)

<u>Deviant Princess</u> #5 (Emmie & Theo

<u>Deviant Reign</u> #6 (Emmie & Theo)

<u>One Reckless Knight</u> (Jodie & Toby)

<u>Reckless Knight</u> #7 (Jodie & Toby)

<u>Reckless Princess</u> #8 (Jodie & Toby)

<u>Reckless Dynasty</u> #9 (Jodie & Toby)

<u>Dark Halloween Knight</u> (Calli & Batman)

<u>Dark Knight</u> #10 (Calli & Batman)

<u>Dark Princess</u> #11 (Calli & Batman)

Dark Legacy #12 (Calli & Batman)

<u>Corrupt Valentine Knight</u> (Nico & Siren)

Corrupt Knight #13 (Nico & Siren)

Corrupt Princess #14 (Nico & Siren)

Corrupt Union #15 (Nico & Siren)

Sinful Wild Knight (Alex & Vixen)

Sinful Stolen Knight: Prequel (Alex & Vixen)

Sinful Knight #16 (Alex & Vixen)

Sinful Princess #17 (Alex & Vixen)

Sinful Kingdom #18 (Alex & Vixen)

Knight's Ridge Destiny: Epilogue

Harrow Creek Hawks

(Reid, Maverick, JD & Alana)

Merciless #1

Relentless #2

Lawless #3

Fearless #4

Ruined Series

Ruined Plans #1

Ruined by Lies #2

Ruined Promises #3

Never Forget Series

Never Forget Him #1

Never Forget Us #2

Everywhere & Nowhere #3

Chasing Series

Chasing Logan

The Cocktail Girls

<u>His Manhattan</u>

<u>Her Kensington</u>